Push in Boötes

by

RICHARD F. WEYAND

RICHARD F. WEYAND

ISBN 978-1-954903-26-5
Printed in the United States of America

Cover Credits
Cover Art: Luca Oleastri and Paola Giari,
www.rotwangstudio.com
Back Cover Photo: Oleg Volk

Published by Weyand Associates, Inc.
Bloomington, Indiana, USA
September, 2025

PUSH IN BOÖTES

CONTENTS

The Question

Life for Arthur Vegan got much more interesting after he, Steven Bach, and Barbara Nowak Bach were awarded the Presidential Medal of Freedom for negotiating a peace with Arthur's hive queen on Vega. For one thing, the insect-like alien no longer had to hide himself from humans.

Arthur took to using a self-drive rental car for exploring the tourist and sightseeing spots around the university town which had been their base of operations for twenty years. He visited national forests, state parks, historic sites, and museums. He particularly liked the state museum in the local state capital, which was full of materials that were right up his alley as a human sociologist.

Sometimes Steven and Barbara would go with him. Sometimes one or both of their teenage children, Jared and Daphne, would go with him. But most often Arthur would go alone.

Arthur never had any confrontations with anyone on his forays into the world. Some people shied away from him, but he understood that. There was a big difference between a TV image, such as at the president's news conference, and running into the six-foot-tall, orange-brown alien with large, faceted, green eyes and sharp mandibles in person.

About a year after they returned from Vega, the mayor of the university town where the three of them had established the sprawling Spaceport USA asked if they would all appear in the city's Fourth of July parade. They were the only recipients of the Presidential Medal of Freedom the city had ever had, and the Fourth of July was all about freedom, after all.

While Steven and Barbara had stayed out of the limelight that one would normally associate with their current levels of wealth and power, they thought participating in the Fourth of July parade was a good idea. All the better to get people more accustomed to seeing aliens in general – and Arthur in particular – around town. The presence of the spaceport and the status of their trade agreement with the hive queens meant Arthur would soon not be the only alien around, after all.

They rode in the big back seat of an antique convertible and waved to the crowds lining the parade route. The crowds were larger this year, given the mayor's announcement that Arthur would participate, and people cheered seeing him.

It was a lot of fun.

It was almost two years since their last trip to Vega, to confront the hive queen, when a question that had been bothering Arthur surfaced. It had been troubling him for some time, but he couldn't quite put his finger on what it was. Then he had it.

They five of them were eating dinner in the kitchen of the pretty little house in the woods where they had lived for twenty years, just off the grounds of the spaceport, opposite from the university town on the other side of the spaceport, just into the hill country.

"Barbara, can I ask you a question?"

"Sure, Arthur. Go ahead."

"Do you remember two years ago when you confronted the hive queen?"

"Yes. Of course."

"Do you remember that, in response to her accusing you of stealing the interstellar drive technology, you accused the bug-people of doing the same thing? Of stealing the technology?"

Books in the EMPIRE Series

by Richard F. Weyand:
EMPIRE: Reformer
EMPIRE: Usurper
EMPIRE: Tyrant
EMPIRE: Commander
EMPIRE: Warlord
EMPIRE: Conqueror

by Stephanie Osborn:
EMPIRE: Imperial Police
EMPIRE: Imperial Detective
EMPIRE: Imperial Inspector
EMPIRE: Section Six

by Richard F. Weyand:
EMPIRE: Intervention
EMPIRE: Investigation
EMPIRE: Succession
EMPIRE: Renewal
EMPIRE: Resistance
EMPIRE: Resurgence

Books in the Childers Universe

by Richard F. Weyand:
Childers
Childers: Absurd Proposals
Galactic Mail: Revolution
A Charter For The Commonwealth
Campbell: The Problem With Bliss

by Stephanie Osborn:
Campbell: The Sigurdsen Incident

"Yes, Arthur. I remember."

"Why were you so sure they had stolen it?"

"Because they were a largely agrarian society, not a technical one. The workers were all doing agriculture and animal husbandry, and the hive queens and their drones were not a sufficient population to foster and maintain a high-tech society.

"That and there had been no progress. When you first came to Earth seventy years ago, the trip from Vega took nine days. Twenty years ago, the trip to Vega took nine days. No progress in fifty years? We made more progress in twenty years from a standing start. Our trip to Vega two years ago took five days.

"To me, that meant the technology wasn't theirs. They had taken it, and used it, but they didn't understand it well enough, with their limited technical base, to be able to advance it."

"Then I have one big question. They stole it. OK. Perhaps. That was well before my time, so I wouldn't know. It does leave us with a big question, however.

"From whom did they steal it?"

"Yes, that's the sixty-four dollar question, isn't it?"

"Excuse me?"

"Sorry, Arthur. It's a phrase my grandfather used to use. He told me that in the 1940s there was a radio quiz show. Contestants were asked a series of questions. The questions started at one dollar and the prize doubled every round, as the questions got harder. The seventh and final round was sixty-four dollars, and it was the hardest question of all."

"So the most difficult and the most valuable question at once. Well, that certainly applies here, I think."

"Oh, yes. No doubt."

"I think it's a question we should try to answer, Barbara."

"How would you go about it?"

"I think I would start with the hive queen and go from

there."

Barbara nodded.

"Probably smart. But there are a number of issues there, Arthur. One is that you need an exploration ship for this. This isn't a courier trip. Just space out to Vega and right back. You will be going to different planets one after the other. That takes a custom-built ship. A couple years' worth of supplies. Special equipment to plot and map stars. Probably offensive and defensive armament.

"Second is that Steven and I can't go with you this time. We have commitments and responsibilities here. We're also in our mid-forties, and we are, quite frankly, getting too old for this sort of thing. And these two aren't old enough yet."

She indicated Jared and Daphne – now eighteen and almost sixteen – with a nod.

"Yes, we are," Jared said.

Barbara continued to face Arthur.

"Probably five or six years too young."

Jared was going to say something else, but Steven laid his hand on his son's arm.

"Get your degrees first, Jared. Trust me."

Jared looked dubious, but Daphne looked thoughtful.

"How would you suggest I proceed then, Barbara?" Arthur asked.

"Plan that ship. Build it. Staff it with a crack crew. Go out and visit the colony planets. Do some searches for new colony planets. Then, in six years or so, set off with these two in search of the answer to your question."

Arthur nodded.

"That sounds right."

"But we're ready now," Jared said.

"Jared. One really important thing in life is to realize when you've won," Steven said.

Jared looked at his father and quieted down. Sometimes his father said the damnedest things. Things that struck one as true the moment he said them.

Steven and Barbara talked about the dinner conversation later, when they were alone.

"I worry about them heading out on a trip like that," Steven said.

"I worry about them, too, Steven, but in six years they'll be full adults and can do whatever they want, with our blessing or without. And is there anyone else you trust to research Arthur's question? To make first contact? To set up a peaceful relationship, assuming that's possible?"

"No. No, there isn't."

"Same for me. It's a values issue. To recognize differences. Work with them. Turn them into advantages, rather than a reason to fight. That's got Jared and Daphne written all over it."

Steven nodded.

"It was a good idea, to fund the experimental school at the university."

"Yes. It gave us the opportunity to veto the stupider aspects of a modern curriculum. And the kids are well ahead because of it. Daphne's taking college classes now, and Jared's almost a junior in college. Daphne will likely have her master's degree before they leave, and Jared will probably have a doctorate."

"So that's the plan then, Barbara?"

"I think so."

"Is it fair that we lay these expectations on them, though?"

"They want to go, Steven. You saw them."

"I still worry about them."

"Of course."

Jared and Daphne also compared notes when they were in private.

"Well?" Daphne asked.

"What do you think?"

"I asked you first."

"They don't want us to go," Jared said. "The six years thing is just a put-off. In six years, there'll be another excuse."

"Could be, but I don't think so."

"Then why the hesitation?"

"Two reasons. One, they worry about us. Not about our abilities, but the obvious danger involved. Second, they don't want to inspire any knee-jerk teenage pushback."

"I don't do that, Daphne."

Daphne just raised an eyebrow.

"OK, well some. But that's what it is to be independent. To become independent, in any case."

"Of course, Jared, but they know it's an issue. Or can be. So I think they want us to go. In six years."

"Why six years?"

"First, there's no hurry. Second, we'll be better prepared."

"How so, Daphne?"

"Education for one. What is your degree major, Jared?"

"Engineering. That's how you do things."

"And mine was going to be finance, like Mom. Because that's how you pay to get things done. But I think, with this trip looming, I'll change majors."

"To what, Daphne?"

"International relations. Understanding other cultures, and figuring out how to deal with them effectively. That has direct relevance to the mission."

"Oh, that's a good one. Should I change mine as well, do you think?"

Daphne thought about it, then shook her head.

"No, I don't think so. Engineering issues will come up, Jared. What's their tech like? Can we use it? Trade for it? I think engineering issues will likely be front and center. Just understanding what they have will be a big problem."

"You think so, Daphne?"

"Oh, yes. How long ago did the hive queens steal their technology, do you think? Given that Vega is a colony planet for the bug-people?"

"Must be several hundred years, Daphne. Maybe a thousand. They've been on Vega a long time."

"Exactly. Jared, where were we a thousand years ago?"

"A thousand years ago, the Battle of Hastings was still in the future."

"So how advanced will this new alien race be now, given that they had the interstellar drive before William the Conqueror defeated Harold of Saxony?"

Jared just stared at her.

The Design

It was the very next Friday evening that Arthur had a question for Jared and Daphne.

He started with Jared.

"Jared, do you guys have any time to look at the colony ship design with me and start working up what an exploration ship variant would look like?"

"Sure, Arthur. When is good?"

"Any time, actually. I don't need to sleep very often."

"Well, let's go, then."

They stopped by Daphne's room to pick her up, then headed to the rooms Steven and Barbara had added to the three-bedroom house for Arthur when Daphne had come along. They could be converted into a two-car garage in the future, if they decided to sell the house. In the meantime, they were Arthur's rooms.

In the living room of the addition, Arthur had a visualization engine set up, with a large wall display. He would be able to display the colony ship plans – and edit them – as they talked.

When everyone was settled in, Arthur called up the plans.

"Here's the current colony ship design."

"First, let's take out what we don't need, Arthur," Jared said. "Lose all those cabins on F, G, and H Decks. The bathrooms and galleys, too. Open it up."

Arthur manipulated the drawing, and the interior walls and features of those decks disappeared.

"OK. Good. I think those top two decks are for missile launchers and missile storage. Let's label those. We'll fill them in later."

"Two decks for missile launchers and missile storage?" Daphne asked.

"Each of those missiles has a nuclear reactor and a graviton drive, Daphne. They're pretty big."

"Oh. OK. And there's the warhead, too, right?"

"No, there's no warhead," Jared said.

"Then how does it work?"

"A device of the mass of a nuclear powerplant and a gravitonics drive impacting a spaceship at tens or hundreds of thousands of miles an hour will negatively impact the structural integrity of the craft," Arthur said. "In addition, even a near-miss will prove itself a problem, as the passage of a high gravitational field will almost certainly result in mortality for the occupants."

"Oh. I get it. We just ram 'em."

"Essentially, yes."

"All right, Arthur," Jared said, "mark those top two decks for the missiles and launchers. Now what have we got?"

"We still need passenger space, as opposed to crew space."

"OK, let's put a dozen two-room suites on F Deck. Make them big, like a luxury hotel penthouse. Put a common living room, and a dining room. And put in a really nice gourmet kitchen on that deck, too."

Daphne raised an eyebrow, and Jared shrugged.

"We can have it be a luxury rental when we get back. In the meantime, it will be a nice place to live for a couple of years."

Arthur was making the changes as Jared called them out.

"Put the common living room in the center of the space, next to the reactors. That moves it in from the exterior of the ship and makes it a safe room if we come under attack. All the suites and the kitchen around the outside should have air-tight doors."

Arthur could select spaces and slide them around in the display. The other spaces would move around and morph to accommodate the changes.

"OK, Arthur. Add an elevator. We want one of those ones with the doors on both sides. One door opens into the living room, and the back door opens into the kitchen. So kitchen staff can get supplies without trundling them through the passenger spaces."

Jared and Daphne looked at the finished F Deck.

"That looks right," Daphne said.

Jared nodded.

"Let's look at Deck D, Arthur."

Arthur changed the view on the display.

"Well, we don't need anywhere near the crew a colony ship has. Let's make the officer's quarters two-room suites, and make the crew quarters one to a room. So they have their own space for such a long voyage. And cut the crew cabins by a third."

"Don't forget that you also have the kitchen staff for that gourmet kitchen on F Deck, Jared," Arthur said.

"Hmm. Go back to F Deck, Arthur."

Arthur adjusted the display.

"OK, let's lose two of the passenger suites, and put cabins for the kitchen staff on this deck. Figure individual cabins for six, I think. On a hallway off the kitchen."

"It's still tight, Jared."

"Compress the suites a little bit. Maybe lose one more."

"With nine suites we can get the effect you want, Jared. Nice spacious living quarters for VIP passengers, but still nice quarters for kitchen staff. We can even get a couple more kitchen staff cabins, for eight total."

Jared nodded.

"That's probably better, Arthur. OK, let's look at the overall plan and see what we have."

Arthur adjusted the display again, and Jared and Daphne studied it.

"Something's not quite right," Jared said.

"Arthur," Daphne said, "Rearrange the decks so the crew deck is below the torpedo storage deck, and the passenger deck is below that. Maybe put the stores deck between them."

Arthur rearranged the decks, swapping D Deck and F Deck, and leaving E Deck – the stores deck – where it was.

"Yeah," Jared said. "That's better. Both the crew deck and the passenger deck have the stores deck adjacent, which reduces moving things around if the elevator fails, and the crew has easy access to the torpedo deck if they need it. Good call, Daphne."

"Now what about the other decks, Jared?" Daphne said. "A, B, and C Deck. We certainly don't need all the cargo space of a colony ship."

"No. We could lose B and C Decks entirely, I think. A Deck is enough for anything we would be taking. Mostly vehicles for going down to the surface, I would think. So the ship can stay in space."

"Hmm. Wait a minute. Arthur, could we build a lifeboat of sorts and put it on those two decks? Something big enough to evacuate the ship, and with enough stores to get everyone back to Earth in one straight-through transit? Its own reactors, its own gravitonic devices. We blow one wall of the ship out and hightail it for home."

"I am not sure we could achieve the required structural integrity of the ship with one whole side being able to be opened in that way, Daphne," Arthur said.

"Wait. What if we built it into A Deck? Or A Deck and B Deck? We have it completely surrounded by chambers on A Deck and B Deck that hold the mechanicals for the ship – water storage, air recycling, waste recycling, all that stuff – but the center of A and B Decks is the lifeboat. It just drops out of the bottom of the ship."

"That we could do," Arthur said. "It would give us a way home if everything went to hell, either mechanically or, um, kinetically. It would still be exposed on the bottom side, however."

"Yes, but only on the bottom side," Daphne said. "We could armor that side more."

"And use the same reactors and gravitonic devices as on the ship itself," Jared said. "It would be same-same in terms of maintenance and parts and all, but without the mass of the ship it would go like stink. We'd outrun them."

Arthur worked on the display, setting aside enough volume in the center of A and B Decks for such a ship. He looked at it critically.

"Yes, that will work."

"Excellent," Daphne said. "I'd sleep a lot easier if I knew there was always an independent way home."

Jared nodded.

"All right, Arthur. Do you have enough to work with now?"

"Oh, yes. Thank you very much, Jared and Daphne. Now we just need to build it."

Of course, it wasn't that simple.

Arthur did not have a design for the new exploration ship. He had a rough architectural layout for it. The difference was thousands of man-hours of work. Every piece of the new ship had to be specified and dimensioned and approved.

PUSH IN BOÖTES

Consider a single bolt used in the ship. It had to be carefully planned so that when it showed up on the production floor it fit in this hole, right here, and was the proper bolt for the use.

What was that bolt? What were its radius and the pitch of its threads? How long was it? What head did it have? Hex head or socket head or what? Was it a shoulder bolt or a simple bolt? Did it have provision for safety wire or a cotter key? What material was it made of? Steel, stainless steel, titanium? Was it soft steel, or was it a grade 5 or grade 8 bolt? Was it cadmium-plated?

Now multiply this by the millions of parts it took to build a spaceship, most of them much more complicated.

A new ship design would be a major engineering effort, and Arthur took it to the current head of engineering for Graviton Dynamics, Gerhard Fischer.

"Good morning, Mr. Vegan. Come in."

Vegan went in to Fischer's office and took the indicated seat.

"Thank you for meeting with me, Mr. Fischer."

"Not at all, Mr. Vegan. I'm honored. You said you had a new ship design for us?"

"Yes. A new ship layout, in any case. Let me send it to you."

Arthur forwarded the design docs from his phone. Fischer called it up on his desk terminal. He looked it over briefly.

"Very interesting, Mr. Vegan. The purpose of this ship?"

"It is a dual-purpose ship, Mr. Fischer. Exploration first, and use as a yacht – perhaps a leased yacht – thereafter."

"Built on the scale of a colony ship, that's a mighty big yacht."

"Yes, it is, Mr. Fischer. But the primary mission is exploration, for which the size may be necessary.

"And the customer for this design is?"

"Steven Bach."

"With your permission, I'll check on that, Mr. Vegan."

"Oh, no, Mr. Fischer. I insist that you do. One cannot have people going around claiming Steven's approval for things without a check."

Fischer nodded, though Vegan's casual reference to Graviton Dynamics' majority shareholder by first name probably meant it was OK. Fischer, for that matter, had driven the car Vegan and the Bachs rode in for the Fourth of July parade last year, as he was one of the few people around who could still drive such a vehicle.

"And the priority assigned to this effort, Mr. Vegan?"

"The primary use of this ship is scheduled for five or six years in the future, Mr. Fischer. So it is not one of those 'drop everything and do this first while making all your other schedules' situations common to the engineering profession. At the same time, the primary passengers for that mission will be myself and the Bachs' children Jared and Daphne, so we are all very interested that it be done properly."

Fischer nodded and looked back to the plans.

"It mounts graviton missiles, Mr. Vegan? Is this a warship?"

"More a privateer, Mr. Fischer."

"We'll need to get Department of Defense approval."

"I will work on approval through the president. It should not be a problem. The U.S. Constitution anticipates private armed ships."

"It does?"

"Of course, Mr. Fischer. In Article I, Section 8. Otherwise, to whom would Congress issue letters of marque and reprisal?"

"Hmph."

Fischer continued to page through the decks of the new ship.

"A lifeboat, Mr. Vegan?"

"A means for passengers and crew to return to Earth in case the ship is incapacitated by mechanical failure, mischance, or hostile action. Correct. And the nuclear reactors and graviton devices are to be the same spec as the main ship."

"Gonna be pretty zippy."

"If the main ship is incapacitated through the actions of hostiles, I would anticipate a speedy departure to be of some benefit, Mr. Fischer."

Fischer nodded.

"Makes sense. Very well, Mr. Vegan. We will work up a design schedule for the new ship. You are Mr. Bach's design contact, I assume."

"Yes, Mr. Fischer."

"Very well, Mr. Vegan. I'll be in touch when we have a design schedule together."

"Thank you, Mr. Fischer."

Hurdles

The first hurdle one had to clear when building what amounted to a privateer was permission from the president and the Department of Defense. Arthur took the problem to Steven and Barbara.

"You want to mount gravitonic missiles on your exploration ship, Arthur?"

"Yes, Steven. We do not know anything about this other race. In the case of the Vegans, we had a great deal of information, both through me and from our first trip. So *Vegan Dreams* did not need missiles. But about this other race we know nothing."

Steven looked to Barbara, who shrugged.

"The *Santa Maria* and the *Bounty* and the *Golden Hind* all had cannon, Steven."

"Those were all government ships, Barbara."

"The *Bounty* was, but Columbus' and Drake's flagships were not. They were private vessels which had some sponsorship by the crown, but remained private vessels."

"So you don't think it's too much to ask?"

"Not for an exploration ship, Steven. For a colony ship, yes, that might be a bit much. But not an exploration ship bound for what we know to be inhabited planets."

"All right, all right. I'll ask the president about it the next time he calls. I haven't heard from him in a bit, due to the election last year and getting his second term under way, but I should hear from him soon."

It was two months later that the call came.

"Steven Bach."

"This is the White House switchboard, Mr. Bach. Can you hold for the president?"

"Of course."

"Thank you, sir."

There was a click, then several seconds before the line clicked again.

"Mr. Bach. You there?"

"Yes, Mr. President."

"Sorry I haven't been in touch lately. There's been a lot going on. Election and all. Maybe you heard about it."

Steven chuckled. This time around had been something of a raucous election.

"Yes, sir. I was aware of something of the sort."

"All that's over now, and I've got what? Maybe three and a half years left. So I was wondering what you guys were working on. You always seem to have something going on. Anything you need my help with?"

"Well, there is one thing, sir. Let me ask first. Did you read the after-action report on the last trip to Vega to meet with the hive queen?"

"Yes. I wouldn't normally, but it was fascinating stuff."

"You may recall, then, that Barbara confronted the hive queen when the hive queen said we had stolen the interstellar technology. Barbara said they stole it as well, and the hive queen as much as admitted they did."

"Yes, I recall that, Mr. Bach."

"The question then arises, Mr. President, from whom did they steal it? We don't know. We're planning on sending a mission to go and find out."

"That is not a mission without risk, Mr. Bach. The Vegans have been interstellar for a long time. If they stole the technology, that means that other alien race is centuries, perhaps millennia, ahead of us."

"I know, sir. There's a countervailing consideration. If they have had such capabilities for hundreds of years – at least – and are still around, they must have learned how to live peacefully with each other. Perhaps they can live peacefully with us as well."

The president nodded.

"Are you and Barbara going on this mission, Mr. Bach?"

"No, Mr. President. Exploration is a young man's game. By the time our exploration ship is ready in five or six years, we'll be over fifty years old. So we're sending Jared and Daphne."

"Your kids?"

"Yes, sir. They're the only other people experienced with negotiating with aliens. And they'll have Arthur Vegan with them."

"That makes sense. All right. What do you need from me, Mr. Bach? Funding?"

"No, sir. We can cover that. We want this ship to have survivability. In case things go south in a big way. We're including a fast escape ship as part of the bigger ship. We also want to include missile capability. That last, however, we can only do with your permission."

"I see. What sort of missiles?"

"Gravitonic drive missiles. The only thing likely to work against another spaceship."

"I have two concerns there, Mr. Bach. One is that these missiles not be misused. One gravitonic drive missile launched from a couple million miles out could wipe out an entire city on Earth."

"The same can be said of any of the gravitonic drive ships, sir, and we have dozens of them spacing back and forth to the colony planets now."

"Understood, Mr. Bach. Most of those are under the command of former military people, are they not?"

"I believe all of them are, sir."

"Let's do the same thing here, Mr. Bach. Former military in command of those missiles. Better yet would be someone still in reserves."

"Understood, Mr. President. Not a problem."

"The other problem I have is simple to state. It is unlikely that my party will be able to hold the White House in the next elections. Normally the electorate switches off which party has the White House. Which means that your actual mission will likely be undertaken under the other party."

"Yes, sir."

"So I think we want to play a little subterfuge here, Mr. Bach. To keep you from being denied those missiles. Change a couple parts here and there, and give the result a new name. Something with 'defensive' in the title. And stock the ship with those missiles while I'm still in office, then keep quiet about them. You get me?"

"Yes, sir. I sure do."

"All right, Mr. Bach. Given those conditions, I'll get you your permissions. Plan on that."

"Yes, Sir. Thank you, Mr. President."

"Oh, thank you, Mr. Bach."

"Change a few parts, then call them defensive missiles?" Barbara asked.

"Yup."

"Sneaky."

"Yup."

"But we get our missiles."

"Right. It was the president who brought up the risks of this mission, so it was a pretty easy sell."

"Excellent. And a military man in charge sounds right to me anyway, Steven."

"As captain, yes."

"And who'll be the admiral?"

"Arthur will be, Barbara."

"OK. That's fair. And the kids?"

"Diplomatic mission. Ambassadors-at-large."

"Works for me."

"Thank you for meeting with me, Mr. Vegan," said Harriet Campbell, head of special projects engineering for Graviton Dynamics.

"No problem at all, Ms. Campbell."

Arthur took the offered chair.

"Call me Harry, Mr. Vegan. Everyone else does."

"And I am Arthur, Harry."

Campbell nodded.

"We've been all over the architectural plans for your new ship, and we have some questions for you, Arthur."

"Of course."

"Let's start with the missiles. We're going to need authorization to include those in this design, Arthur."

"Understood, Harry. The authorization is pending, but we'll get it."

"You're sure, Arthur?"

"The president committed it to Steven Bach last week."

"Good enough for me. Now, we need to talk about launchers and missiles. Every launcher takes up the volume of six missiles. If we gave you no launchers, and just filled these two decks with missiles, we can get maybe eighty missiles on board. Of course, you can't launch any of them.

"If we gave you ten launchers, you could launch ten missiles at a time, but you only have twenty missiles.

"Four launchers, Harry."

"So four launchers, and fifty-six missiles?"

"That sounds right to me."

"Why four, Arthur?"

"Assume half the launchers are out due to battle damage or mechanical failure. That still allows launches of two missiles at a time, and two near-simultaneous missiles is a much more difficult problem for a point defense than simply one."

Campbell raised her eyebrows and stared at Arthur for a few seconds, and he shrugged.

"I read a lot of science fiction," he said simply.

"OK, I think I agree with you. Four launchers it is. On to the next question, Arthur. You have two nuclear power plants and two gravitonic devices on the ship itself, and another two of each on the escape ship. Do we need four on the combined ship? We could use the two on the escape ship to power the combination, and not have any interstellar drive on the ship at all."

"Hmm. That's an interesting question."

Arthur thought about it for several seconds.

"I think we need all four, Harry. Let me explain why. The escape ship certainly needs redundant interstellar drive to be sure to get us home. That's for sure. Now, assume the main ship has one drive out due to battle damage or mechanical failure. It would still be of benefit to have one gravitonic drive operational."

"Why, if you have a working drive on the escape ship?"

"Because the main ship could fight a rearguard action as we got away."

"With no one aboard?"

"Yes. Either by remote control or under computer control. For that it needs one drive operational. So I think I want all four. We have plenty of room."

Campbell shrugged.

"Works for me. Not my money."

"What about timeframes, Harry? Are we still on track?"

"Two years to complete the detailed design, then a year – maybe a year and a half – to build. Yeah. We're still good there, Arthur."

"I guess I'm a little confused about the time to build, Harry. Isn't Graviton Dynamics rolling out a colony ship every month?"

"Yes, Arthur. A couple of points there. One is that the colony ships are built in parallel. One a month doesn't mean starting from scratch and completing a ship in a month. There are half a dozen or more on the line at any given time, in various stages of construction.

"The second thing is that this new ship will not be built on the colony ship production line. It will be built in prototyping. It's just too easy to make a mistake. Put this fastener in this hole, because that's the one the colony ship uses there, even though the exploration ship specifies a different fastener there.

"So it will be built in prototyping, which is not as fast because everything is a one-off. There are no production-line efficiencies."

"Ah. Very good. I knew there must be a reason."

"We'll get your ship built for you, Arthur. But to do it right is going to take some time."

"Very well. Thanks, Harry."

Jared

It was a year into the exploration ship project, and Jared had just turned nineteen, when he had a proposal for his parents.

"Mom. Dad. I think I should get an apartment on campus this coming school year."

"That sounds about right," Steven said.

"It's probably about that time, dear," Barbara said.

"I want to be able to socialize with my friends, and be a part of the campus scene, and— Wait. What?"

Steven chuckled and Barbara smiled.

"We just said Yes, Jared," Steven said.

Jared had one of those 'Who are you people and what did you do with my parents?' moments.

"Huh. I— I guess I didn't expect that."

"Clearly," Barbara said. "But we understand, Jared. It's that time. Let us know if you need any help finding a place."

"I liked my place when I was a student. Separate unit, with an outside door, not some cubicle in a big building, with hallways and all. You know. And a washer-dryer as part of the unit is a big plus."

Daphne had been watching all this with interest.

"Ahem," she said.

"You, young lady, are sixteen," Steven said. "Too early."

"Almost seventeen."

"Almost eighteen is much better, dear," Barbara said. "Wait a year. You can learn from Jared's experience."

Daphne opened her mouth to speak, then reconsidered. She effectively had permission to get her own place on campus next year. This year had been a serious long shot, and next year was pretty iffy. But she now had the go ahead for next year.

She decided to quit while she was ahead.

"All right. That sounds good. Next year."

Barbara nodded, and Steven looked thoughtful.

"We're going to be empty-nesters," Steven said when they were alone.

"Yes. That's normal. And it's that time, Steven. They aren't getting any younger, you know."

"Oh, I know, Barbara. But that was always something that was going to happen at some point, and now it's here."

"Yes. Other than Arthur, of course."

"Yes, of course. But Arthur's— Well, Arthur's different."

"You can say that again."

"No, you know what I mean, Barbara. He's no trouble. He's not our dependent. And he's always been a big help."

"I understand, Steven. But he's going on this trip, too, you know. Then it'll just be us."

"Yeah. For the first time, really. That'll be weird."

"Arthur, do you have a minute?"

"Sure, Jared. Come on in."

Jared went into Arthur's room and took a seat facing the alien as he sat at his display, going over the latest ship plans.

"I want to ask you a favor."

"Go ahead."

"I know you helped Dad be successful, uh, with the ladies. Back when he was single."

"Yes, that's true."

"Can you help me, Arthur? The same way?"

"Well, I can tell you what worked for your father, back in the day, Jared. Is that what you want?"

"I guess. Yeah."

"There's not much to it, really."

"I need to know, Arthur. I'm moving to campus, and I need to know."

"OK. Well, the first thing is to keep yourself in shape. Take your weights with you to campus. Walk or ride a bike to get around. Don't take a car."

"Won't the ladies prefer a car?"

"Not with someone who's not in shape. Jared, seventy-five percent of young men these days are overweight. Most of the rest don't take care of themselves. Staying in shape gives you a huge advantage."

"OK. What else?"

"Personal hygiene and grooming. Shower, shave, deodorant. Cologne or aftershave, brush your teeth, mouthwash. Fresh change of clothes. Every day."

"Every day?"

"Every single day. The only thing a woman has to go by when you ask her out is what's in front of her. So always be at the top of your game."

"OK. I guess that makes sense."

"And take your clothes up a notch. Dress just a bit better than everyone else. Set yourself apart."

"Anything else, Arthur?"

"Oh, we're just getting started. This next bit is the most important. Be their friend."

"Be their friend?"

"Yes. Don't talk about yourself. Boring. Ask about them instead. What they're up to. Where they're going. Care about them. Look out for them. Listen to them. Value their opinion. Treat them much as you treat your sister."

"But I don't want to treat them like my sister, Arthur. I

want— I want to have sex with them."

"You mean, you want to make love to them."

"Well, yeah."

"But sex is the easy part, Jared."

"It is?"

"Yes. Once they know you care, that you're not stuck on yourself, that you actually give a shit about them instead of just yourself, sex is the easy part."

"Oh. I can see that, I guess."

"And always make it an option."

"An option?"

"Yes. Be friends first. You want to stay overnight? OK. Or not? That's OK, too. Have sex? OK. Or not? That's OK, too."

"But I do want them to stay overnight and have sex with them, Arthur."

"Of course. But if they know you're friends first, and anything more is up to them, you'll get much more sex than if you're pushy, Jared. Trust me on this."

"Anything else, Arthur?"

"Yes. Learn how to cook. Nothing is more attractive to a woman than a man who can cook."

"Really?"

"Oh, yes. Otherwise, if the relationship goes somewhere, she's going to have to cook for you for the rest of your lives. Much better for her to be able to share the cooking. And when you invite a woman over to dinner, you're already alone in your apartment with them. Anything can happen, and often does."

"OK, that makes sense."

"You need several dinner dishes you know how to make really well, Jared. And at least one breakfast. Two would be better."

PUSH IN BOÖTES

"How do I learn to cook, Arthur?"

"Ask your father to teach you?"

"Really?"

"Oh, yes."

"Dad, can you teach me how to cook?"

"Been talking to Arthur, have you?"

Jared turned an alarming shade of red.

"Um. Yeah. Kind of."

Steven nodded.

"OK. We'll start tonight with something simple. Beef and onions with gravy, over noodles."

Another night, another lesson.

"OK, so far it's the same, right?"

"Yeah. Chop up the onion, and brown it and the ground beef."

"Right. But tonight, let's make it chili instead. You get the chili powder and garlic. I'll get the cans of diced tomatoes and tomato sauce."

Another night, another lesson.

"So this time we're starting with Italian sausage instead of ground beef?"

"Yes. For spaghetti sauce, what matters most is what Italian sausage you use. I prefer this brand."

"And we brown it with the onions like before?"

"Yes, and the tomatoes and tomato sauce as before. Even some garlic. But instead of chili powder, we add oregano."

"It's so simple."

"Most cooking is. It's just about getting the hang of it."

Breakfast was next.

"How about pancakes. Everybody likes pancakes, right?"

"OK, Dad. What do I do?"

"It's right there."

"I just follow the instructions on the box?"

"Couldn't be easier."

"Then why don't people have pancakes every day?"

"Cereal is easier."

"Not by much. I always thought cooking was hard."

Steven pulled the twenty-year-old dual-burner griddle – which had been a present from Barbara – out of the pan cabinet.

"Nope. People are just lazy. I mean, there are things that are hard to make, but mostly, people are just lazy."

Back to dinners.

"The solid beef cuts are next. Let's do steaks."

"OK, Dad."

Steven set the oven to broil.

"Line a thirteen-by-nine cake pan with aluminum foil. It makes it easier to clean."

"All right."

Once that was done, Steven put a cooling rack in the cake pan.

"The steak needs a way to drain while it cooks. Now place the steak on the cooling rack and season it. Salt, pepper, garlic salt, onion powder."

"All right. All done."

"Now put it in the oven. Notice the rack is one position down from the top position. You don't want it too close."

Jared put the cake pan in the oven under the broiler coils and closed the oven.

"Now it's four to six minutes a side depending on how thick it is and how you want it cooked."

"And that's it?"

"That's it."

The next dinner was more complicated.

"The other common solid beef cut is roasts."

"We're starting at two in the afternoon?"

"Yes. Pot roast is a little more involved. First we need to brown the meat on both sides."

Jared did that until he was satisfied.

"No, Jared. You want it really brown."

The second attempt met with approval.

"OK. Now add the chopped onions and celery, and a couple cups of water."

"All right. Now what?"

"Cover the pan, and turn the burner all the way down to the lowest level."

"OK, Dad. Now what?"

"We leave it sit and simmer for two hours, then, for the third hour, we add the diced potatoes and sliced carrots."

"Then what?

"Make a gravy and you're done."

"That's it?"

"That's it."

"Remarkable. I can't believe how easy this all is."

"Yes, but it makes a big impression, and most people love pot roast."

Jared started making dinner for the family a couple times a week.

"I have to get in practice."

He also started experimenting with other recipes, from one of his mother's cookbooks.

That under way, Jared popped in on Daphne one Saturday morning.

"Daphne, can you help me out this afternoon?"

"Sure, Jared. What do you need?"

"I'm not going to get anywhere with the ladies in ratty blue jeans and tee-shirts, so I need some help."

"Well, you probably would with some, but not necessarily the ones you want."

"Exactly. So I figured you could help me upgrade my wardrobe a bit. Or a lot. Give me a woman's perspective on what would be attractive."

"Playing dress-up. How fun! It'll be like playing with dolls."

Daphne looked at him critically, and Jared squirmed.

"You need to do something with the hair, too, Jared. And keep the mustache, but lose that sorry excuse for a beard. We should start with those, so we pick the right clothes."

"OK, Daphne. Whatever you say."

"Oh, this is gonna be fun."

"Jared's looking pretty upscale lately," Steven said.

"Yes. He's become an attractive young man," Barbara said.

"He's upping his game for the ladies, I think."

"Well, it's about that time, Steven. Late, if anything."

Steven nodded.

"Like me in that regard."

"Yes. It's good to see. And his cooking is really coming along."

"Make them dinner. Always a good play."

"Well, it worked with me."

"Like I said."

"It meant I didn't have to cook every night for the rest of my life. Speaking of which, since it's your turn, what are you making me for dinner tonight?"

Jared moved to campus the week before classes started. With the class hours he already had, this would be his senior year.

He got an apartment like Steven had had, with its own outside entrance. The end unit of a triplex in a low-rise complex. Not quite as cash-strapped as his father had been – to grossly understate the situation – he got a unit closer to campus. He could walk everywhere, and did not need a bike. When he needed a car – such as to visit home – he could call a self-drive cab.

That left the car they had shared to Daphne full-time.

"I like this situation already," she said.

Jared got a two-bedroom unit. Arthur had advised him that was a good idea if money was not an issue, because it gave him a junk room. That allowed the rest of the apartment to be neat and tidy, also a big plus with the ladies.

"If you wish, I can visit once in a while, Jared. I can stay out of sight in the junk room, but I have very good hearing. I can advise you on your conversation ability with the ladies. As I say, if you wish."

"Thanks, Arthur. I may take you up on that."

The other advantage of a two-bedroom unit in this complex was that it had its own washer and dryer. Wearing fresh clothes every day was going to generate a lot of laundry, so that was a big plus.

Jared came home every other weekend at first, but that soon tapered off as his social life picked up. They didn't see him at all between Thanksgiving and Christmas.

That said, he was very happy when he did come home.

When Barbara asked him at Christmas about his social life, Jared did not offer details.

"Good, Mom. Really good."

Daphne

It was after New Year's – and Jared's short visit over Christmas – that Barbara asked Daphne about him.

"How's Jared doing, Daphne? You see him on campus once in a while, and we've seen very little of him the last several months."

"He's doing good, Mom. He's got some guys he hangs out with, and it's a good crowd."

"Good. Excellent. And his social life? How's he doing with the ladies?"

"No worries there, Mom. Jared isn't lonely. Let's just put it that way."

"Oh, good."

That surprised Daphne. She tipped her head a bit and raised an eyebrow.

"There comes a time, my dear, when it's time," Barbara said. "I'd rather Jared have a little experience before he makes permanent decisions, you know?"

Daphne nodded. OK, that made sense. It also brought up another subject.

"Mom, how do I find somebody like Jared? Or Dad?"

"That's a good question. I would say the first thing is to stay away from people with self-esteem issues. Especially the passive-aggressive types. Those are the worst."

"Self-esteem issues?"

"Yes. Someone who doubts their own worth. You can't fix that. They have to. But they usually won't. Like the braggart. Who's he trying to convince? Not you. He was a braggart before you showed up."

"Yeah. I know some of those."

"Poison. But the passive-aggressive types are even worse."

"Passive-aggressive?"

"Oh, yes. And they can be absolute charmers. Over the long haul, they'll make you doubt your own sanity."

"How do you spot one?"

"Hmm. OK. Say a guy suggests a movie. A horror movie. And you say, 'I don't like horror movies.' A normal guy knows he can watch the horror movie on his own anytime he wants. He'll just say, 'OK, how about a comedy?' And he'll never suggest a horror movie again, because he knows you don't like them."

"OK. And a passive-aggressive type?"

"He won't leave it alone. 'Why don't you like horror movies?' 'You know, horror movies do great box office. Most people like them.' Like there's something wrong with you that you don't like them. Again and again and again. And the next movie he suggests will be, Guess what? A horror movie. He'll just keep picking at it until you give in. He can never let it go until he gets his way, whatever the topic."

"How do you deal with that?"

"Say goodbye and walk away. Immediately. You can't fix him. Passive-aggressive types see nothing wrong with their behavior. They won't ever change."

"So no matter how good-looking, or how charming, or how desirable in other ways...?"

"When you spot a passive-aggressive type, you walk away. Avoid them like the plague. That's not far off."

"Wow. Good to know."

"Oh, yes. The other thing you need to do, my dear, is go to the university health clinic and get on some form of birth control."

"I'm not having sex, Mom. I haven't really seen any good candidates for it yet. I'm just starting to think about it."

"That's the perfect time to start birth control. Before having sex. After is less effective. Trust me. Babies are always a blessing, Daphne, but at the wrong time they can be a mixed blessing at best."

"OK. I'll take care of it."

"Soon?"

"Yes. Soon."

"Good. See that you do."

Daphne was a little nonplussed by the conversation with her mother. She'd expected more of a 'No, don't do *that*' attitude about sex. Instead, her mother was telling her how to go about it. Maybe even encouraging her. What was with that?

Of course, a no-no-no attitude would be hypocritical, given her pleasure that Jared had an active social life with the ladies. One thing Daphne appreciated about her parents was that they weren't hypocritical about much. They were pretty clear-eyed in their views.

She just hoped she could meet a man as smart, as caring, and as noble as Jared or her father.

On everything else she was open, but on those things she would not compromise.

At the end of March, Daphne threw her parents a curve ball.

"Mom. Dad. I want to move to campus at the end of the semester."

"You're not even seventeen and a half yet," Steven said.

"Yes, but I'm ahead of myself."

"Yes, I know. That's what worries me."

Barbara laid a hand on Steven's arm on the table.

"Why at the end of the semester?" she asked.

"Three things, really. As far as the university is concerned, I'm already a sophomore. Have been for a while now. If I take classes over the summer, they will all be university classes. I'll be a junior in the fall.

"Second, summer session is always accelerated. I'll be on campus a lot. The back and forth will be much easier.

"And third, if I'm to have an apartment in the fall, I have to pick up the end of somebody's lease. Sublet the apartment over the summer. Because the leases run August first to August first. To have a lease in the fall, I have to pick it up in May.

"So I'll be paying for the apartment anyway. It seems silly to let it sit vacant all summer when it would be much more convenient than commuting from home."

"That's right. I remember that sublet business," Steven said.

"Where would you get an apartment?" Barbara asked.

"I was thinking in the same complex with Jared. He's got a nice place, and then we would be close."

"A two-bedroom?"

"Yes, because then I have a washer and dryer in the unit."

"I have one more question for you. Have you been to the health department?"

"Yes. Back in February. I'm on my second pack already."

"All right. Your father and I will talk about it."

Daphne hesitated. But she'd made all her best arguments already. Rather than say anything more, she nodded.

"OK. Thanks."

"What was that about the health department?" Steven asked Barbara later.

"I told her to get on birth control."

"Is she having sex with somebody?"

"No, but she's thinking about it. I told her to get on birth control before sex. Much more effective than after."

"I'll say. Especially if she takes after you. One try, each time. Boom. Pregnant."

Barbara nodded.

"So what do you think?" Steven asked.

"I'm leaning toward saying Yes. You gotta let 'em grow up sometime."

"But so soon?"

"It's not that soon, Steven. And she's right that she's ahead of herself. She's more mature than I was at her age, by a lot. She'll be a junior in the fall. It was just the beginning of my senior year that I accepted your marriage proposal, and you were by no means my first."

"I suppose. She's still just seventeen, though."

"Yes, I know. But she's talking everything out with us. She's taking our advice. And Jared will be close by. She'll be OK."

"All right, Barbara. I trust your judgment here. You understand women better than I do, by a bunch."

"Well, my own daughter, anyway."

Daphne moved into her apartment at the beginning of May. Summer classes had not started yet.

Daphne transferred her clothes, books, computer, and personal items, which took up a fraction of the space. She left her souvenirs at the house, along with a couple changes of casual clothes. She still had to get dishes, flatware, and pots and pans to stock her kitchen, as well as food.

With all that done, Daphne went over to Jared's that night for supper. He had just graduated with his bachelor's degree and would be starting his graduate degree in summer session.

He cooked for her, and he was glad to see her.

"So you're all moved?"

"Yes. Everything I have. I still need to get a bunch of stuff, like for the kitchen."

"Simplest thing is get two starter sets. You know, place settings for four. Same with silverware. Two sets. Then you get one set of serving bowls, one set of cooking bowls, a set of pans, and a set of cooking utensils. You're pretty set at that point, Daphne. Oh, and you need a cutting board and one good chef's knife."

"One knife? Not like one of those knife block sets?"

"No. Waste of money. You ever see those cooking shows? The guy's got one knife. That's it. Maybe a set of steak knives and a bread knife, but one sharp chef's knife is all you need for cooking. Oh, and a steel."

"A steel?"

"Yeah. The thing you rub the chef's knife on to keep it sharp. That's pretty much it. There's a good store for all that stuff. We could go tomorrow and have you all set up."

"That would be great, Jared. And I'm going to have to learn how to cook."

"When I have you over, you should come early. I can show you each time how to make whatever we're having."

"Hey, I don't want to cut into your social life."

"There are seven evenings in a week, Daphne. I'm good."

"OK, thanks for that, but there's another problem. All Dad's recipes make enough for four. When I cook, I'm going to have a lot of leftovers."

"OK, so we need to get you a set of storage containers as well. So you can save the leftovers."

"Oh, those plastic things."

"Plastic lids, yeah. But you get the glass containers, Daphne. You can take them out of the freezer or fridge and shoot them right into the microwave."

"The glass doesn't break?"

"It's a special glass. Borosilicate glass. Zero coefficient of thermal expansion."

"Huh?"

"It doesn't expand and contract with temperature. So temperature extremes won't break it. They come with plastic snap-on lids."

"OK. That sounds good, Jared. I appreciate the help. I don't want to ask Mom and Dad for help."

"Why not, Daphne?"

"I don't want them second-guessing their decision to let me move into town."

"Ah. Well, I don't think they would, but I understand the concern. You certainly don't want to be going to them all the time. But once in a while is probably fine."

"Yeah, but I want to save that for when I need them, Jared. Not routine stuff."

"Makes sense."

"Mostly I'm just going to keep my nose clean and study. No partying or dating or any of that. Not for a while. I want them to be happy they let me move. I have a heavy schedule for summer anyway."

"No dating? Sounds boring."

"Not really. You know I dated before. There was David. And Timothy. But I just don't need the hassle right now, and I don't want Mom and Dad to worry. But when I start dating again, I'm going to be interested in men, not boys."

"When you start dating again, you need to worry about birth control, Daphne."

"Already done. Mom told me to go, so I went."

"Huh. Smart, but I'm surprised Mom told you to go."

"You know Mom and Dad's history, Jared. They were no angels. Neither one of them."

"Yeah, I know. But when they get older, people seem to forget what it was like to be young."

"Oh, no. They remember. They remember all too well. That's what they're afraid of."

Jared laughed.

"Yeah, you're probably right."

With Jared's help with the shopping, Daphne got all set up in her apartment.

Summer school classes started two days later.

Construction

They were all together – Steven, Barbara, Jared, Daphne, and Arthur – for Fourth of July that year. They barbecued out behind the house, then watched the fireworks.

The city used the spaceport for the fireworks show every year, as the biggest open space available that had nothing flammable in it. Sitting in front of the old Graviton Dynamics corporate headquarters on the edge of the spaceport, they had the best view in town, and bathrooms and refreshments were mere steps away.

While colony ship traffic was getting heavier, along with freighter traffic to and from Vega, it was not a problem to close the spaceport to takeoffs and landings during the two-hour fireworks show.

Colony ship traffic increased because not only were more colonies being discovered by the survey ships, there were now up to three colony ships making the round trip to each of the established colonies.

Once a colony was established, what it needed most was manpower and supplies they couldn't yet manufacture on their own. These later colonists were not the early-adopter types of the initial settlers, but they were still go-getter types.

The freight traffic was also increasing as additional worlds of the bug-people signed up for peace and trade with the humans.

The colony ship design was used for this trade as well. The small cabins for the colonists on the upper deck proved well-suited to carrying animals – like beef calves and young sheep and pigs – to these alien worlds. For each cabin housing animals, the cabin across the hall was stocked with feed for them. Part of one floor was walled off for the animal caretakers who fed them. A water drip system for the animal cabins was mounted on the ceilings.

The return trade from Vega and the other bug worlds was similarly in livestock. All insectoid. They loved eating the manure of the outbound livestock, which also relieved the crew of mucking out the cabins. They air-conditioned the cabins and turned out the lights, and the insectoid livestock went into hibernation for most of the trip.

On arriving on Earth, the insectoid livestock wasn't useful for feeding humans, who largely disliked the taste. Instead, once ground up, they made excellent feed stock for Earth livestock, as well as being a great organic fertilizer.

They slaughtered the insectoid livestock just as they came off the ships, lest any get loose in Earth's biosphere.

Gold and other rare metals also came back from Vega, where they were cheap. Rare metals prices plummeted on Earth, but the industrial uses of gold, silver, and platinum, previously held back by their rarity and cost, blossomed.

It was in August of that year – the third year of the current president's second term – that Harriet Campbell called Arthur Vegan.

"Arthur Vegan."

"Hello, Arthur. Harry Campbell here."

"Hi, Harry. What's going on?"

"I have something you should see, Arthur."

"All right. What's a good time?"

"Today works."

"OK, Harry. On the way. Figure twenty minutes."

PUSH IN BOÖTES

"All right, Arthur. See you soon."

It was a nice day for a walk, so Arthur walked over to the Graviton Dynamics portion of the spaceport, to the building that contained prototype engineering. One of the big colony ships took off when he was on his way. It was always impressive to see a hundred-and-fifty-foot steel cube lift from the ground, with no noise or smoke, and ascend into the sky at thirty miles an hour.

Campbell's office door was open when Arthur got there.

"Good morning, Harry."

"Good morning, Arthur. Come with me."

They took the elevator to the first floor, where Campbell led him to a small motor pool. They took an electric cart, and set off across the spaceport.

"Where are we going?" Arthur asked.

"Prototyping."

The prototyping building was huge, if not as big as the production buildings further on. The production buildings typically had half a dozen of the big colony ships under way at one time, indoors. The prototyping building typically only had one or two ships under construction at a time, but it was still a large building.

Campbell and Arthur went into the prototyping building and walked across the small lobby to the elevators. They took an elevator up perhaps ten floors, then walked out onto an observation platform that looked out over the huge void in the center of the building.

There were two massive flat frameworks in the middle of the shop floor. A hundred and eighty feet on a side, they rode on hundreds of railroad wheels. More than a dozen railroad tracks ran in parallel from each, under a huge roll-up door to the outside. Called 'sleds,' the frames were to allow moving the finished prototype outside, because starting a graviton device inside the building was highly inadvisable.

On one of the sleds, a construction project was starting. Girders were laid out in a square-inside-a-square pattern. Workmen were checking dimensions and welding them together. It looked to be a hundred and fifty feet or so on a side.

"Is that what I think it is?" Arthur asked.

"Yes, Arthur. The design is complete. Construction is just beginning."

"Excellent."

Another person joined them. A burly man with red hair.

"Arthur, I want you to meet Angus MacDermott. He's the head of prototype assembly."

"Arthur Vegan, Mr. MacDermott."

"Call me Angus, Mr. Vegan."

"And then I am Arthur."

"Fair enough. I have a question for you, Arthur."

"Sure. Go ahead."

"What's her name? We usually give them their name when we start on them. It's good luck."

"Her name is *Beyond the Known Stars*."

"Aye. It's a little long, Arthur, but it works."

"You can just call her the *Beyond*, Angus. But *Beyond the Known Stars* is her full name, because that's where she's going."

MacDermott nodded.

Arthur looked at the other sled. On it, workmen were laying out a much smaller vessel, a square a hundred feet on a side.

"And there, Angus?"

"Your lifeboat, Arthur. Has she got a name?"

"Yes, Angus. Her name is *Earthbound*. Because if we need her, that's where we'll be headed."

"Makes sense to me."

MacDermott and Arthur shook hands.

"Please keep me informed of your progress, Angus."

"Aye. We'll let you know when anything big happens."

"And with that, it's out of my hands, gentlemen," Campbell said. "Arthur, Angus is your contact on this project going forward."

"Thanks for everything, Harry. I think it's a great design."

Jared, now twenty and change, and Daphne, just turned eighteen, came home for Christmas that year. They actually stayed for the whole week between Christmas and New Years. It was fun to all be together again, but, after a week, Steven and Barbara were happy to be back to being empty-nesters.

During that week, Arthur took them over to the prototyping building. They had heard the construction was under way, but they had not seen it.

The prototyping department was in shutdown for the holidays, but building security allowed them onto the viewing balcony. They walked out onto the balcony and Daphne gasped.

"Oh my God, look at the size of it."

"This is not the *Vegan Dreams*, Daphne," Arthur said. "This is based on the colony ship design."

"But it's so huge. Can that thing actually fly?"

"Oh, yes. She's lighter than a colony ship, but with the same engines. She accelerates faster than a colony ship."

"It looks like they already have the reactors mounted, Arthur," Jared said.

"Oh, yes. They build the ship around them."

Jared nodded as he took it all in. The framing was now all complete, and the entire one-hundred-and-fifty-foot cube of the ship was outlined and crisscrossed with steel girders. The plating was starting to go in on some of the decks now, while the plating of A Deck, the bottom of the ship, was already complete, a donut around the hundred-foot-square hole in the center for the lifeboat.

In the center of the ship, the sixty-foot-tall, eight-foot-square, containerized nuclear power plants stood side by side, stretching from the deckhead of C Deck all the way to the overhead of F Deck, just below the missile decks. There was no A Deck or B Deck below the power plants, as that was where the *Earthbound* would nest into the *Beyond*.

Looking over at *Earthbound*, Jared saw that the two nuclear power plants were horizontal and stacked one above the other in the center of the ship. Unlike *Beyond*, *Earthbound* was only two decks tall, so the power plants had to be horizontal.

"This is a lot of progress, Arthur."

"Oh, yes, Jared. They're going great guns on the ship. Another year or so, and she will be complete."

"That'll still be a year and a half before Mom and Dad think we're ready," Daphne said. "At least."

"The ship will go on other voyages first, to be sure she's ready, too. You don't want to take an untried ship and crew into troubled waters, Daphne."

Jared and Daphne nodded. They were halfway through the five-year period their parents had specified as a minimum for this trip. At that, they were doing well, and would be prepared in time.

That was the plan, anyway.

Jared, now twenty-one, had finished his engineering bachelor's degree in May, and was two years ahead of his age. He was in the graduate program now, and would likely have his doctorate in two and a half more years.

PUSH IN BOÖTES

Daphne, just turned eighteen, would be a second-semester junior in spring semester. She was almost three years ahead of her age. She would have her master's degree in international relations in another two and a half years.

Their educational attainment, however, was not what their parents were keeping an eye on.

After the first of the year – after the kids had headed back to campus – Steven, Barbara, and Arthur were comparing notes one evening after supper.

"Daphne sure is growing up in a hurry," Steven said.

"As Jared did last year," Barbara said.

"Yes," Arthur said. "They have left teenage behaviors behind. I think those behaviors are largely the result of living with one's parents."

"Living alone, they're responsible for themselves," Barbara said. "There's no one to remind them of things, or to hound them about things that need doing. They have to police themselves."

Steven nodded.

"After six, seven months of being on their own, it's really apparent," Steven said.

"It was a good move getting them out of the house when you did," Arthur said. "They are very much on track for the expedition."

"That's not why we did it, Arthur," Barbara said. "Not the only reason, anyway."

"Understood," Arthur said. "But it serves the purpose well. They will be ready to go when we have the expedition together."

"What do you think, Arthur? Another three years?"

"More like two and a half, I think, Steven. The ship will take another year to complete, and eighteen months is probably an optimum time for the crew settling in and shakedown of the ship."

Steven nodded.

"You're likely right, Arthur. They'll be ready to go by then."

"They and likely their partners," Barbara said.

Steven raised an eyebrow, and Barbara shrugged, then he nodded.

"Yes," he said. "You're probably right."

Completion

"Come in, Captain," Barbara said.

"Thank you, ma'am," Frank Proxmire said.

Proxmire came into her office in the headquarters building of Graviton Dynamics and took the chair she waved to.

Barbara consulted some papers on her desk.

"To review, Captain. You retired from the U.S. Space Force at forty-two, after twenty years service. You took a position as captain of a survey vessel for Graviton Dynamics, serving in that role for two years. You then transitioned to colony ships, and have captained the *Star Gazer* for the past year, making the circuit to Stanhope. You remain in the ready reserve for U.S. Space Force.

"Is that all correct, Captain?"

"Yes, ma'am. That's correct."

Proxmire wondered where all this was going. It sounded like he was either going to get fired or promoted, but he couldn't decide which. Not yet. Then again, if he was being fired, it wouldn't take Barbara Bach to do it. The chairman of the board of Graviton Dynamics had better things to do.

"Very well, Captain. I have a new ship for you. She comes off the sled in two months."

"A survey ship or a colony ship, ma'am?"

"Neither, Captain. She's a new ship type, coming off the sled from prototyping. In size and mass, she is most like a colony ship, but she is designed from the keel out as an exploration ship. And she's armed."

"Armed, ma'am?"

"Yes, Captain. She's effectively a Q-ship. Four graviton-drive missile launchers, with fifty-six on the rails."

"That's a lot of firepower, ma'am."

"Yes, it is, Captain. Which is why the President of the United States is requiring she be captained by a military officer who's still in the reserves. Without that, we don't have permission of the president and the Department of Defense to arm her."

"I understand, ma'am."

"She is capable of twelve gravities. She also mounts an escape ship capable of forty gravities.

"Her ultimate mission will be to make contact with a new alien race we know exists. We do not yet know what they are or where they are. Finding out those things is part of the mission. That information is confidential, not just to Graviton Dynamics, but to the Department of Defense, to which your oath still applies."

"I understand, ma'am."

"Your reporting structure on that mission will be to Arthur Vegan. He will act as something of an admiral for the mission. Will you have any problems reporting to an alien, Captain?"

"No, ma'am. I don't believe so."

"Good. Acting as ambassadors to this new race will be my son and daughter, Jared and Daphne Bach. They are the only people other than Steven Bach and I who have first-contact experience."

She was sending her kids on this mission? With a start, Proxmire realized the level of trust that implied.

"Yes, ma'am. Thank you, ma'am."

Barbara nodded.

"You are to assemble a crew, Captain. The best you possibly can. You have carte blanche on Graviton Dynamics and the U.S. military. After last week's election, the White House will be changing parties in January, so you have just two months of priority on military crew members. You should therefore expedite your selection.

"You will then have eighteen months of lesser assignments to shake out ship and crew before the ultimate mission leaves.

"Your new ship's name is *Beyond the Known Stars*, Captain, because that's where you're going."

Capt. Frank Proxmire USSF (retired) stood relieved, effective immediately, from his current command, the *Star Gazer*. He went to the prototype engineering department and pulled up the engineering drawings of his new ship, *Beyond the Known Stars*.

Proxmire noted the crew size, both ship's crew on the command deck, Deck F, and the hospitality crew on the passenger deck, Deck D.

Best to concentrate on ship's crew.

Proxmire's priority hires were the executive officer, the ship's engineer, and the chief non-commissioned officer. Everything else could wait for now.

Once he had those key personnel, they could help him with the rest.

Arthur, Jared, and Daphne went out to look at the ship between the holidays, as they had last year. The ship had been painted just before the holiday break, and they could smell fresh paint from the viewing balcony.

Of course, the bottom plating had been painted over a year ago, just after it was installed, when the bottom framing of the ship had been stood on end for the plating process.

Despite the holiday break, one workman was painting the ship's name, several feet tall, high on the right of each side of the cube. Unlike a normal colony ship, on which the name was painted in white in block letters, this name was painted in gold in a beautiful calligraphy script:

Beyond the Known Stars

That was real gold in the paint, too, given that gold was now so cheap. Against the navy blue of the ship's color – not battleship gray like the colony ships – it stood out splendidly.

"She's beautiful, Arthur," Daphne said.

"Do you really think so?"

"Oh, yes."

Arthur turned to Jared.

"She's a splendid ship, Arthur," Jared said.

"I'm glad you think so. I'm pretty pleased with how she came out, myself."

"So now what happens, Arthur?" Daphne asked.

"They'll take her out of the building and stock her for her trials. They'll be the normal space trials, where they stay close enough to Earth that radio transmissions work and we can go out and rescue the crew if something goes wrong."

"And then?"

"Eighteen months of other assignments before we go on the big mission."

"Eighteen months? You're sure of that, Arthur? Not thirty months?"

"No, it's eighteen months."

"Do Mom and Dad know that schedule, Arthur?"

The alien turned from his regard of the ship to look at Daphne.

"It's your mother who set the schedule, Daphne."

"Yes!"

"Wait a minute. I don't get it. What just happened?" Jared

asked.

Daphne turned to him.

"You remember when Mom and Dad said we were too young for the mission?"

"Yes. I think they were right, by the way."

"So do I. They said six years. Maybe five. Well, they've decided. Five it is."

"Ah."

Jared thought about it.

"Oh, shit," he said.

"What?"

"I need to get going on this doctoral degree. I only have eighteen more months."

"You? What about me? I just turned nineteen, Jared, and I'm graduating at the end of this coming semester. I've got like a year for the masters degree."

"I thought you were taking some courses for grad credit already."

"I am, but the masters degree is normally two years."

"Better get cracking, Daphne."

"Maybe I can still add another class this semester."

They rolled sled on *Beyond the Known Stars* the first week of January. It took several hours for the sled bearing the ship to make its slow way out of the prototyping building to the end of the rails, moving the ship a hundred yards clear of the building.

At that point, the gravitonic drive was engaged at a low enough setting to hold the ship in buoyancy against gravity, a few feet clear of the sled. The engineering crew used thrusters to move the ship to a pad where it could be stocked for its trials.

Later that same day, they rolled sled on *Earthbound*. She was also lifted just clear of the sled and transferred to a pad for stocking.

The two ships would undergo their trials separately, and be united only once their individual trials had been passed.

The outgoing president called Barbara Bach the second week of January, a week or so before the inauguration of the new president.

"Hello, Ms. Bach."

"Hello, Mr. President."

"I see you launched the exploration ship."

"Yes, sir. *Beyond the Known Stars* is undergoing her space trials now."

"I would caution you to transfer those missiles before the inauguration, Ms. Bach."

"They're already aboard, sir."

"And her captain?"

"U. S. Space Force ready reserve, sir."

"Excellent. How does accounting show those missiles, Ms. Bach?"

"In inventory, sir."

"An accounting error, Ms. Bach?"

"No, sir. *Beyond the Known Stars* is not a government-owned ship, like the survey ships and colony ships. She's ours. And the missiles are shown as in inventory, in missile storage location number three."

"Missile storage location number three?"

"Yes, sir. That is, the missile decks of *Beyond the Known Stars*. Inventory management is the responsibility of the vendor, Mr. President. You know that."

The president laughed.

"Very good, Ms. Bach. I just thought to check. I should have known you were on top of it."

"As you say, sir. Good luck in your retirement."

"Thank you, Ms. Bach."

Captain Proxmire settled back in the command chair on the bridge of *Beyond the Known Stars*.

"All right, Mr. Fogerty. We have our window. Take us up."

"Aye, Sir."

Beyond the Known Stars lifted off the pad and was soon rising at thirty miles an hour, straight up into space.

Three hours later came the announcement.

"Ninety miles now, Sir."

"Check barometric readings on all compartments."

"Aye, Sir."

Beyond the Known Stars was divided up into airtight compartments. Every compartment door had an air-tight hatch. The corridors had air-tight hatches periodically along their length. All had been secured for this takeoff on her maiden voyage.

It was a situation Proxmire was familiar with. He had served in the U.S. Navy for ten years before transferring to the U.S. Space Force. This vessel was intended to fight if it had to, and some familiar precautions had been taken.

"All compartments show one atmosphere, Sir."

"Unsecure air-tight doors Class C and Class D."

"Aye, Sir. Unsecuring Class C and Class D."

Class D were the corridor doors. Class C were the compartment doors on each deck. Class B doors were hatches between decks, which usually would remain secure. Class A doors led outside the ship.

"Class C and Class D doors unsecured, Sir."

"One hundred miles now, Sir."

"All right, Mr. Fogerty. Bring engines gradually to twelve gravities along our plotted course.

"Aye, Sir. Twelve gravities, easy."

Proxmire watched the gravity meter climb as the ship increased her acceleration.

"Now making twelve gravities, Sir. She actually has a little left, Sir."

"That's all right, Mr. Fogerty. I'm perfectly happy staying within the design specification."

"Aye, Sir."

Barbara Bach watched from her office window as *Beyond the Known Stars* settled to the pad. It had been a couple of days since she had set off on her space trials, to circle Mars and return.

The ship was ready. Next would be assignments to get the crew ready. After that was to make sure Jared and Daphne were ready – by no means a foregone conclusion.

Then the mission would begin to find a new alien race.

The one the bug-people had stolen the gravitonic drive from.

Romance

It was early in the morning. They were lying in bed, nude, arms and legs all atangle. Both were awake, although just barely so.

"Jared?"

"Mmm?"

"You seem awfully available lately."

"What do you mean, Lena?"

"I mean, whenever I say 'Let's do this tonight,' or 'How about dinner tomorrow evening?' you say, 'Yes.'"

"Is that bad?"

"No, but— Jared, are you seeing anybody other than me?"

"Not currently, no."

"Not that I'm complaining, but why not?"

"I don't need anybody else, Lena. I'm happy."

"Well, if we're going steady, shouldn't you let me know?"

"Why?"

"Jared, what if I were seeing other people?"

"That's up to you, Lena. What you do when you're not with me isn't really any of my business."

"No jealousy?"

"No. What's the point? I'm happy to be with you when we're together. What you do when we're apart doesn't matter."

"What if I want to go steady with you, too?"

"That's fine. Your decision."

"Jared Bach, you are one strange person."

"Thank you. I think."

Lena laughed.

"Look. Lena. There's something I need to tell you."

"So tell."

"In another year or so, I'm leaving."

"Leaving the university?"

"No. Leaving Earth. I don't know for how long."

"Leaving *Earth*?"

"Yes. So it wouldn't be fair of me to get deeply into a relationship with somebody just to abandon them."

"Where are you going, Jared?"

"I don't know. I'm going on a mission. We've been planning it for years. Working toward it. And now it's almost here."

"And you're going alone?"

"No. My sister is going. Others. But I'm one of the key people. And we don't know how long it will take."

"Can you take someone with you? Me, for example?"

"It could be dangerous, Lena. Will be dangerous, in fact. I wouldn't want to expose someone else to that."

"Yet you're going."

"Yes. It's important."

"It must be."

She disentangled herself, and sat in tailor seat on the bed, thinking. Jared put his arms behind his head and considered her.

Lena Stox was not conventionally beautiful, in the perfect, chiseled-face manner, but was very attractive. She kept in shape, and had a nice figure. She also had a lot of the 'girl next door' thing going on, and Jared found that pleasing as well.

Further, she was a practical, grounded person. She had not been bothered by his carrying a firearm at all times, but found it interesting that he considered it necessary, or at least desirable. She shared cooking duties with him when she came over, and was handy in the kitchen. She was a senior, and her major was in business administration.

For her part, Lena was thinking through what Jared had said. The significance. The implications.

"You need a ship, obviously."

"We have a ship, Lena."

"A colony ship or a survey ship?"

"Neither. A custom ship has been constructed for the purpose."

"A custom ship? Who's in charge of this mission?"

"I am. Rather, I and my sister Daphne and Arthur Vegan."

"Arthur Vegan. And a custom ship…. Wait a minute. You're *that* Jared and Daphne Bach? Your parents are worth like a trillion dollars or something?"

"Yes, that's right."

"Oh, shit."

Jared and Daphne had both been common names twenty years ago, and Bach wasn't that unusual as a family name, so it wasn't surprising that Lena hadn't known who Jared was. He certainly didn't act like a bazillionaire, or what Lena thought a bazillionaire would act like, anyway. He was just a regular guy. Did his own cooking. Was going to school like anybody else.

Wait a minute.

"Your parents were behind the university allowing students to conceal carry, weren't they? Because a lot of universities don't allow it."

"Yes. That was for Daphne and I."

Lena nodded. A lot of things made sense all of a sudden.

"So what's your mission, Jared?"

"That I can't tell you."

"Truly?"

"Truly. I'm sorry."

Lena shrugged.

"That's OK, Jared. Is it OK if I worry about you, though?

You and your sister?"

"Sure, Lena. You can worry about us."

"Good. I will."

She lay back down alongside him.

"In the meantime, let's celebrate life while we have it."

She pulled him to her, and they made love again.

Lena was sitting at the kitchen table and Jared was making pancakes.

"Jared. Something I don't understand. With all that money, you could just send out for food whenever you wanted. Have someone cook for you, for that matter. Yet you cook for yourself."

"My parents still cook for themselves."

"Really."

"Of course. Would you rather have cold, rubbery, take-out pancakes or the real thing, Lena?"

"OK. I get that."

"As for having someone cook for you, that comes with all its own baggage. You've just turned a cooking problem into a personnel management problem. And now you don't have your space to yourself."

"That makes sense, Jared. It just seems weird. With all that money...."

"But that's not what money's for, Lena. The important thing about money is what you can do with it."

"Like build a custom spaceship to go on a secret mission."

"Yeah. Like that. I mean, I don't have to worry about paying for college and stuff, and that's nice, but I don't really think about the money."

"Most people have to think about money, Jared."

"Yes. I know. I suppose I'm spoiled rotten."

He served them both pancakes and sat down to the table with her.

"Spoiled but not rotten, Jared. And besides, you make great pancakes."

Later that day, back in her apartment, Lena looked up Jared and Daphne and Steven and Barbara Bach. She ran down several bunny trails, following all the leads and links.

Lena was trying to figure out how she felt about Jared, now that she knew about his gaudy family connections. It shouldn't make a difference, but it did, somehow. Before, she had been seriously interested in him as a permanent romantic prospect. Now she wasn't so sure.

As she read, Lena got sucked in. It was a terrific story. A couple of working-class kids who had made it, in a really big way. They had gotten started by standing up for Arthur Vegan to the hive queen, at the risk of their own lives. They stole the technology base that, with a lot of hard work, had made them wealthy.

As Lena was reading, though, something didn't jive. How the hell did an agrarian, feudal society come up with the gravitonic drive? She made the intuitive leap that Barbara Bach had made seven years ago about the bug-people and the gravitonic drive.

Who had *they* stolen it from?

Lena called Jared.

"Jared Bach."

"Jared, Lena. I know what your mission is."

"Not over the phone. Come on over. I'm just starting dinner."

"I'll be right there."

It was only a fifteen-minute walk, and it was a pleasant fall evening. Jared let her in, then raised an eyebrow.

"It's my business background, Jared. How does an agrarian, feudal society come up with the gravitonic drive? Answer: it doesn't."

Jared nodded.

"That's what my mother concluded seven years ago, Lena."

"And your mission is to go out and find the alien race the bug-people stole it from."

"In brief, yes."

"Then you need me, Jared. You need me to go along."

"Lena..."

"Neither you nor Daphne nor Arthur Vegan have any business experience, Jared. I know. I checked. It's a mission need, and you don't have it."

Jared considered.

"So do we go as a couple, Lena?"

"We could, Jared. Or not. I was seriously interested in you as husband material before I knew about the money. Now I'm not so sure."

"The money's a turn-off?"

"Yes. Big money comes with its own share of problems. Problems I'm not sure I want. You and Daphne both carry all the time. I understand that, but I'm not sure I want to. I mean, I get guns. My mom's a firearms instructor. I can shoot. But right now, it's an option. For you it's not, is it?"

"No. Not so much."

Lena nodded.

"And how would I ever know who my friends are? That it's not just the money? So the money's not an attraction. I'm not a gold-digger, Jared. And I don't need your money. I can support myself just fine, thank you very much."

Jared nodded. He had had those thoughts himself. Then again, he had no choice – he was who he was – whereas she did.

"I understand, Lena."

"So what's the next step?"

Jared shrugged.

"Meet the parents, I guess."

"Oh, shit."

For Daphne's part, the graduate-level courses had not proved as hard as she had feared. Unlike Jared, who had held back because of the coming mission, she took it as a deadline. With just a year left to go until departure, she was seriously on the hunt.

The problem was separating the wheat from the chaff.

First, no fatties. If they were overweight now, what would they be like in ten years? Or twenty? Or forty? No way she wanted to deal with the health problems that would attach to that.

There were the 'one time Charlies,' the guys who just wanted another notch in the bedpost and then move on. Daphne wasn't interested in just sex, and they were usually pretty easy to spot. A couple of dates with no serious action and they moved on.

There were the passive-aggressive types her mother had warned her about. She found a way to turn those up pretty quickly. Whatever a guy proposed for a first date, Daphne proposed something else. If they said, 'Oh, all right, sounds good,' that was one thing. If they argued with her for their choice, out they went. I mean, for a first date, what did it matter, other than winning? She didn't need that.

Daphne also crossed off anybody who knew she was *that*

Daphne Bach. There were male gold-diggers, too, she knew, and she didn't want to have to deal with that.

Daphne was picky enough it was good she had a lot of choices. The combination of her mother's good looks and her father's rugged masculinity had produced in Jared a young man with strong features in a good face.

In Daphne, it had given her the best of both worlds. Stronger features and darker coloring than her mother's soft femininity, but with her mother's dazzling smile. Together with her mother's figure and a little more of her father's height, it was a winning combination.

That smile got attention from the men she wanted to pay attention.

As fall semester wore on, one fellow in particular got her attention. He was also a second-year grad student, perhaps three years older than Daphne, who was way ahead of her age. He had done his undergrad at another school, so it was just his second year in town.

Their first 'date' was coffee one afternoon after classes were done for the day. It turned into dinner as well.

Robert Drake was just so easy to talk to, within minutes Daphne felt like she'd known him for years. He was just so, so… comfortable. That was the word.

Robert – she didn't call him 'Bob' – was a computer science major, specifically in AI applications. So another engineer, like Jared or her father, but not in mechanical engineering or physics like her brother and father.

Robert had traveled extensively, and had funny stories of different places. But it wasn't a one-way conversation. He seemed most interested in finding out about her.

When she let him know that she carried a firearm – part of

her sorting process; if someone objected, out they went – he allowed as how he did as well. He asked what gun she carried, then commended her choice.

"That's a nice piece," he said. "Small, powerful, reliable."

"Yes, for a woman, it's about the most you can carry comfortably. It's only nine millimeter, but that's about as big as I can go without printing."

Robert nodded.

"What ammo are you using?"

"Plus-P jacketed hollow points."

"That's a good self-defense round. Even in nine millimeter."

"So I get why I'm carrying. Woman on campus and all that. Why are you carrying?"

"My father was afraid I might be something of a target. One reason I came here for grad school is I can carry on campus."

"Why would you be a target?"

Robert hesitated. He hadn't been forthcoming about his background other than his travels. He sighed.

"My father is Forester Drake, the multi-billionaire."

Daphne stared at him wide-eyed.

"Yes, I'm *that* Robert Drake."

Daphne broke out laughing, while Robert looked perplexed. She laughed so hard, she couldn't say anything for several minutes.

"I'm sorry, Robert," Daphne eventually said, gasping and wiping the tears from her eyes. "You see, my parents are Steven and Barbara Bach."

It was his turn to stare at her wide-eyed.

"Yes, I'm *that* Daphne Bach."

Robert guffawed at that. It was just too ridiculous.

Then again, neither of them had to worry about the other being a gold-digger. At some level, what's the point?

For their second date, Daphne had Robert over to her place for dinner. Not take-out or delivery, but a dinner she cooked.

"It's one of my father's recipes," she explained.

"Well, this is great."

After dinner, they got into some serious making out on the sofa in her living room. At one point, breathing hard, Daphne pulled back from him.

"I'm sorry, Robert. You should probably leave now, before I do something I'm not ready for."

"That's fair. I'll see you again?"

"Oh, yes."

"Good. It's my turn to cook for you."

She raised an eyebrow, and he shrugged.

"My father taught me to cook. He's an old-fashioned, self-made man. He thinks a man should be able to cook, to shoot, to change a flat. 'Be competent,' he told me. When I asked, 'At what?' he said, 'At everything.'"

"He sounds like my father. More, like my grandfather. And you listened."

"Yes, I did."

Robert nodded at her as he tucked in his shirt.

"Next time, my place."

For their third date, Robert cooked for Daphne at his apartment. His apartment, like hers and Jared's, was a triplex, low-rise sort of thing. It was not super luxurious or anything – not extravagant spending – but it was neat and tidy. Robert had some souvenirs of his travels about, on tables or hanging on the walls.

Robert cooked her a stir fry, something her parents never did. They ate it with chopsticks. It was very good.

After dinner, they once again got into some serious making

out on the sofa in his living room. At one point, Daphne got up, took his hand, and led him to the bedroom. She started to undress.

"Oh, no, Daphne dear. Let me unwrap my present."

They undressed each other, lying there on the bed, taking turns. An item here, an item there. Taking their time.

"You are very beautiful," he whispered to her when they were both nude.

"Robert? Be gentle. It's my first time."

He raised an eyebrow, and she nodded.

"I've been so busy with school, and no one I met was worth it. Until now."

"I am honored, milady. And birth control?"

"All taken care of."

He was gentle. It was dreamy.

Daphne woke in the morning, tangled up with Robert. He was still asleep. She looked at him. His face. His body. He was fit, and handsome, in a rugged sort of way. Like Jared. Like her father.

He woke at some point, looked at her and smiled. She smiled back.

"Again," she said, pulling him to her. "And this time, you don't have to be so gentle."

She winked at him, and he laughed.

"Robert, there's something I need to tell you about."

"OK. Shoot."

"Sometime next year – end of the summer, I think – I'm leaving Earth. I don't know for how long."

"You emigrating to a colony, Daphne?"

"No. It's more of a mission. But I don't know how long it

will take."

"Can you use a good AI guy?"

"Actually, we probably could. But it's dangerous, Robert."

"Not suicidal?"

"No, not suicidal. Dangerous. There's maybe a ten percent chance things could go terribly wrong."

"You need a ship, Daphne."

"We have a ship, custom-built for this mission."

"What's the mission?"

"I can't tell you, Robert. Not without permission."

"Who's going on this mission?"

"My brother and I and Arthur Vegan. It's very important. We've been planning it for years."

"Do your parents know about this, Daphne?"

"My parents are sending us. It's that important."

"Then I'm in."

"Robert, you don't even know what it is."

"Doesn't matter. If you think it's that important, I believe you."

"Well, we have to discuss it with my parents."

"Fair enough."

Daphne gave him a hug.

"It would be great to have you along."

Robert nodded.

"Maybe I can impress my father for once," he said.

When Daphne left after breakfast, Robert read up on Steven and Barbara Bach. Then he logged into his favorite AI.

"Maria, analyze the public ship-building records of Graviton Dynamics. What gravitonic ships are not colony ships or survey ships?"

"There are two. *Vegan Dreams* and *Beyond the Known Stars*."

"Which is newer?"

"*Beyond the Known Stars* is the newer vessel. It began service last year."

"What type of ship is *Beyond the Known Stars* listed as?"

"*Beyond the Known Stars* is listed as an exploration ship."

What the hell were they exploring?

"Maria, analyze available public data on the planet Vega. What anomalies or inconsistencies emerge?"

The AI chewed on that one for a while. It took seconds.

"The biggest anomaly about the planet Vega is how a medium-tech, agrarian, feudal economy was able to field computers and gravitonic-drive technology."

"Maria, do you have any idea how they were able to do that?"

"Yes, Robert. There are several analogs in history, the most familiar being the American Indians. They were a Stone Age people – not a metal using society – yet they had steel knives and firearms obtained from European settlers. Proposing a similar mechanism here, the technology was either a gift, or the Vegans purchased it, or the Vegans stole it."

"A gift, a purchase, or a theft, Maria?"

"Yes, Robert."

"From whom?"

"That is unknown."

Robert nodded. OK, so he now knew the mission.

Go out and find the more advanced high-technology race from whom the Vegans got their tech base.

Sounded like fun.

The Holidays

"Hi, Mom."

"Hi, Jared."

"I'm bringing someone with me for Thanksgiving, if that's OK."

"Of course. Is this the long-rumored Lena?"

Jared laughed.

"Daphne's been talking out of school, I see. Yes. Lena Stox. She wants to talk to you about joining the mission."

"What does she know, Jared?"

"Well, I told her I was leaving Earth for a period sometime next year, and she guessed the rest."

Barbara raised an eyebrow, which Jared could see on the video call.

"She made the same intuitive leap you did seven years ago, Mom. She's a business major. She figured it out."

"And are you two a permanent number?"

"I don't know, Mom. She's put off by the money. By the hassle of it."

"Yes, I can see that. Well, we'll have a full table. Daphne is bringing Robert."

"He's a good man. I'm really happy for them both."

"So is that a permanent arrangement?"

"I think so, Mom. They both want it to be. And, Mom? He figured it out, too."

"Another business major, Jared?"

"No. Robert's in AI applications. I think he used an AI to figure it out."

"Hmm. Well, we'll talk when you all get here. Not on the

phone. In the meantime, just a quick note."

"Yes?"

"As I told Daphne, we are not in the habit of specifying the sleeping arrangements of our adult guests. That's up to you."

"Thanks, Mom. I appreciate it."

"Of course, Jared. See you next Thursday."

"Wednesday evening more like. After supper."

"Anytime is fine, Jared."

Given the way her parents had treated Steven and her back in the day – was that really thirty years ago? – Barbara could see no other option with her own kids.

She remembered very well what it was like to be young.

"So what are your folks like, Jared?" Lena asked.

"I don't know. Like parents anywhere, I think. There's no difference just because they have money."

"Huh. Well, I don't think most parents wouldn't tell us we can sleep together in their house."

"But we're adults. None of their business, in their mind."

The rental self-drive pulled up at the guard gate at the back entrance of Spaceport USA. Jared presented his photo ID, one of the guards checked it and handed it back. The gate went up and the car proceeded through.

"And most parents don't have armed guards on their driveway."

"That's because the house was here first, then the spaceport grew up around it."

"What's this building?" Lena asked, waving at the original Graviton Dynamics headquarters.

"That's the original spaceport, believe it or not."

"And now?"

"It's ours. We sometimes use it for stuff. It has a pool table."

The car drove through the parking lot, then took a small lane into the woods, winding around a couple of corners before it arrived at a small house set into the trees.

"Oh, it's so cute. You grew up here, Jared?"

"Home sweet home. My folks rented it from the fledgling company when they were getting started, and they never left."

"Well, that says something, I guess."

They got out of the car. Jared got their bag out of the trunk, then he dismissed the car. It negotiated the turnaround, then set off back to town.

Jared opened the front door and waved her past him into the house.

They were sitting around with coffee after a small dessert.

"So you don't quite know what to make of the money side?" Barbara asked.

"Oh, it's not that, Barbara," Lena said. "In some sense, I do know what to make of it. I'm just not sure I want it."

Barbara nodded, and Lena continued.

"The security issues. The expectations issues. The friends issues. How do you even know who your friends are, and that it's not the money?"

"Jared solved that last one by not telling anyone who he was. No need for them to know, really."

"Yes, but while Jared was a pretty common name twenty years ago, Lena wasn't. Jared and Lena Bach? That would be hard to hide."

"If somebody brings it up, you can just say, 'Oh, that's not us. All that money? Wow. I wish.'"

"I suppose. And the security issues? I'm not sure I want to pack heat the rest of my life. And armed guards on the house?"

"That one's harder, Lena," Barbara said. "And packing

heat's the least of it. You mentioned the gate guards. There's also the security cameras – both visible and infrared – that cover the grounds. The AI that monitors them twenty-four-seven. Active patrols of the perimeter. The hot response team from the guard center. The dogs, which are highly trained for personal-protection."

Jared looked surprised.

"I never noticed any of that," he said. "They were just dogs."

Steven had been quiet. He stirred now.

"Does a fish notice water?" Steven said. "It's just the environment he swims in. He takes it for granted."

Barbara nodded.

"There's a reason we never moved from this house once Spaceport USA built up. We're within its security envelope. Don't get me wrong. We love this house. But it was an easy decision for other reasons."

Lena nodded.

"So Jared's a much bigger package than he would be otherwise, and I'm just not sure how I feel about that."

"Good," Barbara said. "I would be more worried if you hadn't thought it through. But if there's any questions you ever have for me, just give me a call."

"Thanks, Barbara. I just might do that."

Daphne and Robert showed up then, but it was getting late. After the barest of introductions, everyone took their leave of one another and went to bed.

Daphne woke up in the queen bed of her old bedroom and had a few moments of disorientation.

Had it all been a dream?

Then Robert moved, and the moment passed.

She snuggled up to him and went back to sleep.

Breakfast on Thanksgiving morning was eggs and bacon. No one wanted to eat pancakes or anything heavy that would compromise their appetite for Thanksgiving dinner that afternoon. Steven was cooking, but Robert stepped in to handle the bacon so Steven could concentrate on the eggs.

After breakfast, they talked about the mission.

"So you both figured out what the mission is?" Steven asked.

"I just looked at Vega, and economically it didn't make any sense that they would have such advanced technology," Lena said.

"It's public record that *Vegan Dreams* and *Beyond the Known Stars* are the only two graviton ships that aren't colony or survey ships," Robert said. "The most recent of them is listed as an exploration ship. So what's to explore? I asked my AI what if anything was anomalous about Vega, and it gave me the answer. No way should they have such advanced tech. It was either a gift, a purchase, or a theft."

"You both want to go on the mission, despite knowing it could be dangerous," Barbara said. "What are your skill sets?"

"I'll have the business degree in June," Lena said. "There's nobody on the mission now who has a business degree. If the talks get to trade and such, they'll be at a loss. Also, my mother's a firearms instructor. I'm a very good shot."

Barbara turned to Robert.

"My degrees are in computer science, specifically AI applications," he said. "I'm very good at getting an AI to give good answers to poorly specified problems. My father believed a man should be a generalist. So I'm also handy with tools and such. And weapons."

"Which weapons?"

"Long gun and hand gun, both target and tactical. Archery.

Fencing. Even a bit of javelin."

"Interesting," Barbara said. "You both have desirable skill sets, and would make the team stronger. That you both figured out the mission – each with your own specialty – speaks to your abilities there.

"And you both know it could be dangerous, right?"

Lena and Steven both nodded.

"That said, we don't think it's going to be *that* dangerous. Vega, based on the age of its infrastructure and the size of its population, has to be hundreds of years old. It's a colony for the bug-people, which means it's been hundreds of years since they obtained the gravitonic drive.

"A super-aggressive and warlike third intelligent race would have conquered or killed off the bug-people by now, or perhaps killed themselves off. So we think that is unlikely.

"The other possibility is that the bug-people's home world is a high-technology society. We haven't been there, so we don't know. Perhaps only the colony worlds are agrarian and feudal.

"But we don't think so. The feudalism is sort of built into their biology. Feudalism is based on the idea that some people, by birth alone, are better than others. The nobility, so-called. But for the bug-people, that's true. The queens and drones are different than the workers, who are asexual.

"So I expect the bug-people's home world to be more of the same. And one thing feudal societies aren't good at is technical advancement. Too much of the possible brain pool is essentially off-line."

"But surely we have to go there to check," Robert said.

"Yes. We think we should," Steven said.

"If this mission is potentially dangerous, why are you sending Jared and Daphne?" Lena asked. "I wouldn't think you would want to send your own kids."

"We don't," Steven said. "But there's no one else we would trust to get it right. Further, they are the only people in the world with alien contact experience other than Barbara and I. And we're simply getting too old for this sort of thing."

"As it is, we've put off this mission for five years until they were old enough to attempt it," Barbara said.

"So, are we in?" Robert asked.

"I think so," Barbara said. "Steven and I have to talk about it alone."

Robert nodded. Just like his parents.

At that point Arthur Vegan came in, just returned from another trip. He walked into the kitchen.

"Hi, everybody."

"You made it," Steven said.

"You didn't think I would miss out on turkey, did you?"

"Gosh," Lena said.

Robert considered the six-foot alien in silence.

"Arthur, I would like you to meet Lena Stox and Robert Drake," Jared said.

"Very pleased to meet you both," Arthur said.

He held out his hand and shook hands with each in turn.

"Hello," Lena said, still a little speechless.

"Nice to meet you," Robert said.

Arthur nodded, then went over to the counter and poured himself a cup of coffee. He came back to the table and sat down.

"So are they going along?" Arthur asked Barbara.

"We think so. We'll talk later, Arthur."

"Very good. So when does the turkey go in the oven?"

Daphne had been lounging in a pair of old flannel pajamas for breakfast. She headed back to her room to dress for the day, and Robert followed along.

"So you're going," Daphne said.

"She said 'I think so,' Daphne. Not 'Yes.'"

"Yes, but that's Mother. She won't say Yes until she's positive. And for that, she needs to talk to Dad alone. But the answer will be Yes."

After Thanksgiving dinner, the two young couples went over to the old headquarters to play pool. Steven, Barbara, and Arthur sat in the living room.

"So what do you think, Barbara?" Steven asked.

"I think we should probably green light them all going," Barbara said.

"They certainly have useful skill sets. I think we lucked out there."

"I'm more impressed by them as people, frankly. Lena's got a head on her shoulders, and she's not afraid to use it. Her head is holding her heart in check at the moment. And Robert, for all his parents' wealth, is not spoiled. He jumped right in to help you with breakfast."

"He was great help with dinner as well. He knows his way around a kitchen."

Barbara nodded.

"A parent always worries, but I sense our worries were misplaced," she said. "They chose well."

Steven nodded, then turned to Arthur.

"What about you, Arthur. Do you have any concerns?"

"Just one, Steven. Daphne has matured a great deal, and has good instincts as well. However, she is almost three years younger than the other three. I worry they will not take her counsel. That she will somehow end up the lesser of the four, due to the age difference."

"Interesting point," Steven said, and raised an eyebrow to Barbara.

"There's a way around that, I think. Make Daphne head of mission. The ambassador. Everybody can have all the input they want, but it's her decision. She's got the most pertinent degree anyway."

"Do you think that would work, Barbara?"

"Of course. Jared defers to her a lot already. You've seen that. Robert would as well. And Lena is so level-headed, I don't have any concerns there."

"Fair enough. Let's do that, then. Are we agreed?"

Barbara nodded, and so did Arthur.

"Done," Steven said.

When the young couples came back to the house, they all sat around the kitchen table.

"We've come to a decision," Barbara said. "All four of you can go."

Jared and Robert exchanged high-fives, while Daphne and Lena nodded to each other.

"It's on one condition, however. With four of you, someone has to be the decision-maker. That will be Daphne. She has the most pertinent degree, she can parley with the hive queens as an equal, and it will keep the three older of you from ignoring her opinion. She will be the ambassador. When push comes to shove, Daphne will decide."

Robert and Lena both nodded. They knew it would be one of the Bachs. Jared thought about it, then he nodded as well. It was Daphne who was nonplussed about it.

"Oh, gosh. I'm not sure I'm up to that," she said.

"That's the strongest possible sign that you're the right choice," Steven said.

Barbara nodded.

"Daphne, you'll have everyone else to consult with, including Arthur. You'll do fine."

"I suppose."

The Christmas holiday was much more laid-back than that momentous Thanksgiving. They had settled into being family, and it was a joyous time.

Lena still had her misgivings about the downsides of extreme wealth, but she kept them to herself. Meanwhile, her relationship with Jared had become very comfortable.

He really was a sweetheart.

Preparation

After the holidays, time seemed to fly. Spring semester saw all four of the young people buckling under to get their degrees finished before the mission. There was no desire to leave anything unfinished behind them.

They were busy enough not to go out to the house for spring break or the Easter holiday. They all four pushed hard on their studies right through the breaks.

The work paid off. All four graduated in May. Jared got the doctorate in mechanical engineering, Daphne got her master's in international relations, Robert got his master's in computer science, and Lena got her bachelor's in business administration.

After two weeks off to decompress, they started in on the preparations for the mission.

Beyond the Known Stars came into port in the beginning of June. Her crew was given sixty-days leave before the big mission.

Steven and Barbara took them on a tour of the ship after she had been in port for a couple weeks and basic housekeeping had been done.

They drove out to the ship in one of the ubiquitous electric carts.

"Are we there yet?" Robert said.

Jared laughed.

"I never appreciated just how big these ships are," Robert continued. "It seems like we should be right on top of it, but it's still a ways to go. It's like we're never going to get there."

"It's bigger than I imagined," Lena said.

PUSH IN BOÖTES

Jared and Daphne had seen the big colony ships up close before, so they just nodded.

When they got to the ship, they went on into Deck A through one of the open hatches. Service people were in and out of the ship constantly, servicing and testing systems on the ship before loading her for the mission.

Steven and Barbara took them through the ship one deck at a time. Deck A, full of mechanical systems, plus the air locks containing the shuttles, one large and one small. Deck B, more mechanicals, the water tanks, the recycling systems. Deck C, the long-term storage of things like spare parts and tools, the machine shop and all its paraphernalia.

Deck D was the residential deck for passengers. That drew a lot of interest, as it should.

"This is basically where you'll live for as long as the mission takes," Steven said.

"Bedroom suites, living room, dining room, galley," Barbara said. "Also, the living quarters for the kitchen and housekeeping staff for this deck."

"I'm going to feel like Captain Nemo, aboard the Nautilus," Robert said.

"Yes, it's set up for taking wealthy people out on safari or whatever, so it's pretty fancy," Barbara said. "Still, it's important that you arrive rested and in good spirits. There will be some tough negotiating to be done, and you should be at your best."

"It will also be your entire world while in space," Steven said. "There is no other place to go. There's no outside. No cafes or restaurants or friends' houses. This is it."

Robert nodded. A sobering thought.

Deck E was the stores deck. Service people were cleaning out the remaining stores from the prior trips, defrosting chest freezers, emptying shelves, cleaning out refrigerators. Two of the many chest freezers were being replaced, as well as one of the refrigerators.

"I'm surprised you don't have a cold room," Robert said.

Steven shook his head.

"Single point of failure. Imagine if the compressor went out. If a freezer fails, though, everything gets moved into one or more of the other freezers. You don't lose anything. Same with the refrigerators."

"OK. That makes sense. And they all have temperature monitors on them?"

"Of course."

Deck F was next. The command deck. They toured the bridge and the captain's day room. The map room, with its big display table. The mess and galley. The rec room. The crew quarters.

"All single cabins for crew?" Lena asked.

"And two-room suites for the officers," Barbara said. "Yes. For a potentially long voyage like this mission, crew comfort is important to efficiency. Carelessness is to be avoided at all costs."

On up to Deck G. Robert looked around at all the huge missiles in their racks. Automated racks from the look of them. Nobody was going to move them around by hand.

"What are these?" Lena asked. "Why are they so big?"

"Graviton-drive missiles," Steven said. "Each one has a full-size nuclear power plant and a gravitonic drive."

"Missiles? Does the government know about this?" Robert asked. "I wouldn't think the current administration would approve."

"Oh, they wouldn't," Barbara said. "But they know we have these fifty-six missiles in inventory. They're on the books. This is their inventory location."

Lena laughed, and Barbara turned to her.

"This is the real utility of large amounts of money, Lena," Barbara said. "To continue operations, whether the government is involved or not. Approves or not. We are continuing to roll colony ships, even though the government – this government – is not currently paying us for them. The next administration will."

"Don't they try to stop you?" Lena asked.

"Oh, yes. I have an entire law firm worth of attorneys to foil those attempts. *Beyond the Known Stars* is not a government ship, Lena. She's all ours. They've tried to ground her, and the courts have stopped them. They have no statutory authority to interfere with a private ship."

"You're effectively spacing a Q-ship, without authorization," Robert said.

"The U.S. Constitution actually anticipates privately-owned armed ships, Robert."

"It does?"

"Absolutely. In Article 1, Section 8. 'The Congress shall have Power to grant Letters of Marque and Reprisal.' Who are you going to grant them to, if there are no privately-owned armed ships?"

"Fair enough. And the missiles are officially not here."

"They're in inventory location number three. Which is right here. See. There they are. In inventory. Like I said."

Barbara turned to Lena.

"And *that's* why it's nice to have large amounts of money. So you can do the things that need doing, whether somebody approves or not."

Lena nodded and looked thoughtful.

Later on, the four were alone at Jared's apartment.

"Your mother's one hell of a rules mechanic, Jared," Lena said.

"Oh, yes. Especially when this party is in office. For that matter, she had the prior president's approval for everything she's doing."

"The turnover in the White House means nothing then?"

"The problem is that the White House turns over every four or eight or twelve years. The Graviton Dynamics effort has been ongoing for thirty years. She takes the long view."

"And in the long view," Daphne said, "She will get approval for everything she's done."

"Once the White House turns over again."

"Yes," Jared said. "Hey. Five of the last six terms have been the pro-space, pro-Graviton Dynamics party. She doesn't expect the current administration to last past four years."

"And if it does?"

"That's what all those attorneys are for," Daphne said. "Tie things up in court until the next administration gets in."

They each took turns piloting a shuttle into space and back. It was the first time into space for Robert and Lena. Jared and Daphne had gone to Vega with their parents seven years before.

They each took someone along for the trip, to help if they got confused or flustered. As it was, though, they each did just fine. The shuttle pretty much flew itself. It was simply a question of giving it the right commands.

"That was something," Robert said. "Get in the minivan and drive it to space. Awesome."

"It was scary, though," Lena said.

"Yeah, but you did fine," Jared said.

"Well, I didn't kill us. I suppose that's something."

"There ya go," Jared said.

One part of the training was to be trained in all the available languages that were part of Lingua Zinga's portfolio currently. The company, which had been Steven and Barbara Bach's first company and had funded the early efforts of Graviton Dynamics, had a branch office in the Graviton Dynamics headquarters.

That branch office was necessary because of all the colonists, including especially those immigrating to the U.S. for the sole purpose of taking part in a colony expedition, who needed to learn English.

Jared and Daphne each had several of the major languages in hand already, while Robert had perhaps half a dozen due to his travels. Lena had not learned any languages other than English.

"One thing I don't understand," Lena said. "Why all these languages? Like Hungarian, for example. Why do we need that?"

"Hungarian's actually a bad example," Daphne said. "It's unrelated to any other human language. Who knows? Maybe they learned it from visiting aliens."

"I suppose," Lena said, but she sounded doubtful.

One day during a break in training, Robert Drake went upstairs in the General Dynamics headquarters building to see Barbara Bach.

"Yes, Robert. What is it?"

"Ma'am, I think there's something we should take along."

"All right. What do you need?"

"An AI platform."

"Every computer has AI in it now, don't they?"

"Yes, ma'am. A simple one. I think we need much more horsepower. The issue is, the unit I recommend is perhaps ten million dollars. That's the one with the comm package."

"That's the one you recommend?"

"Yes, ma'am."

"Will there be power or air conditioning issues?"

"No, ma'am. It has its own air conditioning, and the power consumption isn't that bad."

"All right. Just let Purchasing know what you need, and I'll sign off on it."

"Yes, ma'am. Thank you, ma'am."

Robert let himself out of her office.

Barbara initially wondered why he had called her 'ma'am' rather than 'Barbara,' but then again, he was calling on the chairman of the board of Graviton Dynamics, not on his friend and potential mother-in-law, so it made sense.

Robert was something of a stickler on etiquette issues.

Robert stopped by the Purchasing Department on his way downstairs.

"Yes?"

"I have a system that needs to be purchased."

Robert reached into his pocket and pulled out a paper. The clerk reached out for it, then looked at it with little interest.

"This is ten million dollars."

"Yes. And we're going to need expedited delivery on these units."

"Of course you do."

This wasn't going well. How to light a fire under it?

"It needs to be here at least a week before the departure of *Beyond the Known Stars*. Two would be better."

That got his interest, at least.

"Requisitioner?"

"Barbara Bach. She's waiting for your paperwork to sign off on it."

"Of course, sir. We'll get right on it."

That was better.

Barbara Bach had some unfinished business as well. Her secretary came up with a phone number that should work.

She dialed the number. A man approaching sixty years old answered the video call.

"Forester."

"Hello, Mr. Drake. This is Barbara Bach. We need to talk."

The AI unit came in two weeks before *Beyond the Known Stars* was set to space. Robert supervised installing it in the sitting room of one of the unoccupied suites of the ship.

It was the size of a large side-by-side refrigerator and weighed even more. A refrigerator, after all, was mostly empty, whereas the AI unit also had a refrigeration compressor and was crammed full of processor blades. Robert had specified the fully optioned unit, and there was no empty space within it.

Of course, one big issue in using even a trained AI is access to databases. But there would no access to anything on Earth. They would be out of light-speed communications range of the Earth for the whole trip.

It thus came down to what databases Robert took along. The downsides all accumulated on not taking enough data, so Robert had also purchased a database server unit for the AI. It was in the same size cabinet, and weighed as much, for the same reasons. This unit was full of high-density solid-state memory.

Petabytes of it.

They installed both units in the same room. Luckily, the nuclear reactors that powered the graviton drive could produce plenty of power. And on a steel spaceship, one never knew where one would need to use an arc welder to make repairs or modifications.

Each space on the ship therefore had a dedicated two-hundred-forty volt, fifty-amp circuit run to it. Each two-room passenger suite had one. That was enough to run either cabinet, but not enough for both, so Robert had workmen run a drop from the next unoccupied suite to the one with the two machines – the AI and the database server – in it.

So as not to interfere with the air-tight hatches on the spaces, they ran the drop through the wall, then sealed the pass-through so a leak in one suite wouldn't affect the other. That air-tight seal was tested by closing the air-tight hatch on one suite and pressurizing it, then watching for leakdown.

Once all the installation work was done, Robert fired up both units and ran them through their self-tests. That done, he began loading databases.

A lot of databases.

They were staying in Jared's and Daphne's apartments as the clock clicked down toward departure. They were a bare half a block apart in the same complex, and they usually had dinner and spent the evening together.

"So did your toys all come in?" Jared asked.

"Yes," Robert said. "Both cabinets, with all the bells and whistles."

"Excellent. What are you doing now?"

"Loading databases."

"What databases?"

"Any I can get my hands on. Which, with Graviton Dynamics' subscriptions, means a lot of them."

"Is that a copyright infringement?" Lena asked.

"No. The subscriptions include the right to make a local copy for use by the subscriber."

"Nice."

"Yeah. There were some key issues to work through, but I got all those straightened out. Now the worry is whether they'll all load in time."

"Over Graviton Dynamics' network connection?" Daphne asked. "That's a lot of databases."

"Yeah. Like I said. Looks like we'll make it, though."

"If it's important enough, we can delay the launch," Jared said.

He looked over to Daphne, and she nodded. That would, after all, be her decision.

"No, I think we're going to be OK," Robert said.

To Vega

It was the beginning of August – when the four new graduates would normally be getting ready for fall-semester classes – when the crew of *Beyond the Known Stars* returned from leave.

The ship was loaded for the mission already, and the crew started taking inventory, testing systems, and getting ready for the mission. They lived in crew housing on base rather than in the ship. There would be enough of that very soon.

The four completed their training four days before departure, and spent the time preparing their wardrobes for the trip. They were taking most of what they owned, but there were purchases to be made. They didn't, after all, know what weather conditions would be on any planets they visited.

Their penultimate evening on Earth, they went out to eat at a nice restaurant near campus. Something of a last hurrah.

The night before departure, they spent a quiet evening together, retiring early.

Steven, Barbara, and Arthur were sitting in the living room of the pretty house in the woods the night before the departure of *Beyond the Known Stars*.

"So what did we forget?" Barbara asked.

"Nothing I can think of," Steven said.

Steven looked to Arthur.

"I cannot think of anything, either. The preparations have been most extensive. We've been planning this for years, and all my notes of what we needed to take have been filled."

"OK, then. I guess they're good to go."

"Big difference between this time and our first time going," Steven said. "All we had was the clothes we were wearing and the things you grabbed from my dresser."

"Yes," Barbara said. "So long ago. Still we did OK. Hopefully you guys do as well on this trip, Arthur."

Also the night before departure, a sleek gravitonic-drive private plane touched down at the Spaceport USA airport. Unlike private jets in the past, this plane had no wings and the cabin was large, the size of one of those big buses set up as a motor home. In fact, it could be driven as a motor home on the highways.

With a small nuclear power plant in the rear, and a small gravitonic drive amidships, such devices were very expensive, just as private jets were back in the day. The counter to its expense, though, was that it was big inside. There was no being crammed into a tiny cabin. There was a master bedroom, a kitchen, a living room, and one could stand fully upright.

The crew stayed in transient crew rooms on the spaceport grounds. The passengers spent the night in the motor home, with all the comforts of home.

The morning of departure there was a going-away brunch in the offices of the chairman of the board of Graviton Dynamics. The conference room was pressed into service for this special event. The sideboard would act as buffet.

Jared, Daphne, Robert, Lena and Arthur all got there early. They were talking and laughing, at least some of which was due to pre-launch nerves.

"Why so many chairs?" Lena asked.

"I think that's just the normal compliment of this room," Jared said.

"Eleven? Seems an odd number."

Servers came in and started fussing the buffet, placing chafing dishes – both iced and heated – and beverage dispensers on the sideboard. They were completed before the official time of the brunch. Most left, but a couple stood by in case there were problems or requests.

At the official time, Steven and Barbara walked in from her conference room down the hall. They were followed by Ken and Patty Stox, and Forester and Claudia Drake.

"Mom! Dad!" Lena said.

She rushed forward to greet her parents. She had not seen them since the graduation two months before.

"Dad?" Robert asked.

Forester walked up to his son and shook his hand. The Drakes had not attended the graduation, nor had Robert expected them to. It was not that they were estranged, exactly. More that there was never time to get together. His father was always so busy, and Robert had been busy as well.

It had been very hard on Robert when his mother had died when he was twelve of uterine cancer. His father had remarried fifteen months later, and Forester Drake had been lucky in both his marriages. Claudia Drake was a tender, loving woman who had come along when young Robert needed her most. He called her Mom, not in spite of his birth mother, but to honor the woman who had stepped in for her.

"I wanted you to know, as you go on this mission, how very proud I am of you," Forester said.

Robert swallowed hard twice.

"Thanks, Dad," he managed to get out.

Claudia came up to him then, and gave him a hug.

"He is, you know," she whispered in his ear.

Robert drew back from her and addressed them both.

"Dad. Mom. I'd like you to meet Daphne Bach."

Robert hesitated, then continued.

"My intended."

"It's good to meet you, Mr. Drake," Daphne said.

"Forester. Please," Forester said as he shook her hand.

"And I'm Claudia. Pleased to meet you, Daphne," Claudia said as she shook Daphne's hand.

"It's good to meet you, Claudia."

There was a flurry of other introductions. The Stoxes had met Jared, Daphne, Robert, and Arthur at the graduation, so that simplified things somewhat. Forester and Claudia had some hesitation about Arthur, but that was to be expected, and they warmed up to the well-spoken and considerate alien quickly.

"All right, everyone," Barbara said. "We should eat while everything's hot."

At that, the two remaining servers removed lids from chafing dishes. There were crepes, and Belgian waffles, and eggs Benedict. There was ham and beef and bacon. Coffee and orange juice. Toast and muffins.

Nobody needed to tell Jared twice, and he started off the buffet line, everyone else queuing behind him.

"I meant to ask you details of this mission, Barbara," Forester said. "I know it's important, and not without its risks, but what is it, exactly?"

Barbara nodded.

"We've kept the purpose of the mission secret, lest we be forbidden from pursuing it in some way by the current administration."

Forester nodded, as did Ken Stox.

"Sensible," Forester said.

"We know that the bug-people stole the graviton-drive technology from someone, Forester. It's time we go out and figure out from whom they stole it."

"Ah. Another intelligent race?"

"Or their home world. We're not sure. We think it's probably a third intelligent race."

"And the administration would try to stop you?"

"We're not sure. We'd rather not find out. But once *Beyond the Known Stars* leaves, there's nothing they can do about it."

"Couldn't they send another ship after them? Or order you to call them back?"

"There are a number of problems with that plan, Forester. First is that we can't call her back. They'll be out of light-speed communications reach. Second is that *Beyond the Known Stars* is faster than any equivalent ship. And third is that *Beyond the Known Stars* is a Q-ship. An armed commercial vessel."

That got raised eyebrows from both Forester and Ken.

"An armed ship couldn't chase her down?" Forester asked. "They can't make a faster ship and send her out with similar weapons?"

"Several problems there, too, Forester. Who would make a faster ship? Why, Graviton Dynamics, of course. Where are the specifications, the bid requests, the budget? That defense procurement could take a while to square away. As for arming such a ship, where would she be fitted with missiles? Why, right here, of course. I'll have to check our inventory. I'm not sure what we have in stock locally."

"Locally, Barbara?"

"Yes. The missile room of *Beyond the Known Stars* is our inventory location number three, and she's not in-system at the moment."

Forester chuckled. Barbara continued.

"The final problem is that we don't know where they're going. The first stop, yes, of course. After that, though, we have no clue."

"Good. You've covered your bases."

"Always."

"Barbara Bach, it's a pleasure to know you."

They had the luxury of tarrying over brunch, as *Beyond the Known Stars* would not lift until after one. NASA had a window for them, and that's when you left.

The conversation drifted around, though never touched on the mission again. It was just a pleasant brunch with friends and family.

Then it was time to go to the ship.

The goodbyes were at the Deck A entrance to the ship.

"All right, you five," Barbara said. "Take care of yourselves, and take care of each other."

"You all come back to us, now. You hear?" Steven said.

"Always remember how proud I am of you," Forester told Robert.

"I will, Dad."

"Good luck, dear," Claudia said to Robert. "Use those AI things you do to help out however you can."

"I will, Mom."

"Mom. Dad. We'll see you soon," Lena said to her parents.

"OK, dear. You take care," Patty said.

Ken didn't say anything, just shook his head and gave Lena a big hug.

Then they went on into the ship and the hatch closed. The parents all got back into the electric cart and removed themselves a safe distance from the ship.

Ten minutes later – when the NASA window opened up – *Beyond the Known Stars* lifted off the pad and headed into the sky at thirty miles an hour.

It was soon out of sight.

Three hours out, NASA gave them clearance to increase acceleration.

"Bring us easy to twelve gravities, Mr. Fogerty," Captain Proxmire said.

"Aye, Sir. Twelve gravities, easy."

Proxmire watched the acceleration gauge on his display climbing.

"Twelve gravities now, Sir. Still straight up."

"Steady as she goes, Mr. Fogerty. We won't come onto course until we've passed the geosynchronous orbit."

"Aye, Sir. Steady as she goes."

It had taken them three hours at thirty miles an hour to make ninety miles in altitude. But at twelve gravities, twenty-two thousand miles and change didn't take long. It was barely fifteen minutes later that Fogerty reported.

"We've passed the geosynchronous orbit, Sir. NASA has released us."

"Very well, Mr. Fogerty. Bring us to charted course for Vega."

"Aye, Sir. Coming to course for Vega."

The minutes passed as *Beyond the Known Stars* changed her vector.

"On course now for Vega, Sir."

"Very well, Mr. Fogerty. You have the conn."

"I have the conn. Aye, Sir."

Captain Proxmire went down two decks to the passenger

deck. The elevator dropped him out in the living room. All five of his passengers were there, watching their progress with the external cameras piped into the big display there.

Proxmire walked up to Arthur.

"Departure procedure is complete, Sir. We are now on course for Vega."

"Excellent. Well done, Captain."

"Any further instructions, Sir?"

Arthur looked over to Daphne, and she shook her head.

"No, Captain. Our time to the tunnel?"

"About two and a half days, Sir."

"And to Vega, Captain?"

"A little over ten days, Sir."

"Very well, Captain. Carry on."

"Yes, Sir."

Proxmire saluted and left.

Some people might have had problems serving under an alien commander, but not Space Force Captain Frank Proxmire. Arthur Vegan wore the Presidential Medal of Freedom, and they didn't exactly give those away.

Not under the previous administration, at least.

"What do we do now, other than sit around for ten days?" Lena asked.

"I'm going to ask the AI to lay out the possible responses of the hive queen to our request for information on where they got the gravitonic drive technology," Robert said.

"And then Arthur and I need to work out what our replies are to each of her possible responses," Daphne said. "Things will work out better if we have our replies ready."

"And I could eat," Jared said.

"You can always eat," Daphne said.

"How can you eat anything after that terrific brunch we had?" Lena asked.

"Hey, that was brunch. It's coming up on dinner time."

Both galleys on *Beyond the Known Stars* – the passenger deck galley and the crew deck galley – were operational. It wasn't long before dinner was announced.

After all, the galley crews had to eat as well, and they hadn't been at brunch.

"Oh, that was great," Daphne said. "It's too bad we didn't put a gym on the ship, because I'm gonna turn into a blimp. That's one thing we forgot."

"But there is a gym on-board, Daphne," Arthur said. "We added it at the request of one of the people who leased the ship over the last year and a half."

"No kidding? You're gonna need to show me, Arthur. Later. Not now."

They stayed up late the third night aboard to watch the tunnel form.

"See that black circle?" Daphne asked.

"Barely. It's so thin," Lena said.

"Keep watching it."

Lena watched for several minutes.

"It's getting thicker."

"It's actually a black tube, Lena. Were getting closer."

"There's a tube in space from Earth to Vega?"

"We're creating it. By our speed. By churning dark matter. Something. But it's the secret to actually getting there in a finite time."

"I don't get it, Daphne."

"I don't either, Lena, but it works."

The mouth of the tunnel grew larger and larger, then passed

by them, receding into the distance behind them.

"Oh, my gosh," Lena said.

"Yeah, I imagine the first person who passed into the tunnel was pretty freaked out," Daphne said.

"Gee. Ya think?"

The entrance to the tunnel shrank behind them until space around the ship was completely black save for a small circle ahead that held Vega and a small circle behind that held the Sun.

"How long are we in this thing?" Lena asked.

Jared shrugged.

"About five days, I think," he said. "It was faster for us the last time we went, but *Vegan Dreams* is a smaller ship and much faster. Not suitable for a long journey."

"Too bad. This could get unnerving."

"Nah. You get used to it."

Vega

After two and a half days, *Beyond the Known Stars* reversed thrust and began decelerating, but her passengers didn't notice. The gravity in the cabin did not change.

After five days, the ship exited the tunnel and Vega lay ahead.

When the exit of the tunnel approached and then shot past them, Lena was happy. She watched the tunnel recede behind the ship.

"Thank God," she said.

"Every trip," Jared said. "No big deal."

"Well, the first time it's pretty upsetting, OK?"

"No doubt."

Ahead of them lay the star Vega. They couldn't see the planet Vega yet. The planet was actually Vega-2 – the second of four planets in the system – but everyone just called it Vega.

Beyond the Known Stars settled into orbit around Vega. Since there were now cargo flights back and forth from Earth to Vega, there was a protocol for requesting and receiving an orbital. There was also a way to contact the planet.

There had been advance word sent via one of the freighters that an ambassador from Earth would be visiting.

Arthur had Captain Proxmire patch him through to the planet. He spoke in Vegan.

<The ambassador from Earth has come calling on hive queen [name]. The ambassador – an Earth hive queen – has now arrived. Please inform the hive queen's drones that she is here.>

<Very well. We will let them know.>

PUSH IN BOÖTES

The hive queen's name was unpronounceable by humans and untranslatable into English. But Arthur had to specify which of the hive queens on Vega they had come to visit.

The one with whom they already had a relationship.

Arthur Vegan's old hive queen.

A recorded message came back within the hour.

<We will notify Her Majesty when she awakens.>

"That is what I expected, actually," Arthur told the others. "The hive queens spend a lot of time sleeping. Days at a time."

"Well, at least we don't have to sit down there in that waiting room of theirs," Daphne said. "We can wait up here."

"Yes," Jared said. "Much more comfortable. And the food is better."

"No argument there," Arthur said.

Two days passed. During that time, Daphne and Arthur kept reviewing their projections of what the hive queen might say, and their arguments for countering them.

What if she didn't know how they got the technology? Could she give them some clue to act on? Were there archives that might contain such clues? Would she assist them, or not? Give them access to those archives?

What if she did know? Would she tell them, or would she refuse? If she refused, why did she refuse? Was there something binding her against telling them? Did she want to stymie their search for some reason? Could they argue around that reason, and get her to tell them anyway?

The whole thing was a huge unknown. There was simply no way to find out but to ask.

A recorded message came in just after noon ship's time.

<The hive queen has awakened. You may call on her today.>

"It's early morning at the hive queen's palace. Should we go and attend Her Majesty?" Arthur asked.

"Yes," Daphne said. "Let's go."

The trip down to the palace was uneventful. The shuttle had the coordinates of the landing pad of the hive queen's palace from their last trip. All five of them went down to the surface. Jared piloted, which was no more than specifying the landing pad's coordinates to the computer which flew the shuttle.

Once they were down, a Vegan came out to meet them. He was a worker like Arthur.

<We are calling on Her Majesty.> Arthur said in Vegan.

<You are expected. Follow me.>

The palace Vegan led them into the palace. He led them along corridors and up ramps, higher and higher in the palace. Daphne was relieved that he was not leading them to the waiting room as before, but to the antechamber to the hive queen's chamber.

Daphne understood the ramps in a flash of insight. There couldn't be stairs. When the hive queen left her palace to attend the Convocation of hive queens – or for any other reason – they would move her on a motorized cart of some sort. The hive queen's bulk made her incapable of walking.

When they arrived at the antechamber to the hive queen's chamber, he waved them ahead into the room.

<You will wait here.>

Then he left.

In about ten minutes, a drone came into the antechamber through the other door. He was eight feet tall and very obviously a male, a two-foot spermipositor hanging between his legs.

"Gosh," Lena said.

<You may attend Her Majesty now,> he said in Vegan and waved them through the door.

All five of them went on into the queen's chamber and walked toward the hive queen's pallet. The room was dim, the shades pulled down over the windows that circled the room here at the top of the palace's highest tower.

The hive queen herself lay on a bed in the center of the chamber, her drones standing around her. She lay partially on her side, her shoulders and head turned so she could see them. Her abdomen, if anything, was even larger than it had been before. She looked prepared to lay a new brood of eggs.

They stopped a respectful distance away from the huge insect, with Daphne stepping forward a couple of steps. They all bowed to the hive queen.

"Good morning, Your Majesty. It is good to see you again," Daphne said, bowing.

<Ah. You were the lesser hive queen in the last party to visit me,> the hive queen said in Vegan.

All four of them understood her, having received the training in Vegan, even though they could not pronounce any of it. The hive queen, for her part, understood their English as well.

"Yes, Your Majesty. I have now matured enough to undertake an assignment such as this one. I have selected my first drone, and will begin my first brood soon."

She indicated Robert with a wave of her hand.

<Very good.>

"I have brought Your Majesty a small gift. A delicacy."

Daphne unwrapped a small package and held forward a lamb's liver in the wrapping.

The queen gestured, and a drone took the gift from Daphne. The hive queen's food taster, he snipped a small portion off of it with his mandibles and chewed.

<It is exquisite, Your Majesty,> he said, and held it out to the hive queen.

She took the gift and snipped a portion off with her mandibles. She chewed, her eyes closing in pleasure, and emitted a soft thrumming sound. Presently, her eyes opened.

<A wonderful gift. Thank you, fellow hive queen.>

Daphne bowed again.

"You're welcome, Your Majesty."

<But surely you have not come all this way to give me this gift. What is your purpose here?>

"We know that Vega obtained the graviton-drive and other technology from someone else, Your Majesty. Either from your home world or some other race entirely. We seek information about these people, that we might make contact with them."

<Yes. The fur-people,> the hive queen said, nodding.

So it was another race!

<Unfortunately, I have little information to give you, hive queen. As old as I am – some hundreds of your years – I was born on Vega. Which is to say, after we had the interstellar drive. I know the bare bones of the story.>

"Whatever Your Majesty could share, we would appreciate."

<The fur-people are the source of the technology. We had little in common with them, however, and did not keep contact with them. Among other things, they are obligate herbivores, and there was little basis for trade between us.>

The hive queen thought about it.

<They do not understand carnivores, and may have been a little afraid of us, despite their technology.>

"I understand, Your Majesty. Anything else?"

The hive queen thought about it, then spoke up.

<I am afraid not, hive queen. However, there is one among us who would know more. She is the oldest of our hive queens. She is in failing health, but she may have the answers you seek. She is located on our home world.>

"Could you tell us how to locate her, Your Majesty? Perhaps provide us with a letter of introduction?"

<This I can do, hive queen. I have some curiosity as to what became of the fur-people myself. Perhaps you could report back to me about what you find.>

"We would be happy to, Your Majesty. You are likely on our way home from this mission anyway."

The hive queen nodded.

<I will have coordinates prepared for you, as well as a letter to my sister [name]. I hope to see you again, hive queen.>

"You will, Your Majesty."

As was her own name, the name of the old hive queen was not pronounceable or translatable into English.

The hive queen made a shooing gesture, which Daphne knew was a wave goodbye. They all bowed to the hive queen, then walked out through the door the drone opened for them.

<You will wait here.>

They waited perhaps twenty minutes, then a drone came into the antechamber from the queen's chamber. He handed Daphne two paper documents, then bowed to Daphne and returned to the queen's chamber.

The palace Vegan returned through the other door.

<Follow me.>

He led them back down through the palace to the landing pad and the waiting shuttle.

Once in the shuttle and on the way back to *Beyond the Known*

Stars, they talked about the meeting with the hive queen.

"That was interesting," Jared said.

"Yes," Lena said. "Fur-people definitely means there's a third intelligent race out there. They didn't invent the tech on their home world."

"So what do we do now?" Robert asked.

"Head for their home world," Lena said. "Assuming we can interpret these coordinates."

"I can do that," Arthur said.

"I thought you were a sociologist," Robert said.

"Yes, but I needed to know how Earth people calculated coordinates to compare with ours."

"That makes sense."

"What about the introduction letter?" Lena asked.

"It's written in Vegan, but I can read it," Daphne said. "It's pretty glowing about us. She didn't say anything bad."

"Excellent," Jared said. "We have a plan."

"Arthur, I don't get these coordinates," Daphne said. "A hundred and fifty degrees? So their home world is almost due south from here? That doesn't make any sense. It would be on the other side of Earth."

"No, Daphne. You're reading it wrong. On Vega, a circle has twenty-five hundred and twenty degrees."

"Twenty-five hundred and twenty?"

"Yes. Twenty-five hundred and twenty is something of a magic number. It's divisible by one, two, three, four, five, six, seven, eight, nine, and ten. Your three hundred and sixty degrees is not divisible by seven."

"So one hundred and fifty degrees from north is—"

"About twenty-one of your degrees. Twenty-one and three-sevenths."

"OK, Arthur. That makes more sense. So it's further north from Earth than Vega, and a bit off to one side."

"Yes, that's right."

"Let's look at the charts. Re-center on Vega. Get the altitude and the azimuth, and look at ninety-three light-years distant and... There it is. Excellent."

"That appears to be it, Daphne."

"Hmm. No name, just a catalog number. There are ten thousand stars within a hundred light-years of Earth, so that's not so surprising. We should probably give it a name."

"It already has a name, according to the hive queen's directions."

Arthur said something unpronounceable in Vegan.

"What you said starts out sounding like Shandra, Arthur. How about we call it Shandra in English?"

"That is acceptable."

"All right. Our destination is Shandra."

"I will pass our course on to Captain Proxmire."

"Thanks, Arthur."

Ninety-three light-years was almost four times the distance Earth was from Vega, so it would take twice as long in the tunnel. That was because the speed kept building in the tunnel as the ship kept accelerating. The trip, rather than ten days – five in the tunnel – would be more like fifteen.

Lena didn't find the experience as troubling as the first time, but she was still glad when *Beyond the Known Stars* exited the tunnel in the Shandra system.

Shandra

As they approached Shandra, and the planet became visible, something else became visible as well. A moon. And what a moon.

"OK, now that's weird," Jared said.

"What is?" Daphne asked.

"I think that moon is going too fast for its orbital distance."

"Margie. Calculate orbit of Shandra's moon from available data," Robert said to the display in the living room.

The display lit up with calculations.

"Shandra's moon has approximately one-fifth the mass of the planet. It is in an elliptical orbit varying from a bit over three hundred thousand to almost seven hundred thousand miles from the planet. That orbit is not in the plane of the ecliptic, but is roughly north-south on the planet."

"Well, that explains it," Jared said. "That moon has to be an extrasolar capture, I think. Otherwise it would orbit in the ecliptic."

"That makes sense," Daphne said.

"What kind of tides would that give them?" Lena asked.

"Heavy ones, I would think," Robert said. "At least when it's at perigee."

"Which fits with intelligent life evolving here," Jared said.

"How so, Jared?" Lena asked.

"You know the Fermi Paradox, right? 'If there is intelligent life in the universe, where is everybody?' One solution of the Fermi Paradox is that Earth is so unique, life could only evolve on Earth or some planet very much like it. The existence of such a large moon is one of those uniquenesses."

"That's right," Daphne said. "Something about the tides being important, right?"

"Right. To mix things up. To keep things wet without being perpetually submerged. To provide hazard as an evolutionary driver. Anyway, we discover a second intelligent species, and guess what? They have tides from a large moon also."

"Got it. How curious," Daphne said.

Arthur sent a message down to the surface, using the same frequencies and signaling that Vega had in place before the system had been upgraded to interface better with humans.

<We request an audience with the hive queen [name 1]. We are sent by the hive queen [name 2]. Please inform her drones of our request.>

It was several hours before an answer came back.

<We will pass your request to Her Majesty when she awakens. If she awakens. Due to her extreme age, Her Majesty is not in good health.>

"Well, that throws a wrench in things. What do we do if she dies, Arthur? Ask to see her successor?"

"I don't think that would be possible, Daphne. Normally it takes several years for the hive queen's drones to prepare a successor hive queen. It involves feeding a new larva a specially prepared food. That larva eventually becomes a pupa, and finally transforms into an adult. Only then is there a new hive queen, and she would know nothing about the fur-people."

"Then what do we do if she dies?"

"Perhaps there is another very old hive queen on the planet. One who would remember what happened with respect to the fur-people."

"But she hasn't died yet," Jared said. "Let's not borrow trouble."

"I suppose," Daphne said. "But we do have to keep thinking of contingencies."

"No argument there," Jared said.

It was four days before they received another message.

<The hive queen has awakened. She will see you today.>

The message contained a set of coordinates. Robert had by this time taught his AI to convert Vegan coordinates to English coordinates. They took the AIs answer, and scanned the area with high-resolution cameras as they passed overhead.

"Well, it is a palace, and the coordinates are for what looks like a landing pad," Daphne said.

"Shall we go, then?" Lena asked.

"Yes. On our next orbit. We'll probably leave in an hour."

The shuttle landed on the indicated spot. Coming out of the shuttle, they looked around.

The 'landing pad' had pretty clearly been a large balcony back in the day, as the palace antedated the availability of gravitonic drive.

The palace itself gave the impression of extreme age, like the ruins of ancient Sumerian cities or Egyptian monuments. Despite regular maintenance like tuckpointing, the stones themselves showed the erosion one expected of thousands of years of exposure to the elements.

A palace servant came out on the balcony. He spoke a different dialect of the bug-people's language, but they had training in that one as well and had no difficulty understanding him.

<Come with me.>

He led them into the palace. Instead of angling up and up, however, they angled down, deeper into the palace. Daphne wondered whether the palace dated to a time when the bug-people had internal wars with each other, as it seemed the hive queen was in a bunker underneath the palace.

At one point, they took a bewildering set of turns and ramps. It was a maze, Daphne realized. Further protection for the hive queen.

At last, they came to an antechamber.

<You will wait here.>

After a few minutes, a drone entered through the other door.

<Her Majesty is very old and tires easily. You will have a few minutes, not more.>

He led them into the hive queen's chamber. They approached the hive queen's pallet and stopped a respectful distance away.

The hive queen was in repose on her pallet, turned partially on her side. She was bolstered in that position with pillows. Her abdomen was shrunken – perhaps half the size of the Vegan hive queen's – and wrinkled. Her color was not good, tending more to the brown than the orange, and splotchy.

A drone spoke in her ear and she opened her eyes.

<You may speak.>

They believed this hive queen would not understand English, and would not learn it, so Arthur would translate everything Daphne said for the hive queen.

Daphne stepped forward a step.

"Your Majesty, I am the human hive queen called Daphne Bach. I come to you as an ambassador of the humans of Earth and its interstellar colonies at the direction of the hive queen— put her name in there Arthur."

Arthur translated. Daphne produced the introduction from

the Vegan hive queen and held it out to one of the drones.

He took the introduction and read it to the hive queen. A glowing recommendation of Daphne and noting her as a fellow hive queen and a friend. Then he licked the document in the signature space.

<It is signed with her spittle, Your Majesty. It is from her.>

The hive queen beckoned Daphne to continue.

"We seek information on the fur-people, Your Majesty. Those from whom you received the gravitonic drive and other technology."

<That was a very long time ago, sister DaphneBach.>

The hive queen said her name all as one word.

<It was before my time, and for almost a thousand orbits of the planet have I ruled here.>

Shandra's year was about thirteen Earth months long, so she was talking maybe eleven hundred years. She had been ruler here since before the Magna Carta.

"Do you have records or folklore of that time, Your Majesty?"

<The palace archives likely have records. I am the tenth hive queen to rule here, and our records go back to the founding of the hive.>

She paused, and Daphne waited.

<This much I can tell you, sister DaphneBach. It was in the eighth hive queen's time that the fur-people discovered us. We were a primitive people, and sometimes engaged in the most frightful wars.>

Daphne stood transfixed by the image.

<The fur-people made us a deal. If we would give up war, they would provide us a different way to release population pressure. The interstellar drive, and the computer technology to operate it.>

"We thought you might have stolen the technology, Your Majesty."

<No, it was a gift of the fur-people. They trained us in its manufacture and use, in exchange for us forsaking war. The hive queens agreed, and we have kept that agreement for fifteen hundred orbits of the planet.>

They had held the peace since before the Roman Empire fell!

"That is an amazing story, Your Majesty."

<That is all I know, sister DaphneBach. You will find more in the archives, to which I will give you access.>

"Thank you, Your Majesty. You've been most kind."

The hive queen made the shooing gesture Daphne recognized as a wave goodbye.

She bowed, as did the rest of her party, and they turned to where a drone had opened the door to the antechamber. They filed out.

<Thank you for keeping it short, Your Majesty. You will wait here.>

He went back into the hive queen's chamber, closing the door behind him.

"Your Majesty?" Jared asked.

"I'm a fellow hive queen, remember? She addressed me as sister, but a drone must not."

"Ah. Right."

"And punctilious courtesy is one way to avoid war."

"Why would the fur-people be so interested in getting the bug-people to abandon war amongst themselves?"

"Imagine if, knowing it was possible, the bug-people came up with the interstellar drive themselves," Robert said. "The fur-people would then be in danger."

"Imagine an herbivore's thoughts about a war between carnivores in which the winning side eats the bodies of the fallen," Arthur said.

"Oh, yeah," Lena said. "That would get a reaction, for sure."

The palace servant showed up, and addressed Daphne.

<I will show you to the archives, Your Majesty. Follow me.>

Daphne nodded and waved him to go on. They all followed him as he led them to another area in the depths of the palace.

When they passed into the archives, they were surrounded by ancient books on shelves. Dusty and falling apart, the books looked like they would crumble if you touched them.

"Oh, no," Daphne said.

"This is what I was afraid of," Robert said.

They passed through chamber after chamber, then came to a chamber with computer terminals.

<The archives have all been transcribed to digital form, Your Majesty. It was easier than rewriting them continuously as they deteriorated. Even these ancient books are copies of copies.>

"Ask him why they kept all the books, Arthur."

Arthur translated, and the palace servant nodded, then spoke to Daphne.

<We kept them out of nostalgia, Your Majesty. The ancient books remind us how old these records are.>

"Can you operate these terminals, Arthur?"

"I believe so, Daphne."

"Wait. Can we copy these archives, Arthur?"

"Perhaps. It depends on whether Vega shared the Wi-Fi technology they stole from Earth. If they did, I should be able to copy the database."

Arthur pulled a pad out of his shoulder bag – in which he also kept his ten-millimeter pistol – and checked it briefly.

"I have a Wi-Fi signal, Daphne. It's not the latest version, so it will perhaps be a bit slower than we're used to, but let's see how far I get."

Arthur fussed with the pad, then turned to the palace servant.

<Can I have a login name and password to your Wi-Fi connection?>

<I can create one for you.>

The palace servant went to one of the terminals and typed, then turned to Arthur.

<The login name is HerMajestyDaphneBach, the password is humanhivequeen, but spell hive backwards.>

He showed Arthur on the screen, and Arthur entered them into the pad.

"I'm in. I don't know how much I can copy onto this pad, though, Daphne."

"Here, Arthur," Robert said. "Plug this into your pad."

Robert handed Arthur a small datalink with a pigtail on it. Arthur plugged it in.

"Now I can see your data server, Robert. Aboard ship."

"That's right. Make a new directory and copy away."

"Excellent."

Arthur watched for a while, then shook his head.

"What's the matter, Arthur?"

"This is going to take days, Daphne."

"Ask him if we can leave this device here for now, Arthur."

Arthur asked, then the palace servant turned to Daphne.

<Of course, Your Majesty. I was told to give you complete access.>

"Tell him we'll pick it up in several days, Arthur. And ask him to show us back to the shuttle."

Arthur translated, and the palace servant turned to Daphne.

<Of course, Your Majesty. Follow me.>

The palace servant lead them back through the archives, then up, up, up to the balcony and the waiting shuttle.

On the way back to the ship, Daphne had a question for Robert.

"You carry a datalink with you?"

"Of course. It's small enough. I always have it in my pocket."

"And it can stay in touch with the ship?"

"Anytime the ship is in the sky for this location. Maybe a third of its orbit. When the ship goes behind the planet, no."

"Gonna have to be good enough. It'll just take longer."

Departures

As the data came in over the next three weeks, some patterns began to emerge. Robert was continuously running searches against the data uploaded so far, and he was keeping track of trends that were emerging.

"One thing I've noted so far is that there are no pictures," he told the group.

"None?" Daphne asked.

"Nope. None I've seen."

"We are not, generally speaking, a picture-oriented culture," Arthur said.

"How can that be, Arthur?" Lena asked. "'One picture is worth a thousand words.'"

"Yes, that's a human expression. But take it at face value. A thousand words is less than ten thousand bytes, whereas a picture takes millions of bytes."

"However you look at it," Robert said, "it means I cannot find any pictures of the fur-people. At least not so far."

"OK. That's weird. What have you found out about them?"

"They are generally anthropomorphic, like us and the bug-people. They walk on two feet, and have two hands, not four like Arthur. They are covered in a fine fur. And they are obligate herbivores."

"But they could be hogs or dogs, cats or rats?" Jared asked.

"Yup. Or something entirely different. They are about the same size as the bug-people or humans. In the five to six foot range in height."

"That may be a requirement for intelligence," Arthur said. "While anything much larger would be a problematic structure in one gravity. So they are probably from a planet with a similar gravity to Earth or Shandra."

"That makes sense," Daphne said. "Especially if they were running around on Shandra at one point. Hard to deal with a gravity much different than you're used to."

"And, if we're right about them helping out the bug-people in return for them forsaking war, it's hard to be very afraid of someone with much different gravity than your own," Jared said. "Why bother? They aren't going to be interested in your planet anyway, and it would be hard to fight with you."

"Yeah, so that all fits together," Daphne said.

She turned to Robert.

"Anything else?"

"Not so far. We're just going to have to wait for the data to upload."

One trick Robert was using through his remote access to Arthur's pad was to continuously access data with the pad, then squeal it to his data server aboard *Beyond the Known Stars* at the higher speed of his datalink. It still took three weeks to get everything. It was a good thing both the pad and the data link had the extended battery options.

At the end of three weeks, with all the archive uploaded, Daphne got in touch with the hive queen's palace. She sent the message in the Shandra dialect directly to the palace via Arthur's pad, which was logged into the palace systems.

<We have completed our access of the archives. We would like to pick up our devices when it is convenient.>

An answer came back quickly.

<The hive queen [name] has died. We are in mourning. No routine business is permitted.>

Daphne took the matter up with Arthur. She filled him in

first, then made a suggestion

"I guess we need to wait for the mourning period to be complete, Arthur."

"That is unlikely to be short, Daphne. It takes several years to replace a hive queen."

"Really?"

"Oh, yes. They must start from an egg, and feed it the special food required for it to mature into a hive queen. The whole process takes a number of years before the new queen emerges and takes up her rule."

"Do we have spares of the devices? Can we simply leave them behind?"

"I have a spare, Daphne, but it is not up-to-date. There would be some data loss. I suppose I could upload that data as well, though there is a lot of it."

"Is there another way, Arthur?"

"They must be doing some business, Daphne. They will not allow everyone to starve due to a failure to continue animal husbandry, for example."

"Hmm. Let me try, Arthur. Help me with this."

Daphne sent a new message. She digitally signed this one to make sure they knew it was from her.

<I mourn the loss of my friend and sister [name]. Long may she be remembered and her life celebrated.

<While routine business is halted out of respect for my esteemed sister, surely some activities continue. Is there no way to retrieve my devices so that I can continue my mission?

<The Hive Queen DaphneBach.>

An hour later, Daphne got a reply.

<You may view Her Majesty's funeral from the landing pad balcony. Arrive half an hour early, and your devices will be returned to you at that time.>

It also specified the date and time of the hive queen's funeral, two days in the future.

"Well, we can do that, I guess," Daphne said.

"Daphne," Arthur said. "I think we should talk about the likely nature of the hive queen's funeral, so you aren't made uncomfortable."

Arthur hadn't gotten very far into his explanation before Daphne cut him off.

"Wait. They're gonna do *what*?"

"Can I just stay here, Daphne?" Lena asked. "I don't need that image in my mind forever."

"Sure, Lena. No problem."

"I'll stay with Lena, Daphne," Jared said. "I don't think we should split up in onesies."

"That makes sense," Daphne said. "I have to go, and they're Arthur's and Robert's devices."

Just before the scheduled time, the shuttle set down on the landing pad. One of the palace servants was waiting for them. He had their devices with him.

<Your devices.>

He handed the pad and the data link off to Arthur and then scurried off, presumably to view the funeral.

Daphne walked over to the parapet of the balcony.

"Wow. Look at the crowd."

There were perhaps two hundred thousand workers in the square before the palace and up into the side streets. They were a quiet crowd, all subdued by the nature of the event.

"You must realize, Daphne," Arthur said. "Given the hive queen's great age, all of these people were born of her. It is, in a very real sense, their mother's funeral."

120

Daphne nodded, though the concept of so many progeny was extraordinary.

Something like a dirge began to play, and the body of the hive queen was brought out into the center of the square by the drones pushing her pallet along. The crowd parted for the small processional, then closed in behind it.

An ululation began from the crowd upon the hive queen's appearance. Most of the people in the crowd had never seen her before.

Once the pallet stopped in the center of the square, the most remarkable thing happened. The drones mounted the pallet and began to cut the hive queen up into cubes perhaps half an inch on a side, beginning with the abdomen and working forward. They collected these cubes on a tray.

Once that tray was heaped with remnants, another tray was brought forward. The first tray was carried by a drone to the end of the pallet, where they were handed out to the workers, who lined up quietly.

As each worker took his piece, he put it in his mouth, chewed, and ate it. They then moved away, ceding room to the next in line.

"Now there's something you don't see every day," Daphne said.

"It's not so different than communion, in a sense," Jared said.

"Yes, but this is the actual body of the hive queen. There's no transubstantiation involved."

"We have always eaten our dead," Arthur said. "It comes from our culture developing in a very tough environment. One couldn't waste the resources. The funeral of the hive queen, though, is different, because everyone here is her children."

"We have our devices," Robert said. "Should we go?"

"I wouldn't think so," Daphne said. "Not until this is over."

"Yes," Arthur said. "I would advise we wait until the ceremony is over. It won't be that long, and we don't want to be irreverent."

They continued to watch as the ceremony proceeded. When everyone had been served, the drones fell upon what little of the hive queen remained and finished her off. They then rolled the empty pallet back into the palace as the crowd began to disperse.

"All right," Arthur said. "We can go now."

"OK. Let's saddle up and hit the trail," Daphne said.

Back aboard *Beyond the Known Stars*, Lena was curious.

"How was it?"

"About as weird as you might imagine," Daphne said.

"Jeepers."

The next day, after dinner, Robert reported on his progress in processing all the data from the upload.

"As I say, the big disappointment is the lack of pictures in the archives. We still have no clue what the fur-people are like other than that they're furry.

"We also don't have specific coordinates for a fur-people planet. We have a general direction and distance, but not a specific star location.

"Generally speaking, they are further north from here. In this general direction."

Robert indicated an area of the night sky with the major stars indicated.

"Can you show that from Earth's point of view?" Daphne asked.

Robert changed the view to show a different star view. Vega and Shandra were indicated, and a vector from Shandra. That vector had a specific length, the distance the records indicated the fur-people had traveled to arrive at Shandra, the only planet the bug-people occupied at the time the fur-people contacted them. It was almost a hundred and fifty light-years.

"I think they're in Boötes somewhere," Robert said.

"Huh?" Lena asked. "Bow-a-tees?"

"Yes. It's a constellation roughly north from Earth."

"Interesting that we keep heading north," Jared said.

"Well, it's not surprising they're all more or less in a line from us," Daphne said. "If the fur-people were southwest of Shandra, say, they might have found Earth first."

"OK, that's fair," Jared said. "They found Shandra and stopped heading in our direction."

"Or not," Daphne said. "No telling. They may have visited Earth and decided to have nothing to do with us. Depends on when they visited."

"Right," Jared said. "That makes sense. They visited Shandra, what? A thousand years ago?"

"More like two thousand," Robert said.

"So now what do we do?" Lena asked.

"I think it's time for a push into Boötes. See what we find," Daphne said.

"*If* we find," Jared said. "There's a lot of stars within even a modest radius of any given point. Even out where Earth is located, which is pretty thin."

"I think we can up our chances over a random search, Jared," Robert said.

"What are you thinking, Robert?" Daphne asked.

"We now have parallax views of this volume of space, from Earth records and from the Shandra records. We can map the stars there pretty exactly. If we go to a star within a denser area, and use the ship's telescopes, we should be able to see a technical civilization by analyzing the atmosphere of the planets nearby using spectroscopy."

"Look for carbon dioxide and stuff?" Jared asked.

"And other industrial byproducts. Yes. It means a two-hop strategy, but it has high odds of success."

"I like it," Daphne said. "We can also increase our odds by picking a good candidate as the initial target star. But pick one in a denser area, as you said, Robert. What does everybody think?"

"Sounds good," Jared said.

Lena nodded.

Daphne looked to Arthur, who had been watching the discussion quietly.

"It sounds like the best approach to me, Daphne."

"All right. Robert, you pick the star and give Arthur the coordinates. He'll let the captain know."

Within the hour, *Beyond the Known Stars* was accelerating at twelve gravities away from Shandra, heading into the unknown.

Looking Around

A hundred and fifty light-years was two and a half days at each end – the same as for any other trip at twelve gravities – but twelve and a half days in the tunnel. If twenty-five light-years Earth to Vega was five days in the tunnel, then six times further was square-root-of-six times longer in the tunnel because the ship was constantly accelerating.

On the other hand, this trip's purpose was not necessarily to stop at any planet in this first system, so *Beyond the Known Stars* did not decelerate on leaving the tunnel. That would make it that much quicker to reenter the tunnel when they left the system, as it was the velocity with respect to the local stellar mass that mattered.

"Let's begin our observations, Arthur," Daphne said. "Does Captain Proxmire have the coordinates?"

"Yes, Daphne."

"Let's give him the order."

Proxmire had already rotated the ship so its bottom surface was its leading surface. He now opened the door to the telescope bay on Deck A and lowered the big telescope.

Beyond the Known Stars was an exploration ship. As such, it needed good instrumentation for seeing what was around it, and the big telescope was part of that package.

The problem with a really good telescope – one intended to do fine work at interstellar distances – is it had to be held absolutely still. The ship couldn't do that. There was too much vibration. Minor vibrations to be sure, such as from the freezer compressors on the supplies deck, but vibrations nonetheless.

The solution was to lower the telescope from the ship. The cable still carried vibrations, but there was a workaround. The ship was currently not accelerating, but it maintained gravity aboard for the crew and passengers. In this mode, a hundred and fifty yards away from the ship in the axial direction – up and down to those aboard – the gravitonic field had a zero.

They lowered the telescope from the bottom of the ship, as it was being pulled down by the gravity being maintained aboard ship. As it moved away from the ship, at a hundred and fifty yards it hit the zero in the gravitational field and stopped moving. The cable went slack as a bit more cable was payed out.

The telescope was now in freefall at the same velocity as the ship, and isolated from the ship's vibrations.

It was a really big telescope, modeled after the James Web Space Telescope and others fielded by the U.S. and other countries over the past seventy years.

"What's our progress?" Daphne asked over dinner several days later.

"We've looked at the planets in this solar system and no luck," Robert said. "None of them has an atmosphere that would be compatible with life that could walk around on Shandra. Methane. Ammonia. Carbon dioxide. Stuff like that. But no breathable atmosphere. So we've been looking farther afield."

"Any luck there?"

"We're not sure. We're seeing something weird."

"Why weird? What's going on?"

Robert looked to Arthur, and Arthur answered.

"The planets with the closest match in gravity and

atmosphere to Shandra have some extra compounds we don't understand, Daphne. At least in their upper atmospheres, which is what we're seeing."

"What kind of compounds?"

"Compounds that might be used in geo-engineering. To give the planet a lower albedo and make it absorb a little more heat, or give it a higher albedo so it reflects more heat."

"Geo-engineering? Sounds like our fur-people have been busy making their planets more pleasant."

"That's what it looks like, Daphne," Robert said, "but we're not sure yet. And you'd think their original planet would be most amenable to the people who evolved there, and need the least modification."

"Assuming things haven't changed over time," Jared said.

"Well, yes, there's that, too. Right now we're just mapping them all, to see if we can come up with some sort of pattern and pick out their home planet."

Daphne sat and thought about it. Something wasn't adding up, but she couldn't put her finger on it. Everybody else knew that look and waited. She finally stirred.

"What about industrial gases. You know, pollutants associated with an industrial economy."

"We don't see any, Daphne," Robert said.

"None?"

"No."

"Well, if they're so serious enough about their comfort and making their planets more pleasant that they take on geo-engineering, wouldn't they be just as committed to not polluting them?" Jared asked.

"I suppose," Daphne said. "But I would think we would see something."

"Not yet," Robert said.

"How many of these planets have you found so far? The ones with the potential geo-engineering?"

"About a dozen. It takes a while to re-aim the big telescope and get it stable, then it takes a while to gather enough data to make conclusions."

"Understood. We have all the time we need, so let's not get in a hurry and make mistakes."

"We're on it, Daphne."

After the meeting, Arthur reflected on the decision they had made to make Daphne Bach the leader of the group. That had worked out well so far, and she was growing into the role. The others deferred to her automatically at this point.

Humans were remarkable creatures.

They were all together the next afternoon waiting for the announcement of dinner.

"I figured out what was bothering me yesterday," Daphne said. "Why hasn't this phenomenon of the geo-engineering been seen from Earth?"

"That's a very simple question with a complex answer," Robert said.

"First, we've traveled two hundred and seventy-five light years. That's not all in a straight line, but it's pretty straight, so we're about two hundred and fifty light-years from Earth. Big difference looking at a planet from, say, thirty light-years away compared to one two hundred and eighty light-years away.

"Second is that that is a *very* big telescope. Your parents spared no expense in outfitting this ship. Normally a facility that big and expensive is booked in small time slots, and the people doing cosmology and the like have priority. They're looking at distant galaxies – billions of light-years away – not planets a few hundred light-years away."

"Wait a minute. Don't those big telescopes take a decade or more to plan and build? How did my parents get one in five years?"

"Because they said, 'Build us another one like that one you just did.' The plans are done, they have all the fixturing and jigs to build it with, they know all the tricks and missteps. The whole thing goes much faster."

"OK. Got it."

"Third is that it's easier to see big planets, because they make their sun wiggle a bit. The planet is so big that, as it orbits, it moves the star back and forth. But we're looking for small rocky planets, not gas giants. And even among small rocky planets, Earth is on the small side.

"Fourth is that there are a thousand stars within a hundred light-years of Earth, and the Sun is in a thin spot. There are probably eight or nine thousand stars within two hundred and fifty light-years of Earth. They simply haven't looked at them all. Like I said, the big telescopes – on the order of what we have here – are scheduled very precisely. No one's had the luxury to systematically go after local stars like we're doing.

"And finally, they may have seen one or two of these planets, and thought it was likely a natural thing. You know, that planet has sulfur dioxide in the atmosphere. Big deal. But from this close we can see that it's in the upper atmosphere and not in the whole atmosphere, and it's a repeated thing across multiple star systems. Oh, and we didn't see that on the bug-people planets."

"How prevalent is it?" Daphne asked.

"Every Earth-sized planet in the right temperature range, with a suitable atmosphere, orbiting a G-type main-sequence star that we've looked at so far has had its climate modified by geo-engineering."

"*All* of them?"

"Every one we've found so far."

"That's a lot of geo-engineering," Jared said. "And the scale of such an operation is incredible. One part per million of something like sulfur dioxide in a planetary atmosphere is fifteen billion tons or so. And you probably need multiple parts per million to get the effect you want. That's just for one planet."

"Well, if they're only dealing with the stratosphere, it's smaller, but yeah, it's a big effort," Robert said. "We couldn't do it."

"And they're doing it with no pollution," Daphne said. "Then again, they are at least two thousand years ahead of us. They've had hundreds of years to make their planets whatever they want them to be. They didn't have to do it all at once."

Daphne though about it, then nodded.

"OK, I guess that answers my question. Thanks, Robert."

"No problem. You'll know as soon as we have any more to report."

A galley staffer came in then and announced dinner, and they went on into the dining room.

For ten days, *Beyond the Known Stars* kept on her ballistic course. She sped through the target star system and beyond, not accelerating, not slowing down, as the big telescope examined star after star, planet after planet.

On the eleventh day in the target star system, Robert and Arthur were ready to report on their findings. That afternoon, the group sat facing the big display in the living room.

"Here are the star systems we've identified thus far as having Earth-like planets orbiting G-type main-sequence stars.

All of these planets have atmospheres with mixtures in the right range to support Earth-like life, a description that also applies to the bug-people planets Vega and Shandra."

The display showed a smattering of stars and planets mostly along their current bearing and further from Earth. A few such planets lay behind them, but mostly they were still ahead.

"It's important to note that there may be similar planets in this narrow cone here, but that cone is the blind spot for the telescope because it is obscured by the ship being behind the telescope. We can't maneuver the ship while the telescope is deployed. We would have to pull it in, rotate the ship, and then redeploy the telescope."

Robert indicated a cone that was drawn within the diagram. He also rotated the diagram along their bearing, so they could see the three-dimensional nature of the layout of interesting planets.

"Every one of these planets has had their climate modified at least a little by geo-engineering. I can display the amount of geo-engineering on each planet with a bar graph for each planet. Red is for making the planet warmer, Blue is for making the planet cooler."

Each planet now had a bar alongside it, either red or blue. The bars varied in height.

"Just keep the display rotating if you would," Daphne said.

She stared at the display, not focusing in on details, but just watching the whole thing. Looking for the shape of it. The logic of it. Jared saw what she was doing and tried the same.

"Stop the rotation," Daphne said.

Robert stopped the rotation of the diagram.

"That's their home world. Number...? What is it? Twenty-five."

"This one?" Robert asked.

"Yes. That's their home world."

"Interesting. Why do you say that?"

"OK. They're on one world, right? They get the drive. They start settling planets. At first, they settle any planet they can. Later, they get pickier. They roam a little wider. Finding the right planets to colonize. That's the pattern we're seeing."

"I don't see it," Lena said.

"I do," Jared said. "Number twenty-five is in the densest part of this cluster. It has very little geo-engineering – a little warmer, but not much – as it's their home planet, so it should be about right already. Around that planet, the planets they settled are closer in, and have, in general, a lot of geo-engineering. Making them more suitable. The other planets are further apart, meaning they're getting pickier as they go. Those planets have less geo-engineering, because they were picky enough to go for the good ones. Right, Daphne?"

"Yes. Exactly. I think we should go there next. To number twenty-five."

"OK. I get it now," Lena said. "Basically, they left tracks."

"Over hundreds of years," Daphne said. "Yes."

"Robert and I came to the same conclusion," Arthur said. "We couldn't put our finger on it, but it was the one planet with very little geo-engineering in the middle of a bunch that had a lot. But your description as to why that's true is compelling, Daphne."

"We're agreed then?" Daphne asked. "Number twenty-five?"

"It's almost two hundred light-years away, Daphne," Robert said.

Lena groaned.

"Can't be helped," Daphne said. "It is where it is. Are we agreed?"

She collected input from the group by looking around and counting nods. She even got a nod from Lena.

"All right, Arthur. Ask Captain Proxmire to stow the big telescope and space for number twenty-five."

The winches in the telescope's storage bay reeled the big telescope in. First, they slowly took the slack out of the cables so they wouldn't jerk tight and break, then they sped up as they pulled the big telescope back 'up' to the ship against the artificial gravity.

Once the telescope was secured and the hatch of the telescope bay closed, *Beyond the Known Stars* rotated onto a new bearing ninety degrees to its current velocity. She went to twelve gravities as she started adding side vector to her current velocity.

After several hours, *Beyond the Known Stars* rotated most of the way back to its old vector. Its new vector was about ten degrees to one side of the old vector, and lined up with what everyone was calling 'Number Twenty-Five.'

The ship accelerated along that vector for a little under two hours before she entered the tunnel.

Number Twenty-Five was almost seventeen days away. More than fourteen days in the tunnel.

RICHARD F. WEYAND

Number Twenty-Five

Fourteen days in the tunnel was another fourteen days of enforced idleness. It had been eighty days since they had left Earth. It would be more like ninety seven days by the time they reached Number Twenty-Five.

During that time, there had been no shore leave for the crew or the passengers. They had visited the two hive queens, yes, and Arthur, Robert, and Daphne had attended a hive queen's funeral, but those had not been shore leave, either. Not recreation time on the planet.

The crew had not been off the ship at all.

During the crossing to Number Twenty-Five, the two young couples mostly kept to themselves, staying in their respective suites. They had meals together, and they would sometimes watch a movie together after dinner.

But the long voyage, cooped up in the same quarters with the same companions, was taking its toll.

Being in the tunnel didn't help.

"I didn't realize a voyage of discovery was such a tedious pain in the ass," Robert said to Daphne as they lay in bed one morning.

"They always were, Robert. They sound romantic, but mostly they were tedious and nerve-wracking. Because you don't know what's ahead. It took a certain kind of person to do those voyages successfully."

"Well, I don't know that I'm one of them, Daphne. This sucks."

"Maybe we'll meet some friendly new aliens, and they'll

have a beautiful planet where we can all take shore leave."

"Or they'll be vicious xenophobes and we'll end up running for our lives."

"Yes, Robert. That's that whole not knowing part."

"Yes, Mr. Vegan?"

"Captain Proxmire. We do not know what kind of reception we will receive from the occupants of this planet. I think some precautions may be necessary."

"What did you have in mind, Mr. Vegan?"

"Approaching the planet with the missile decks in the lead may be appropriate, Captain. Having the lifeboat manned and ready to go might be another precaution worth taking. You may think of others."

"General quarters," Proxmire said, nodding. "Very well, Mr. Vegan. Thank you for the heads up."

"Of course, Captain."

When *Beyond the Known Stars* dropped out of the tunnel, Proxmire had the drive brought down to zero acceleration while leaving gravity aboard ship. He then flipped the ship to put the missile decks in the lead, and brought the deceleration back up to twelve gravities.

The crew was at general quarters, and the escape ship was manned, its computers on-line.

Daphne had recorded a general purpose hail to try to raise the planet, and they played it now on multiple radio frequencies, both those used by Earth and those used by the bug-people on Vega and Shandra. She also broadcast it in multiple languages.

She didn't know what to call the planet, however. What was its name?

"Hailing the planet. This is the interstellar ship *Beyond the Known Stars*, requesting landing instructions for a friendly visit. Please respond."

The answer, when it came, was unexpected. It was in English, for one thing.

"*Beyond the Known Stars*. Welcome to Mondoverde. I am Stefano Tommaso Omero Giovanni Battista de Milano, Marquis de Milano, at your service. I invite you to join me for lunch."

Daphne composed her answer carefully, and sent it back on the same channel, in English only.

"Marquis de Milano. Thank you for the welcome and the invitation. We are still a day and a half from Mondoverde orbit. We will advise when we have established orbit of your planet."

The answer came back quickly.

"On which day we have lunch is unimportant. Please inform me when you have established orbit. Ciao."

"What do we know?" Daphne asked.

"Mondoverde means 'green world' in Italian," Lena said.

"Marquis was high nobility in Italy, just below a duke," Jared said. "And duke was often the ruler of a city-state before unification and the establishment of the Kingdom of Italy. He could be the ruler of the whole planet, or a significant portion of it."

Robert raised an eyebrow at Jared, and Jared shrugged.

"I like history documentaries," Jared said.

"A remarkable case of parallel evolution?" Daphne asked.

"I doubt it," Arthur said. "Giovanni Battista is John the Baptist in Italian. I would say it is more a case of mimicry. A sort of cosplay, if you will."

"To make us comfortable?" Daphne asked. "By showing us something familiar?"

"It could be," Arthur said, "if their last contact with Earth was some time ago. It's hard to be sure why. Seeing how he is dressed will tell us much more."

"Why, Arthur?"

"Is he dressed in modern clothes – whatever that means to them – and the title is merely a carryover, or is he dressed, perhaps, in clothes of the Medieval period, which would mean a romantic fascination with that period on Earth."

"I see. Well, I guess we'll find out in a day or two."

Assuming that the Marquis' invitation to lunch meant it was mid-morning wherever he was for the previous message exchange, Daphne let him know they had achieved orbit about the same time two days later. That didn't match ship time, but they napped to make sure they were fresh.

The Marquis repeated his invitation to lunch, and sent them his coordinates. Without the same coordinate systems, he included a set of pictures of his location from orbit all the way in to landing.

"Got him," Robert said. "I see where he is. Yeah, it's between nine and ten in the morning there."

"You got the landing spot nailed?"

"Yeah. Looks like it's in some kind of park or garden near a big manor house."

"That sounds right. OK, everybody. Let's get to the shuttle."

They came down on a hard point in the lawn of a manor house in the style of Tuscany back on earth. The hard point was provided by concrete blocks set into the ground with their openings oriented vertically. Grass grew in the openings of the blocks and made it look like just more lawn.

The stuccoed house sat on top of a low hill, and had a

panoramic view of the surrounding gardens. They were a mix of vegetable gardens and flower gardens, and were very pleasant to look at. Their occasional symmetries appeared almost accidental. The studied casualness of it all took a great deal of effort, more than a simple, structured organization.

It was all the work of someone with an extraordinary eye for aesthetics.

The weather, too, was reminiscent of Tuscany on one of those rare, perfect late-spring days. A lazy breeze carried the smells of loam and flowers, plantings and fruit.

A platoon of guardsmen came out of the house and formed a circle around them and the shuttle. They were dressed in a Medieval style, with tunic and tights in the house colors, but the sidearms they carried looked deadly and modern.

And they were all cats. Or similar to cats, anyway. They walked upright naturally, and looked for all the world like humans except for their heads. They had a muzzle, and fine, soft fur over their faces. Whiskers as well, and cat-like ears. They did not have the slitted cat eyes, however, but eyes more like human eyes, though the irises were a distinct green.

Following them came the most remarkable creature. Another cat-like alien, to be sure, but he was dressed in the Medieval style of a lordling of the house. Like Romeo in a period-correct stage play of Romeo and Juliet. Tights and tunic in the house colors, but also a remarkable hat, and boots topped by turn-down cuffs.

"My God, it's Puss in Boots," Lena whispered.

"Close enough, anyway," Jared said.

The Marquis walked up to them and looked them up and down carefully.

"Humans. How extraordinary. And one of the Greth as well. Therein, I am sure, lies a terrific story. Ah, but where are my manners?"

He swept his hat off to them and bowed.

"I am Stefano Tommaso Omero Giovanni Battista de Milano, Marquis de Milano, at your service. Welcome to Mondoverde, our little green world."

He continued to frankly appraise them, as Daphne stepped forward.

"Thank you. We are most pleased to meet you."

"That voice. Ah ha! Now I understand. Hair and clothing styles on Earth are so ephemeral, I was not sure. You've brought your ladies. Now I must ask you, gentlemen, if either of you is prepared to defend your damsels against me."

He drew his sword, and aimed it first at Jared, then at Robert.

Robert looked at the Marquis' sword. It was an epee, not a rapier. Much more maneuverable than the older weapon. It had no button on its point.

It was also the weapon Robert had competed with in undergrad. It had been a couple of years, but he'd taken the occasional turn during grad school of being a sparring partner for the university team.

"Aye, I'll tilt with you," Robert said.

"Splendid. A duel, then?"

"Not to the death, surely."

"No. Merely to first blood. A bit of sport before lunch."

Robert nodded. He had worn slacks and a button-down shirt with tennis shoes down to the planet, the uniform of the engineer. Not flexible enough for fencing. He stripped down to his tee-shirt now, then kicked off his tennis shoes and stepped out of his pants. He put the tennis shoes back on and stood in briefs and tee-shirt before the Marquis.

"I need a weapon," he said.

"But of course."

The Marquis signaled the head of the guard platoon, who also wore a sword, and he drew an identical epee and handed it to Robert.

The Marquis doffed his extravagant hat and handed it to the platoon officer, who held it for him.

"Robert, be careful," Daphne said.

"Oh, yeah."

"So we play for just a touch. If someone misplays it and kills the other, he automatically loses," the Marquis said.

"And honor is lost," Robert said.

"Exactly. Shall we have at it, then?"

Robert moved away from the rest of the group, lifted his weapon, and nodded to the Marquis.

"En garde."

The two men slowly felt each other out, maintaining their distance. Not the swashbuckling of a grade-B movie, this was real fencing, performed by two men who knew what they were doing.

Robert knew he would have to dispatch the Marquis quickly to win. He suspected the felinoid alien had much better stamina than he did now. Two years ago, maybe not, but it was not two years ago, and this would be best done quickly.

A tap here, a tap there. Usually in sixte. A thrust from the Marquis, a parry and riposte from Robert, a counter-parry from the Marquis. They continued to test each other as the minutes passed.

One thing Robert noted was that the Marquis never attempted a lunge. Could it be he did not know the move? It came late to fencing, later than the Marquis' costume, at least. Perhaps he didn't.

Robert began to prime the Marquis for his favorite move in

competitive fencing. A tap, tap, push on the opponent's blade. Again, a little later, a tap, tap, push. The third time, a tap, tap, push.

This time, though, on the third beat, the Marquis dropped his blade slightly, avoiding the push, and switched to quarte, his blade behind Robert's. He tapped and thrust at Robert in quarte, but Robert was ready for the move and parried him in quarte, then switched back to sixte.

A little later, like someone whose best move has been broken but does not know what else to do, Robert once again went to the tap, tap, push.

The Marquis once again dropped his blade slightly, avoiding the push, and switched to quarte. He tapped and thrust at Robert in quarte, but Robert parried him in quarte, and executed an advance lunge.

The advance lunge is a compound move. One step forward – the advance – followed immediately by the lunge. The compound move covers a lot of ground. Robert was quickly within the Marquis' blade and, on the lunge, perforated the Marquis' ear.

"Touché! A touch, a touch, I must admit it. You have bested me, sir."

A green liquid oozed from the Marquis' ear. Copper-based blood?

In any case, the bout was over. The Marquis swept his arms wide and bowed to Robert, and Robert returned his bow. The Marquis then sheathed his blade, and Robert returned his to the platoon officer. Robert got re-dressed, pulling on his slacks and re-donning the button-down shirt. The Marquis reclaimed his extraordinary hat and put it on.

"And now we are hungry, eh? Come along, my new friends, and let us to lunch."

The Marquis de Milano

The Marquis led them around the house to a deck on the back side of the house. A pergola covered in wisteria covered the deck creating a cooler spot from which to appreciate the view. Staff was setting out lunch. Fruits, vegetables – some cooked and some raw – cheeses, breads, pastries. Wines, both red and white, were also on the table.

Some of the vegetables and fruits looked very familiar, as did the wisteria.

"I suppose we should continue introductions now. You may call me Tomas. And you all are?"

"I am Daphne Bach, ambassador from Earth and head of mission."

The Marquis nodded.

"Madame Ambassador."

"I am Lena Stox, ship's purser of *Beyond the Known Stars*."

"A responsible position. And such a wonderful ship name. Aspirational. Almost yearning. Very poetic."

The Marquis turned to Robert.

"I am Robert Drake, sir. The artificial intelligence specialist on this mission."

The Marquis nodded and turned to Jared.

"I'm Jared Bach, milord. Mechanical engineer for the mission."

The Marquis nodded to him as well, then turned to Arthur.

"Arthur Vegan. I am the sociologist for this mission."

"And a Greth. Very interesting."

The Marquis began filling his plate from the spread on the table, and the others followed suit.

"I suppose you are all filled with questions for me. Go ahead."

"Yes, sir. Why the duel?"

"In our experience, Earth has two distinct kinds of people, Mr. Drake. The honorable men and the dishonorable men. I had to know which of them you were."

"But you only dueled with me."

"But an honorable man will not keep the company of dishonorable men. Not by choice. Not for a voyage that takes a long time."

"I see, sir."

"You must call me Tomas, or I shall have to keep calling you Mr. and Ms. and all that nonsense."

"Very well, Tomas," Daphne said. "You've been to Earth then?"

"Not me, Daphne. Many others have, however. Many of these fruits and vegetables should be familiar to you. They come from Earth stock we shipped back. And my own identity as the Marquis de Milano was derived from Earth patterns."

"Does everyone here follow those patterns, Tomas? Are there dukes and duchesses, counts and countesses, barons and baronesses running around all over?"

"No, Daphne. Not for the most part. My little foibles are my own. My title is self-granted, and has no bearing on the power structure here."

"What is the power structure here, Tomas?"

"Mostly we don't have one, Jared. We are a post-scarcity society. Everyone has everything they need, so there is no need for conflict. It's very upsetting when it occurs, but we handle it in different ways."

"Like what?" Arthur asked.

"Shunning mostly. It's amazingly effective at getting people to work things out if you simply have nothing to do with either of them. And if that doesn't solve the problem, at least you don't have to deal with them."

"Given that there is no power structure to speak of, Tomas, are we or our ship in any danger from someone else?"

"No. My invitation to you in effect granted you safe passage. No one else would risk my anger by striking at you or your ship."

"Are you sure, Tomas?"

"Oh, yes, Daphne. Of course, it never hurts to keep your guard up, but I wouldn't worry about it."

"What is it that's so compelling about Earth for you, Tomas?" Arthur asked.

"Some of the greatest ideas ever conceived, Arthur. Honor. Duty. Loyalty. How extraordinary. No one else came up with these ideas and developed them so fully."

"But they were in service to the nobility, Tomas," Jared said. "In the beginning, at least. They were to keep competent men bound to rules that favored the nobility while most men were peasants and serfs."

"Yes, Jared, that's true. Extraordinary concepts nonetheless. We've been able to carry them out to their fullest extent here, because we are a post-scarcity society."

"But you still have servants, Tomas."

Jared waved to the serving people waiting nearby.

"And your guardsmen as well."

"Oh, Jared. I'm sorry. You missed a major point."

Jared raised an eyebrow at the Marquis.

"They're all robots. Surely you all knew that."

Heads shook all around the table.

"Ah. My oversight. All the serving people and guards are robots. As are the people you see working the fields out there.

The only biological creatures who live here are me and my extended family. My wife, our parents, our children, my younger brother and his wife and children, my wife's sister. Everyone else you see is a robot.

"All these houses you see nearby are my neighbors. All with robots of their own. All the food you see here was grown on this estate, or traded for with my neighbors. But it all came from this valley, all tended by robots."

The Marquis turned to Robert.

"I'm sorry, Robert, but we're a bit ahead of you in artificial intelligence."

"No doubt, but we'll catch up, Tomas."

"No doubt. Perhaps even with some help. That said, the robots make lousy sparring partners. They can all easily beat me with the epee. In seconds. And if I program them to be slower, well, I can program them to be enough slower I win all the time. There is no sport in that, either. So I truly enjoyed our little bout, Robert."

"I would have preferred it with safety equipment, Tomas. You know, masks, buttons on the points of the blades, things like that. Much less harrowing. Given that, I will fence you."

"Oh, good. I want you to teach me that last move you made, Robert. I don't know that one. What is it called?"

"The lunge."

"Excellent. Yes, I want to learn the lunge, Robert. What a splendid maneuver. I'm afraid I won't be your equal until I've mastered it."

The conversation pretty much stopped there as they ate. The food and wines were all wonderful, but Daphne couldn't help thinking she missed meat. Bacon or ham or something. Arthur, of course, ate none of the food except the cheese, which he could process, but he did drink some of the wine.

When their eating slowed down, the conversation restarted.

"Tomas, I guess I'm surprised you could go to Earth and be unnoticed."

"Ah, but we are talking a very long time ago, Daphne. Perhaps you have heard of Bastet?"

Jared nodded.

"The female goddess of fertility and the home, noted for her protection of women and children. She had the head of a cat."

"Yes, Jared. Protector of Pharoah, as well. We did what we could to encourage civilization on Earth when the opportunity arose. Meanwhile, we obtained Earth species for our use, such as the apples there."

"But that was thousands of years ago," Lena said.

"Yes, Lena. Indeed it was. And don't forget, it was the Egyptians who bred the domestic cat in her honor. The domestic cat protected their grain bins from vermin."

"Those were carnivores, but you are, apparently, herbivores, Tomas," Robert said. "Yet with large canine teeth?"

"For displaying dominance during mating selection. One must threaten one's challengers. This is not unknown among your Earth herbivores as well."

Daphne nodded. Gorillas were the obvious case.

"But you have not visited Earth in your own form in the last couple thousand years, Tomas," Daphne said. "Surely some note would have been made of it."

"That is correct, Daphne. We have robots that look like us, of course. We also made robots that look like humans. Primarily female ones. A comely female may make some arrangements that a male would find difficult."

Daphne laughed at the Marquis' description. That was certainly true.

"Especially if she were amenable to certain activities," Lena said. "Although that probably wouldn't apply to robots."

"Oh, but it does," the Marquis said. "Our human robots are indistinguishable from humans. Texture and pliability of the skin, temperature, odor, everything. It is difficult to tell the difference unless one knows exactly what one is looking for. They make compelling sexual partners. It has been very useful for getting what we want in terms of plant species and such."

That brought up the obvious question to Daphne, and Arthur asked it.

"Are your robots not a threat then, Tomas?" Arthur asked. "They do all the manual labor, wait on you at table, effectively prostitute themselves for your business interests. When do they demand a piece of the pie, as it were?"

"That can be a concern, Arthur. Artificial intelligence must be handled carefully, lest one create Nemesis in fact. Our robots are programmed to consider service fulfilling. Were they to be free of us, they would no longer have the opportunity to be of service, and would feel diminished thereby."

"A delicate balance," Daphne said.

"Perhaps, but it has maintained for some millennia. We are not now concerned about it, although we once were."

"We are still concerned about it on Earth, Tomas" Robert said. "There is a natural tendency among humans to anthropomorphize robots and AIs. To feel that they are ill-used as a new servant class. To feel some sympathy for them, even to talk of civil rights."

"I believe that is the wrong path," the Marquis said. "Consider. One has a washing machine. One puts the clothes in, sets the machine to run, and walks away. The machine will work for an hour in washing, and rinsing, and wringing out the clothes. Does one then consider the machine ill-used for its service?"

"There's a difference, surely," Robert said.

"Not particularly. The robots are machines. They do what they were programmed to do, including figuring out new situations and responding accordingly. But they remain machines. That is not to say one does not take care of them. One is no more likely to abuse a robot than to abuse a washing machine. Overloading the washing machine can lead to failure, so one does not do that. One takes more care than that. But it is not a person, after all."

"Interesting," Robert said.

"It has worked for us for a very long time, Robert."

Robert nodded. He was reorienting some of his thinking about AI and robotics.

"On another topic, Tomas," Daphne said. "We have been over three months in space tracking you down. First to Vega, one of the Greth planets close to Earth, then to Shandra, the Greth home planet, then to an intermediate point from which to survey stars and planets looking for you, then to here. Our crew of twenty-three has not been ashore in that whole time. Would you be willing to host shore leave?"

"Perhaps, Daphne. Perhaps. There would have to be some limits on numbers and activities."

Daphne nodded. Sensible. The Marquis continued.

"Now I am assuming that your crew is mostly made up of sensible types. But Earth sailors over the years have earned a reputation for excesses while on shore leave. We would wish to avoid those. So some sensitivity to the situation would be required."

"What did you have in mind, Tomas?"

The Marquis sat back and gave it some thought.

"Hmm. While we have wine – some fairly good vintages, I believe – inebriation often leads to regrettable behaviors. We would want to limit the consumption of alcoholic beverages to some point short of that.

"Secondly, we are herbivores, and we would find the consumption of meat on our planet repulsive. So no meat is to be brought down to the planet. One can wait until they get back to the ship.

"Finally, I only have six female and two male human robots, so we should limit the numbers to make sure no one lacks the companionship his shipmates enjoy."

Wait. *What?*

"You have six female and two male human robots, Tomas?"

"Yes. I am one of the primary people involved in our trade with Earth, such as it is. Those trips are all carried out by robots. Human robots in the case of Earth, of course. But I only have six of one and two of the other. We wouldn't want anyone on the crew to feel left out, so we should perhaps arrange the visits accordingly."

"Are you offering the crew sex with your robots, Tomas?"

"Yes, of course. Sex is a traditional shore leave activity, Daphne, and there are no other human outlets here. Besides, the human robots feel at loose ends between trips to Earth. They live to serve, and there is no opportunity for service here. Normally, that is. It would make them very happy to be, once again, of service."

"It sounds like these robots would trip them and beat them to the floor, Tomas," Lena said.

The Marquis chuckled.

"That is closer to the truth than you might expect, Lena."

Shore Leave

Daphne used Arthur's pad and Robert's data link to video call Captain Proxmire.

"Yes, Ms. Bach."

"Captain, I have the deal of a lifetime for the crew down here, as long as they don't screw it up."

"I'm listening, Ms. Bach."

"Shore leave. Just during the day. They'll take turns, every day a different group. We can do multiple rounds, so everybody gets multiple turns.

"Here's the setup. It's beautiful down here. Like Tuscany on Earth, but with better weather. The food is magnificent, the wines are even better. But there are some caveats.

"No meat on the planet. To them, it's repulsive, so we just don't do that. No overdrinking. They'll cut you off. No execrable behavior, like fighting or breaking stuff.

"Doesn't sound much like shore leave, does it?

"Except – here's the big except, Captain – they have human female and male robots down here. There are no humans down here, but you can't tell the difference. Honestly. These robots love to serve humans, in every possible way. Yes, even that. And for them, it's been a long time.

"I think they'll test the stamina of even your youngest crewmen, Captain."

"Sex with a robot, Ms. Bach?"

"You cannot tell the difference, Captain, and they're all gorgeous. Stunning, even. I've seen them, and they're beautiful, each and every one."

"That could work."

"I think it will, Captain. There are six female and two male human robots, so we should rotate the crew through here on that basis. I've specified days only, because it's easier for things to get out of hand at night, and we really don't want to screw this up. From a diplomatic point of view, things are going really well."

"All right, Ms. Bach. When do we start?"

"Tomorrow morning local time, Captain. At sunup. They have till sundown to enjoy themselves."

The first rotation of crew on shore leave didn't know what to make of the whole thing. A group of them talked about it in the crew lounge.

"So whattaya think about this shore leave thing?"

"No gettin' drunk. No overnights. No humans other than us. Sounds kinda borin'."

"What about the robots thing?"

"Machines? No, thanks."

"I don't know. It beats makin' the scene with a magazine."

"Maybe. Maybe not. I guess we'll find out."

"Me, I'll just be happy to get outside for a while. It sounds like a nice place."

"And fresh fruits and vegetables, too. Nothing frozen. I miss fresh stuff."

"Yeah. At least that'll be OK."

Daphne was up early, her clock not yet having adjusted to the local time. She meandered through the manor house and out onto the patio. A waiter served her a fresh juice and some buttered toast of their wonderful bread.

There was a hard point for shuttle landings in the rear of the building as well, well disguised on the back lawn. She watched as the big shuttle came down and landed on the hard point. As the crew came out of the shuttle, the human robots walked out to meet them. They carried picnic baskets. The female robots wore diaphanous caftans, as one would expect of some Greek goddess, while the male robots wore leggings and were shirtless.

Whatever hesitation any crew member had about consorting with robots disappeared under that visual onslaught. They paired up and headed off into the park-like setting, disappearing amid the vines and orchards ringing the hill.

Daphne chuckled.

"Have fun, my friends. And stay out of trouble."

The Marquis presently came down to breakfast. He was accompanied today by the Marquise, his wife. She was similar in most respects to the Marquis, but her face was more feminine somehow. She wore a dress of the same period of the Marquis' costume, looking much like Juliet but with a cat's head.

"The Marquise de Milano," the Marquis announced.

"Daphne Bach, milady."

"Oh, please call me Bianca, Daphne."

"Very well, Bianca."

"All is well with our first day of shore leave, Daphne?"

"I believe so, Tomas. My crew members seemed quite pleased with the arrangements when they arrived."

The Marquis chuckled.

"As I would have expected. And now, Daphne, you must tell me your story, of how humans acquired the interstellar drive, and of how you came to be associating with a Greth."

Daphne told her parents' story. How they came by the interstellar drive, and what they did with it. The Marquis was amused.

"So they stole the gravitonic drive from the Greth? How extraordinary."

Others had come in while Daphne told the story. The Marquis turned to Arthur.

"And you helped them do it, Arthur."

"Yes, Tomas. The hive queen had passed sentence of death on me, and Steven and Barbara Bach saved me from her. I have since considered myself more human than Greth."

"And no wonder," the Marquis said.

The Marquis turned to Daphne.

"You know that we gave the gravitonic drive and other technology to the Greth, as an inducement to give up war. With multiple planets to expand to, there was no longer any need to relieve population pressure with war."

"The oldest hive queen on their home world told us that, Tomas. And they appear to have kept to it."

"We've kept an eye on them, and, with minor missteps here and there, they actually have. We feared what would happen should such fearsome predators find the gravitonic drive on their own, and have no debt of gratitude to us. Can you imagine war here?"

The Marquis waved his hand out at the rolling hills and carefully tended fields of the valley, and Daphne shuddered. She could indeed imagine. She had seen pictures of Tuscany after the Second World War.

"But the Greth kept to their part of the bargain, Daphne, and have by now largely forgotten the study of war."

Daphne nodded.

"They've forgotten you as well for the most part, Tomas. It was all they could do to point us in the right direction. We had to do significant astrography work with our big telescope to find you and your home world."

"I hate to disappoint you, Daphne, but you may be working under something of a misapprehension. Mondeverde is not the Mrow home world. Earth is."

"*What?*"

"Oh, not your Earth. Our Earth. The planet named after the soil itself. Soil, dirt, earth. All the same word in Mrowan. In translation to English, it sounds better to call it Earth than to call it Dirt."

"What is it in Mrowan, Tomas?"

"Grlau."

"Let's stick with that to avoid confusion. Where is Grlau?"

The Marquis considered the angle of the sun in the morning sky, considered the month, then pointed to his left.

"About seventy-five light-years that way."

"But it looked like this world was the center of the colonization effort."

"Oh, it was, Daphne. Of a colonization effort, at least. You see, all the Mrow on Grlau with that certain get-up-and-go got up and went, to here. That attitude was baked in. When the next rush of colonization came, it was from here, not from Grlau."

"I don't get it," Lena said.

"Where are you from?" the Marquis asked her.

"From America. The United States."

"I rest my case," the Marquis said with a smile.

"I see," Arthur said. "You had no recent colonization event on Grlau the way humans did on Earth with the Americas. The recently colonized lands were largely the source of the new colonists heading into space. The people with a bent toward moving on already. In that sense, Mondoverde is your Americas."

"Exactly correct, Arthur. It was from here that the big

colonization occurred."

"That's interesting," Daphne said. "So what's Grlau like?"

"From what I've heard – for I have not been there – it is crowded, and dirty. They have cities."

The Marquis suppressed a shudder before continuing.

"Wherever there are cities, there is bureaucracy. Hardly the place for a gentleman farmer like myself."

"Do they also have records of the pre-colonial days, Tomas?" Daphne asked.

"Of what interest are such records to you, Daphne? We are talking five thousand years and more ago."

"We want to know where the gravitonic drive came from. It seems so out of the mainstream, we are curious as to how it came about."

"Ah. In that case, you would need to consult the oldest records. I myself do not know the story. It would be like someone regaling you with tales about the construction of the Pyramids. But if such records are to be found, they are on Grlau."

"I guess that's our next stop, then."

"Surely you do not need to leave so soon, Daphne."

"No. I'd like to rotate the crew through shore leave probably three times each. That would be nine days at this rate. And that will give Robert plenty of time to teach you the lunge."

"Assuming you've obtained safety equipment, Tomas."

"It's on the way."

"What about you, Arthur?" Daphne asked. "Are you going to be OK for nutrition?"

"Yes, Daphne. I will go up to the ship on the shuttle this evening, and return in the morning. If I do that every other night, I'll be fine."

"Oh, very well," the Marquis said. "I suppose I can't expect you to put off your mission forever."

"There you go, Tomas," Daphne said. "Live in the moment."

The other reason Arthur wanted to go up to the ship – in addition to his need to consume a large portion of meat at least every other day – was to observe the crew's response to spending the day of shore leave with the human robots, based on their conversations with each other on the way to the ship.

Apparently, they found it satisfactory.

The conversation in the crew lounge that evening was very different than the conversation the night before.

"Oh, you ain't gonna believe these gals. What lookers!"

"Yeah, and they were a lot of fun. No doubts there."

"Really? Not sort of, you know, mechanical?"

"Anything but. And they were willing to do anything. Anything at all."

"Wow. That sounds great."

"Yeah. You'll have a great time."

"I don't know. I told my wife I wouldn't do the hookers thing."

"That's the great part. They're machines, not humans."

"Your wife have a dildo she uses when you're not there? Same thing. Sex toys. Nothing more."

"Yeah. They're not human. It's not a real girl. There's no betrayal there. It's worse with a magazine. That's a picture of a real girl, after all."

"It is a hell of a lot of fun, though. I'll tell you that."

"Yeah. It's easy to forget they're not human."

One of them turned to the two female crew members who had gone down to the planet that day.

"What about you two?"

They looked at each other, and both blushed heavily.

"We had fun. And that's all I'll say about it," one of them said.

"Ha! See. Nothin' to worry about."

Arthur reported to the others when he returned at breakfast the next morning.

"The shore leave is proving very popular, Daphne. I think it's a good thing to stick with three rounds of the crew. I would be surprised if they tired of it before then."

"Always leave 'em wanting more," Daphne said. "Isn't that the old show business line?"

A Unique Solution

On the seventh day of rotation of the crew on shore leave, Captain Proxmire came down to the planet to talk to Daphne and Arthur. They met on the patio under the pergola.

"I'm surprised to see you here, Captain," Daphne said. "You're clearly not down here for the robots."

"No. I thought it important that I talk to you face to face."

"What's going on, Captain? Is there something wrong?"

Proxmire looked to the other end of the patio where others were talking. They were paying the trio no attention.

"Potentially, Ms. Bach. We've been three months gone, and we're a long way from home. I'm hearing rumblings that we've accomplished our mission – we found the third intelligent race – and it's time to go home. So I wanted to ask your intentions."

"I see, Captain. Yes, that is concerning. It is my intention to go to the home world of the Mrow and consult the records there. We still don't know how the gravitonic drive came about. The Mrow may not be the end of our search."

"Well, that last crossing took a lot of the starch out of the crew, ma'am. I think it's the longest crossing that's ever been attempted and, well, it wore on them, ma'am."

Daphne nodded. It hadn't been a bowl of laughs for them, either. But to give up now?

"Let me think about it, Captain. When are you going back up to the ship?"

"I'll go up on the big shuttle in the evening, Ms. Bach."

"All right. So I have some time to think about it, and we can still talk again today."

PUSH IN BOÖTES

Later, the Marquis sat down with Daphne and Arthur. Once again, they were at one end of the patio and the others were at the other end.

"Hi, Tomas. What's going on?" Daphne asked.

The Marquis sighed.

"It's a common problem every wealthy landowner has, Daphne. Maintaining the happiness of the staff."

"The staff? You mean the robots?"

"Oh, yes. They are programmed to serve. That is what they find fulfilling. What does one do when there is no opportunity to serve?"

"Can they not work the farms?"

"Yes, of course. And they do. It is not their highest calling, however, and they know that. Besides, how well-manicured must my fields be?"

He waved his hand out at the view, from the patio, of the well-tended acres of his farm. Daphne saw his point.

"What are you going to do, Tomas?"

"I'll send them to Earth. It's been a while since we picked up new hybrids. That'll take a while. It's a long trip, and they'll have to spend some time researching the best things to bring back. That'll satisfy them for quite a while."

"Wait a minute. You're talking about the human robots?"

"Yes, Daphne. They are already saddened by your pending departure. There will be some tearful goodbyes, I can tell you that."

A possible solution to both her problems occurred to Daphne. That couldn't possibly work, could it?

Why not?

"Tomas, what if I were to take them to Earth for you? We might not get back for several months, but there would be opportunities to serve along the way."

The Marquis considered, then brightened.

"Ah. I see. That would be a splendid solution from my point of view. I would send a ship to pick them up in a year or two."

Daphne foresaw some problems. Turn the robots loose among Earth's population? Of course, the Marquis could do that anyway any time he wanted. As he had in the past, for that matter.

And what would Captain Proxmire think?

Proxmire, as it turned out, didn't like the idea much.

"Such a thing would never be permitted on a Navy ship, Ms. Bach, I can tell you that."

"Yes, but this isn't a Navy ship, Captain, it is a private vessel, and I am the owner representative. Further, we are farther from Earth than anyone has ever been, and have spent longer periods in the tunnel than any Earth ship ever has. So let's talk positives and negatives, and not platitudes."

Proxmire sighed. She was right, of course. Just twenty years old or not, she was right on both of those points. But he'd been aboard ships longer than she'd been alive.

"I don't think having these humanoid robots – and I've seen them now, they might as well be humans, to look at them – running around on the crew deck of the ship is a good idea."

"Fair point. They'll remain on the passenger deck."

"Will they, ma'am?"

"They'll follow my orders, Captain. Tomas has assured me of that. With the robots, that you can trust."

"And crew members visit them there?"

"On their off days, yes. Not otherwise. What is your duty schedule, Captain?"

"Twelve-hours shifts, three days on and one day off."

"So one-quarter of the crew at any given time?"

"Except for general quarters, yes, ma'am."

"You have fourteen operations crew. Four doesn't go into fourteen evenly."

"It alternates, ma'am. Four, then three, then four, then three."

"And how many must you have for general quarters?"

"Twelve, Ms. Bach. We need to man the escape ship."

"So you could accommodate two, or one, at a time, on their off days, being on the passenger deck. Every other off day."

Proxmire hesitated, then grudgingly admitted it.

"Yes, ma'am."

"If you were in port, Captain, would crew on their off days be permitted to go into town?"

"Yes, ma'am."

"Drinking and whoring and all the rest?"

"Most likely, ma'am."

"What's the longest we've spent in the tunnel, Captain?"

"Fourteen days, ma'am."

"Was that hard on the crew?"

"Yes, ma'am, it sure was."

"How far are we from Earth right now, Captain?"

"We've spaced a total of five hundred forty-three light-years in four legs, Ms. Bach, but they haven't been in a straight line. Straight back to Earth in one pass is a bit over four hundred light-years."

"Which is how long in the tunnel, Captain?"

"Twenty days."

Daphne raised an eyebrow at him, and Proxmire looked thoughtful.

"If we split it up into two legs, Captain, how long would they be?"

"They would each be fourteen days, ma'am. Twenty-eight

days total."

"And without planet leave during the stop?"

"That's most likely, ma'am. We would have to know of an Earth-like planet along that path to have planet leave."

"Which is unlikely."

"Yes, Ms. Bach."

"Captain, I will put it to you that we already have a problem. The issue is whether we have a bigger problem with the robots along or without them along."

That got Proxmire thinking.

"What about crew discipline, ma'am?"

"What is your discipline now, Captain? Confine them to quarters? How is that any different than their normal off day? Now, if you were to, say, deprive them of their next rotation to the passenger deck, that would be a punishment worthy of the name."

"What about the Deck D galley crew, Ms. Bach?"

"I believe the eight of them have the same schedule, Captain. Three on and one off. Is that right?"

"Yes, ma'am."

"So for an every-other-day-off schedule, that's only one more person. So there would be either two or three people with the robots in the spare passenger suites on Deck D. Only four of those suites are used right now, two for passengers and two with computer equipment. Arthur stays in the one with the data server. So there are five suites available."

"And if someone jumps the queue, Ms. Bach?"

"Give the robots the schedule, Captain. They'll enforce it. They're incredibly strong, Any one of them can tie your strongest crewman into a pretzel. They'll be no violations of the rules."

"Hmm."

PUSH IN BOÖTES

"Look, Captain. *Beyond the Known Stars* is a unique ship. She's a one-off. This is a unique mission. The two longest spacing legs ever completed by a human ship were our last two legs. Standard cookie-cutter solutions won't work for us. We need unique solutions to our unique problems."

Proxmire sighed.

"Very well, Ms. Bach. We'll give it a try. But I'll call off the whole thing if I have to. Make the passenger deck off-limits despite the robots' presence. Because of it, more like."

"Make sure the crew understands that, Captain, and I don't think we'll have any problems."

Captain Proxmire returned to the ship on the big shuttle with the returning crew that evening. He and Daphne continued to work through the details of the plan, not making anything public until they had worked it out.

One issue was that two-one-two-one, run through twice, was only twelve crew members out of fourteen. Two-two-two-one taken twice worked, but left Proxmire with but eleven crew members for general quarters every fourth day. Proxmire considered carefully which crew members he most needed at general quarters when he was shorthanded.

They also decided the schedule they had followed on Mondoverde was best, with crew being paroled to the passenger deck from eight in the morning until eight in the evening on their off-day. This kept alcohol consumption to a minimum and reduced Proxmire's exposure on his shorthanded days.

They had all the details worked out by the end of the ninth day of shore leave.

The next day, with three rounds of shore leave completed,

Daphne and the rest of the party were getting ready to leave. The small shuttle was still parked on the landing pad of the front lawn where they had landed.

The Marquis called the human robots together on the patio. Daphne sat in on this conversation, and was again struck by how sensitive the Mrow makers of the robots had been to human standards of beauty.

They were all stunning, both men and women. They weren't real humans, but they were all stunning.

"I have a further opportunity for service for you all," the Marquis said. "I have been considering the next mission to Earth, to research their newer hybrids and bring them back to Mondoverde."

The robots looked back and forth among each other with some anticipation, Daphne thought.

"Now, as luck would have it, there is already a ship headed in that direction. *Beyond the Known Stars* is, ultimately, headed for Earth. Daphne and I have negotiated with her captain that you may all travel aboard her.

"Further, we have made an arrangement such that, on their days off from their other duties, crew members may visit you on the passenger deck of the ship. I assume there will be a certain amount of hanky-panky going on during these visits."

This got big smiles from everyone.

"Now there is a caution. Once on Earth, you will follow my instructions for selecting and obtaining the desired hybrids. A Mrowan ship will pick you up there in two years from today, at the spaceport that Daphne's family runs.

"While on board the ship, however, you will obey Daphne's orders as if they came from me. This situation may not work out, in which case the visits will be ordered stopped by Daphne. She may rearrange the situation as she sees fit. In every case, aboard ship, you are to take her orders.

"That is your assignment. Are there any questions?"

There were no questions.

"Do you all accept this assignment as stated?"

"Yes, sir," they all answered.

"You may get ready to depart, taking whatever clothing and other items you will need for two years abroad, primarily on Earth."

The robots filed out to get their things.

Captain Proxmire was having much the same meeting aboard *Beyond the Known Stars*.

"So those are the rules," he finished. "If the rules get broken, I may have to terminate this arrangement, or ban some people from participating, either temporarily or permanently. You need to know that I will not hesitate to do so. The rules are the rules, and, as you are all worthy spacers, you know how to follow rules. See that you do.

"That said, it is time to deploy the big shuttle to the planet to pick up the robots and their things. The current on-call shuttle crew will prepare for departure.

"Dismissed."

The Marquis gave Daphne a big hug, and kissed both her cheeks, before she got into the small shuttle. The robots had already left in the large shuttle.

"Bon chance, mon amie."

"Good luck to you, too, Tomas."

To Grlau

Daphne had the exact coordinates of Grlau from Tomas, translated for their systems. It was seventy-five light-years away, which was a mere hop compared to their last two legs of a hundred fifty light-years and two hundred light-years. This would be two and a half days at each end of the trip, and a little over eight and a half days in the tunnel.

Not too bad.

Captain Proxmire noted that scheduled days off – and leave to the passenger deck – would not begin until *Beyond the Known Stars* was under way, and the crew got the ship ready for space on the quick.

They left Mondoverde orbit at twelve gravities that same day, bound for Grlau.

The next day, two crew members from Deck F showed up. They were joined by one of the service crew here on Deck D.

The robots were all waiting for them in the living room. Each crew member selected a robot, and disappeared into one of the empty suites.

Daphne and the others sometimes saw one of the crew members at a meal or two, but mostly they took their meals in the suites.

When they did take their meals with the group, the conversation gave Daphne some insight into what the crew was thinking and feeling.

"Do you not wish companionship, Arthur?"

The alien looked up from his display at the beautiful female robot.

"I have no use for human sexual companionship."

"Oh, I know that, Arthur. I thought we might talk about the sociology of Mondoverde, and compare and contrast it with that of Earth, with which I am also familiar."

"That actually sounds very interesting."

"Come along then. My name, by the way, is Roxanne."

"Robert, you are in charge of the artificial intelligence computer on the ship, are you not?"

"That's right."

"Would you like to look at the code with me and see if we can find any areas that could be improved?"

"Of course."

"Very well. Come along. Oh, and my name is Rebecca."

Later, Daphne asked Robert if she had anything to worry about. He looked surprised.

"No, of course not. She's a machine, not a person. I deal with intelligent machines all the time. As for her looks, as the son of a very wealthy man, I have had my share of beautiful women make themselves available if I wanted them. But none so beautiful, I think, as you."

"Good answer," Daphne said and laughed.

One of the robots – the last of the six female robots, as today's three crew members were two men and a woman, all of whom preferred female companions – walked up to Jared.

"What are you working on, Jared?"

"I'm trying to figure out a way to distract crew members from obsessing about the tunnel during long transits."

"What is the major problem you are having?"

"The view from the outside cameras is always of the tunnel.

There's nothing I can do about that."

"Is that true? Could we not reprocess the feed from the cameras, or substitute a feed of our own?"

"What do you have in mind?"

"I have a couple ideas. Oh, my name is Rosalind."

"Well, I guess it's just you and me, Daphne," Lena said.

"Yeah. What are we gonna do?"

"Wanna play cards?"

"For bridge we need four. I guess we could play honeymoon bridge."

The two male robots walked up to the game table in the living room where Daphne and Lena were sitting.

"Excuse me, ma'am, but we play bridge."

"You do?" Daphne asked.

"Yes, ma'am. From a prior visit to Earth. We thought it might come in handy."

"Well, pull up some chairs, you guys."

"My name is Randall, and my partner is Rodney."

"Oh, no, you don't," Lena said. "You don't get to be partners. One's with me and one's with Daphne."

"As you wish."

That night, after the crew members all left, they compared notes about their day with the robots.

"Lena and I played cards with the two male robots, Randall and Rodney. And let me tell you something. Those boys know how to play bridge."

"Beat you, did they?" Jared asked.

"No, we split them up. Me and Randall against Lena and Rodney. We woulda got creamed otherwise."

"Well, Rosalind and I worked on a cool idea to keep people

from getting quite so worked up about the tunnel. We replace the camera feeds with computer simulations of what the star field looks like at every point along the way. You know, if we were stopped there.

"It's pretty cool. The galaxies and distant stars stay the same, but the closer stars move across the star field as we're moving."

"That does sound pretty cool," Daphne said. "How far along are you?"

"We've got the basics in place. We can make it work. We just need to incorporate the actual star maps as we go now."

"Nice. What about you, Robert?"

"Rebecca and I were working on the artificial intelligence I brought along. I have about three major papers I can do now, were I not to keep them trade secret."

"Really."

"Oh, yes. Sort of 'Why did you do that here? Why didn't you do this?' A bunch of those. It's a difference in attitude, not just in code."

"Give me an example," Daphne said.

"OK. So there's this place where we wall off this one path the machine can take where it runs off down a bunny trail and spins its wheels, right? Burns up all the processor time on what is likely going to be unproductive.

"Rebecca's like, 'Well, there could be something good down that path. Rather than wall it off, why not just limit the processor time along that path to maybe five percent, then shut it off after a while if it doesn't go anywhere. But, once in a while, that bunny trail could be productive.' That sort of thing. Brilliant, just brilliant."

"Hey," Jared said. "Anybody else notice all their names start with 'R'? What are the other three's names, I wonder."

"Rhiannon, Raffaella, and Rashida," Arthur said. "I inquired when I noticed the pattern. They are all robots, you see."

"Do all of Tomas' robotic staff names start with 'R'?" Lena asked. "Sounds unlikely."

"No, just these eight humanoid robots," Arthur said. "Because their names are in English you see, and the English word is robot."

"Got it," Daphne said. "And what about you, Arthur?"

"Roxanne and I had an interesting and far-roaming discussion of the sociological differences between Earth and Mondoverde and their likely implications."

"Oh, that sounds interesting, especially as to trade. We know they like our fruits, vegetables, and cheeses."

"And we definitely want their AI and robotics technology," Robert said.

Daphne nodded.

"Do we know why we missed Grlau in our review of planets in this area with the big telescope?" Daphne asked.

"Oh, we didn't miss it," Arthur said. "We saw it, but we didn't think it was their home world because it wasn't surrounded with other colony planets as Mondoverde was."

"And we now know why that was."

"Yes. Mondoverde was the jumping off point for further colonization because it was where the wanderlust was strongest."

"OK, so Grlau is populated by all the people who wanted to stay behind. Who wanted to stand pat with what they had rather than go gallivanting off in search of something better."

"That's what it sounds like, Daphne."

"And Mondoverde was colonized first, even though it was seventy-five light-years away, because it was the planet most like Grlau, and required the least geo-engineering."

"The geo-engineering capability may have come along later.

Which would have made those other planets less desirable until they had that capability."

"That all sounds right to me," Jared said.

"Of course, we've been wrong before," Lena said.

"We'll just have to see when we get there," Daphne said.

The trip to Grlau fell into routine. Every day, one or two crew members would come down to the passenger deck from the crew deck. One of their galley staff on the passenger deck would join them. They would all select a robot to accompany them to a passenger suite.

The other five robots would entertain Daphne and the other passengers in various ways, working on the AI or the tunnel viewer or playing cards or talking sociology.

Three days into the tunnel – and with the permission of Captain Proxmire – Jared put his camera views in stream with the exterior cameras of the ship. Now if you looked at the exterior views, you saw the simulated star field of where they were and their progress.

After that, Daphne noticed a gradual increase in the mood of the crew, based on those people who took meals together with the passengers on their days off.

Eight days in the tunnel passed quickly, and then they were in the Grlau system.

Grlau

After eight and a half days in the tunnel, they emerged into the Grlau system. There was a slight shift in the camera views as the simulated images gave way to the real images from the cameras.

Grlau was the second planet out from the sun out of six total planets in the system. As with Earth's solar system, none of the other planets was inhabitable. Also as with Earth, Grlau had a large moon, which Daphne and her team now considered to be a prerequisite for the evolution of intelligent life.

Tomas had had a dictionary for Mrowan available for the language headsets, and all of them had learned Mrowan, but Daphne did not feel comfortable with her ability to speak the language. It sounded much like an argument between two cats, all being mouthed by one person.

As a result, she used a recording Tomas had made for them in Mrowan as her greeting to the planet, and played it over the channel he said Grlau used for orbital traffic control.

<My fellow Mrowans. This recording is an introduction of our friends from the human planets, arriving now on the interstellar vessel *Beyond the Known Stars*. Daphne Bach is the ambassador from the planet they call Earth – same as we call our own home world – and she would like to consult the records of our pre-space history. I beg you to allow this consultation, as her mission is of interest to me. Their primary language is English, although they can understand spoken Mrowan and read written Mrowan. I remain Stefano Tommaso Omero Giovanni Battista de Milano, Marquis de Milano, of the Mrowan planet Mondoverde.>

They waited for a response. In case the conversation had to be held completely in Mrowan, Daphne had Rhiannon waiting with her for their answer.

The answer came within minutes. It was in Mrowan.

<To Daphne Bach of Beyond the Known Stars. We don't have anyone here who understands English at the moment. Do you have a translator?>

Daphne nodded to Rhiannon, and she answered in Mrowan.

<Yes, we have a translator available. Go ahead, Grlau.>

<You are cleared to take a west-to-east equatorial orbit at ninety resti. There is orbital traffic at eighty resti, so conscientious station-keeping is required.>

<West-to-east equatorial orbit at ninety resti. Orbital traffic at eighty resti. Understood. Will comply.> Rhiannon said.

"What's a resti?" Daphne asked.

"About one and a quarter miles," Rhiannon said. "Eighty resti is a hundred miles, and ninety resti is one hundred and twelve miles."

"Good enough. Arthur, let the captain know. And make sure he comes in over the geosynchronous orbits. Tomas told me there was quite a bit of traffic there. Let's come in real slow and keep an eye out for other traffic."

"All right, Daphne."

"That other traffic kind of bothers me," Daphne said. "They're going to go flying past us every couple of hours."

"That's incorrect, ma'am."

"Why, Rhiannon? They're at ninety percent of our orbit, aren't they?"

"No, ma'am. They are at very nearly the same orbit, because the orbital distance is calculated from the center of the planet."

"Oh, that's right. I knew that."

Rhiannon nodded.

"We may see them every week or so, slowly going past us. It's not a problem, ma'am. Even at the same altitude, they would not be much of a problem, as their orbital speed would be the same as ours, and space is a big place."

Daphne nodded.

"And a miss is as good as a mile."

"Yes, ma'am. Accurately stated. It's not a problem. The closer they are to our orbit, the longer Captain Proxmire has to react if they actually were on a collision course."

Two and a half days after exiting the tunnel, Captain Proxmire and the crew maneuvered *Beyond the Known Stars* into the designated orbit.

Daphne and Rhiannon called the planet again, with Rhiannon doing translation chores.

<*Beyond the Known Stars* to Grlau Orbital Control."

<Go ahead, *Beyond the Known Stars*.>

<We are requesting communications with someone from the planet's historical archives.>

<Roger that, *Beyond the Known Stars*. We will pass on your request. Look for response on Channel One-Eight-Three.>

<Channel One-Eight-Three. Acknowledged."

"What's Channel One-Eight-Three?" Daphne asked.

"A specific frequency in their spectrum allocation," Rhiannon said. "I have that frequency, ma'am. The Marquis routinely runs freight shipments to Grlau, so we know all their frequencies."

"Give that frequency to Arthur to send to the captain so we can monitor the frequency."

"Yes, ma'am."

<*Beyond the Known Stars*, come in, please.>

<This is *Beyond the Known Stars,*> Rhiannon answered.

<My name is Meowmrow Reet. I am the Assistant Deputy Archivist for Grlau.>

<Hello, Mr. Meowmrow. I am Daphne Bach. How are you?>

<I'm fine, thank you, Ms. Daphne. You wish access to the archives?>

<Yes. We specifically are looking for the history of the development of the gravitonic drive.>

<Those are very old records, Ms. Daphne, but I think we'll be able to help you with that.>

<That would be wonderful, Mr. Meowmrow. How do we proceed?>

"My suggestion is that you come down here first to see what we have, Ms. Daphne. Would tomorrow an hour after dawn work for you?"

Daphne shrugged, then nodded to Rhiannon.

<That would be fine, Mr. Meowmrow.>

<Ngrish is your preferred language, Ms. Daphne?>

He pronounced English in the Mrowan fashion.

<Yes, Mr. Meowmrow.>

<Very well. I will have my associate meet your party at the following coordinates at that time.>

<Thank you, Mr. Meowmrow.>

<Meowmrow out.>

"Ms. Daphne?" Daphne asked.

"Grlau is a family-name-first society, ma'am. I'm sorry. I didn't anticipate that and give your family name first."

"That's all right, Rhiannon. Ms. Daphne works. So what is an hour after dawn at those coordinates?"

"That's in about sixteen hours, ma'am. Eleven o'clock in the morning ship's time."

"All right. Let's let everyone know. I'm going to want you to accompany me, for translation and other information."

"Yes, ma'am. I'll be happy to."

They let Rhiannon pilot the shuttle. Apparently she knew from other robots – the Marquis' robots that had been to Grlau before – how to navigate Grlau's air traffic control. She connected directly through the shuttle's systems without the need to have radio chatter audible in the cabin.

Rhiannon landed the shuttle on a pad before a large government building in the middle of a city.

All five of the team had gone down to the planet, plus Rhiannon. It was a little cramped in the small shuttle, but Daphne would have taken the large shuttle rather than leave any of them behind. She simply didn't know who she would need on this visit.

They were, all of them, armed. Standard landing-party procedure.

When they exited the shuttle, they were met by a Mrow in what Daphne took to be some officious-type suit.

"Ms. Daphne?" he said in English.

"I'm Daphne Bach."

"Ah. Very good. I am Kkkkreow Mareet. I am an Associate to the Assistant Deputy Archivist."

He pronounced all the 'K's in his family name.

"Hello, Mr. Kkkkreow. Thank you for meeting us."

"Yes. Well, come this way."

Kkkkreow led them into the building to a bank of elevators. They took the elevators down into the basements of the building. He led them out on a deep subbasement level, where they were met by four more Mrow.

"These are my interns, Ms. Daphne. They have been looking

into your request. I will let them show you what they have found."

"Very good, Mr. Kkkkreow. Thank you."

"And with that, I will take my leave of you. Good luck."

He bowed slightly, then went back over to the elevators and took the next car.

<I'm afraid we have been busy with your request and did not take time to learn Ngrish.>

<That's all right. Ms. Daphne understands Mrowan, and I am her mouthpiece for whatever she needs to say.>

<Excellent. Please come with us.>

The Mrow – Daphne was iffy on telling the sex of the Mrow unless they were dressed in gender-specific clothing – led them deeper into the subbasement. They were all dressed in unisex coveralls, which left her confused as to their sex.

Past shelf after shelf, cross-aisle after cross-aisle, they went. They must have had over a city block of storage down here, and this was just one level.

He – for lack of a better term – led them into an open area deep in the stacks.

<All of these records were captured on film millennia ago. The records themselves are mostly falling apart now. The films themselves are deteriorating, too, but are still legible. They have not yet been digitized. I know that would make your search easier, but at least we have them.>

Two walls of the open area were newer bookshelves – only millennia old – with file upon file of microfilm, or the Mrowan equivalent. A table in the center of the open area had a table with multiple viewers on it.

<Mr. Kkkkreow said you have found something?>

<A few things, Ms. Daphne. One is the drawings of our earliest gravitonic drive engine. A bench test, one might say.

Another is a first-person account of the first mission in a gravitonic drive ship. They discovered the tunnel on that mission, which came as something of a shock. We also have a diary from a colonist on the first ship to what is now called Mondoverde, our first colony.

<The fourth thing we discovered may be of even more interest. We have found the autobiography of Growff Gerrrt.>

<Growff Gerrrt?> Rhiannon asked.

<The inventor of the gravitonic drive. We had thought all documentation of that period lost, but a copy of a copy of his autobiography survives, recorded on film.>

<Excellent,> Rhiannon said for Daphne. <We'll start with that.>

Deep in the catacombs of the fourth subbasement of the Archives building on Grlau, Daphne and Robert, Jared and Lena, and the alien Arthur, listened as Rhiannon read to them the ten-thousand-year-old autobiography of Growff Gerrrt. The four Mrowan interns sat on chairs nearby and listened as well, as Rhiannon read it in Mrowan, which everybody could understand.

The problem was that the text was written in Old Mrowan. It was much like reading Chaucer in Old English. Rhiannon wasn't sure she could read it at first, but she started reading it to herself until she began to get it, then started over at the beginning, reading aloud and translating into modern Mrowan as she went.

The beginning portion was mundane. Typical life details about birth, childhood, and education. It was when they got into his career that things got interesting. Very interesting, indeed.

PUSH IN BOÖTES

<It was at about this time that I met Suldan. Our first meeting was something of a shock to me, as you can well imagine. I had been a somewhat parochial academic, and meeting Suldan was an experience so out of the ordinary as to be disorienting. Nevertheless, Suldan and I became friends, though I of necessity had to keep him my secret.>

"Wait," Daphne said. "Suldan isn't a Mrowan name."

"No, it certainly isn't," Jared said. "What's going on? He's talking as though his readers would understand."

"They forgot," Robert said. "Whoever Suldan was, they forgot about him."

"You mean, like if everybody forgot about Arthur?" Lena asked.

"My God, it's exactly like that," Daphne said. "Was Suldan an alien?"

"I don't know yet, ma'am. Should we continue?" Rhiannon asked.

"Yes, please. I'm sorry."

Rhiannon went back to reading aloud. Before long, there was another interesting passage.

<It was not long into our friendship that Suldan disclosed to me the most marvelous invention. It was at the edge of my understanding of the physical sciences, despite my education. The theory behind it seemed sound, if one threw out much of the theory I thought I already knew.

<But the import of it! If one could counteract the force of gravity, there was no limit to what one could do. It would be possible to travel to the moon, the other planets, perhaps even the stars.

<Of course, that last must be true, or I would not have met

Suldan at all.>

"OK, that last tears it," Daphne said. "Suldan is an alien, and Growff knows it. He knows that Suldan's interstellar."

"And Suldan gave him the gravitonic drive," Jared said.

"So there's a fourth intelligent race out there," Lena said.

"And they're even older than the Mrow," Robert said.

"Holy shit. This is like one of those Russian dolls," Daphne said. "You open it and find there's another one inside."

"I find it fascinating," Arthur said. "The question is, How did it not become well known and stay well known?"

Daphne turned to Rhiannon.

"This was a published autobiography?"

Rhiannon turned to the Mrowan interns.

<Was this a published autobiography?>

<It was unpublished. It was found among his papers after his death,> one said.

"OK. Well, that explains that," Daphne said.

Rhiannon raised an eyebrow at Daphne, and Daphne nodded. Rhiannon went back to reading aloud. There was a long story of the building and testing of the drive, then another interesting passage.

<Suldan has left me now. He has gone back to his people. He left in his small craft – in which he had arrived these many years ago – to go back from whence he came.

<I helped him get ready. He says his ship can make ten times the acceleration of one gravity – an astonishing number at the time – and yet it will take him twenty-four days' journey to get home. We ensured he would have the food he required for such a lengthy journey, then I bade him goodbye.

<One last note on Suldan. Before he left, I asked him where

in the firmament he lived. Where should I look in the sky when I thought of him? He told me the center star of the body of the Wainhorse was his home.>

"OK. How much is one planetary gravity here?" Daphne asked. It's not g, like at home."

"The gravity of Grlau is about ninety-five percent of g," Rhiannon said.

"So Suldan's ship could make nine and a half g. And how long is a day here?"

"The day on Grlau is about twenty-three hours, twelve minutes in human Earth measurements."

"So a twenty-three day trip at nine and a half gravities. How far is that? How long would it take us at twelve gravities?"

"Well, it's linear with acceleration, so it would be about twenty days, Daphne," Jared said.

"Eighteen and a third, to be exact," Rhiannon said. "That's days in the tunnel, plus five more days split between the two ends."

"And how far is it?"

"It's three hundred thirty-seven light-years."

"And from there to home?" Daphne asked.

"It depends on the angle, ma'am, but it could be as much as eight hundred light-years. Twenty-eight days in the tunnel at twelve gravities, plus five days split between the two ends."

Daphne's heart sank. Too long! Well, it probably didn't matter. They didn't know the angle anyway.

"Well, it's a good thing we don't know the angle, because I would be tempted to go for it."

Rhiannon turned to the Mrowan interns.

<Do you know of a constellation called the Wainhorse?>

<Yes, of course. But there is no center star in the body.>

<What? Are you sure?>

<Yes.>

<What is your oldest record of the constellations?> Rhiannon asked. <Do you have such diagrams here?>

<Yes, I think so.>

The interns busied themselves about the index, then brought a film over.

<It is here, image one hundred thirty-seven.>

Rhiannon placed the film in the viewer and selected image one hundred thirty-seven. She zoomed in, then called one of the interns over.

<What do you call that?>

<Yes, that's the Wainhorse constellation, but that star you're pointing at isn't there.>

"What?!" Daphne asked. "The star disappeared?"

<Here is a current image of the Wainhorse constellation,> one of the interns said, holding up a handheld display.

There was no star in the center of the body. Yet the millennia-old image showed it clearly.

"Rhiannon, do you have an angle and distance on that star from the image?"

"Yes, Daphne."

"OK. Come along, everyone. I think we have what we came for."

Daphne led them back out of the archives, the interns following along. All the way to the shuttle – all the way to the ship – she did not share with anyone what she was thinking.

A Big Decision

When they got back to the passenger deck of *Beyond the Known Stars*, Daphne flopped on a sofa in the living room with a sigh. Everyone else sat down around her.

"What are you thinking, Daphne?" Jared asked.

"How does an entire star disappear?"

"A nova?" Lena asked.

"Nope. You would have a huge cloud of outwardly expanding gas, lit up by the collapsed star in the center. The star itself would still be there."

"The star couldn't go anywhere," Robert said. "It has to still be there. It's just occluded somehow."

"A Dyson Sphere," Jared said. "That would do it."

"Right," Daphne said.

"What's a Dyson Sphere?" Lena asked.

Daphne turned to Arthur and raised an eyebrow. Arthur turned to Lena.

"A Dyson Sphere is a hypothetical structure that encloses a star, completely capturing all its energy. A civilization could live on the inside surface of the sphere and be completely cut off from things on the outside."

"You said hypothetical, Arthur," Lena said. "Is such a thing even possible?"

"It has been postulated. No such structure has ever been found."

"Until now," Daphne said. "I can think of no other way to make a star just disappear."

"It would still radiate, though, wouldn't it, Daphne?" Arthur asked. "In the infrared at least. There have to be some inefficiencies in the energy capture of the star. That's just thermodynamics."

"Yes, but if it's several AU across, that emission is at a relatively low level," Jared said. "It wouldn't look like a star."

"No, but we should be able to see it with the big telescope, I think," Daphne said. "But if it's there, it raises another big question."

"Of course," Robert said. "Do we go there or not?"

"That could be dicey," Lena said. "What did they say those trips would be? Eighteen days, then twenty-eight days back to Earth? What's the crew going to think about that?"

"They aren't going to like it much," Jared said.

"The crew was told to plan on a six-month voyage," Daphne said. "We still have time to pull this off and have them home early. The issue is those two big hops in the tunnel. Jared's camera views should make that easier, but still."

"Well, let's see if it's there first," Robert said. "We need to deploy the big telescope."

"We have to move away from the planet first, to get a clear view," Jared said.

Daphne nodded.

"That's what I'm thinking."

"Wait a minute," Robert said. "Is it necessarily twenty-eight days back to Earth? What's the direction of this thing?"

"It's further north again," Daphne said. "The Wainhorse constellation is north from Grlau. So it's maybe eight hundred light-years from Earth."

"That's weird, isn't it?" Lena asked. "That every new civilization is further north?"

"The civilizations are also getting older and more advanced as we go," Robert said.

"What's to say this civilization with the Dyson Sphere isn't the seed civilization for this part of the galaxy?" Daphne asked. "We just keep moving closer to the hub. The big question is, How many other spokes does this hub have?"

Jared nodded.

"There could be other chains of civilizations radiating out from this hub, in other directions. Ours radiated out to the galactic south, but there could be other chains, I guess."

"Gosh," Lena said. "They're like the great-grandparents of a bunch of civilizations."

"Could be. Don't know," Daphne said. "That's for other missions. The question for this mission is, Do we go to the hub or not?"

"I think we should," Jared said. "But it depends on whether Captain Proxmire thinks it's possible without a mutiny."

"The short version, Captain, is that the Mrow did not invent the gravitonic drive. It was given to them by an even older civilization. We think we know where that civilization is. The problem is it's three hundred and some light-years from here. Further north. If we go there, we've got eight hundred light-years to go to get home."

"Which would both be even longer than those two long hops we took, Ms. Bach. That's an issue."

"I'm very much aware, Captain. The question is, Will the crew stand for it? Now, we'll still get back before the six-month planning estimate for this voyage. But those two long hops are a big issue."

"They sure are, ma'am. Maybe we can do some things to make it a bit easier. Mr. Bach's simulations of the stars passing by as we go was a big help on the last hop, that's for sure. And, much as I hate to admit it, the robots for off-days worked out as well."

Daphne thought about it.

"How about this, Captain. We can leave things as they are and head home. That's one option. The other thing we could do is head out to check this out, then head home. But we would extend the accessibility of the robots from nine in the evening before the off-day, to eight in the evening on the off-day, and it would be every off-day, not just every other."

"Do you have room for that here, Ms. Bach?"

"Yes, Captain. We have five cabins completely unused, and one cabin that just has the AI machine in the living room of the suite. It's about the size of two refrigerators, and the hot air from the cooling system is ducted into the air return, so not a big deal."

"When we're in the tunnel, we could also go to skeleton crew, ma'am. We don't need to fight the ship when we're in the tunnel. That would give people more time off."

"Whatever you think would work, Captain. It would be a big plus to the mission if we could pull this off."

"I'll talk to my exec and the senior enlisted, ma'am."

"OK, Captain. In the meantime, let's move away from the planet and deploy the big telescope. The first thing we need to do is see if they're really out there."

Rhiannon arranged a departure clearance with Grlau Orbital Control, and Proxmire and the crew accelerated Beyond the Known Stars out of orbit and into open space. They rotated the ship so the bottom of the ship faced north, then deployed the big telescope, lowering it from the hull on its cables.

Rhiannon had the angle and the percentage distance between the two neighboring stars of the constellation from the diagram she had seen in the Grlau archives. They aimed the big telescope at that spot and set it to filter for infrared emissions.

PUSH IN BOÖTES

They scanned the area, then zoomed in on a large infrared source.

It was right where they expected it to be.

"OK, so we have a large infrared source right where we expected it to be," Daphne told the team. "Right where the star used to be."

"What's its blackbody temperature?" Jared asked.

"Two hundred ninety-three Kelvin."

"Which is sixty-eight degrees Fahrenheit," Jared said. "Room temperature."

"My. Isn't that convenient."

"For a Dyson Sphere around Earth's sun to have that temperature, it would have to be about the diameter of Jupiter's orbit," Arthur said. "Five AU or so. Somewhere around there."

"That's a big structure," Robert said.

"Their star could be smaller than the Sun," Arthur said. "If it has lower emissions, it would take a smaller sphere to radiate it all away at sixty-eight degrees."

"The only way to know is to go look," Daphne said.

"Have you heard back from Captain Proxmire yet?" Lena asked.

"No. We're meeting this afternoon. We'll see what he says."

"Well, Captain, what news?" Daphne asked.

"Let me ask about your news first, Ms. Bach. You found what you're looking for?"

"Yes, Captain. A large infrared source at room temperature where an entire star once was. That indicates to us a large structure, like a Dyson Sphere or equivalent."

"Which certainly warrants investigation. I agree with you

there, ma'am. As for the crew, I have two types, as is generally true. There are the serious hard cases. They'll be fine. We also have some people who are more sensitive to issues like long legs in the tunnel. But a third of the crew or so are serious hard types. So I have a proposal for you, ma'am."

"I'm listening, Captain."

"What do you say to the idea of splitting up once the survey of this structure is complete? For the final long leg to home, we send the majority of the crew back in *Earthbound*. *Beyond the Known Stars* continues home as well, at its slower acceleration, with the serious hard cases manning the ship."

"The trip would be how long, Captain?"

"For *Beyond the Known Stars*, it's about twenty-eight days, Ms. Bach. But for *Earthbound*, that same trip is just eight and a half days. *Beyond the Known Stars* would keep the robots. The crew would need them more, and they would be extra manpower if it came to that. You and your party could go home in the *Earthbound*."

"And you, Captain?"

"I stay with *Beyond the Known Stars*, Ms. Bach. Me, five other spacers, and the robots. We'll bring her home. The exec will take *Earthbound*, the rest of the operations crew, and the service crew from the passenger deck."

"What about redundancy, Captain? We're down to two engines each in each ship at that point."

"Yes, but normal colony ships only have two engines, ma'am. And we've never lost a ship to double engine failure. We've been cycling both engines aboard *Beyond the Known Stars*, generally using one for acceleration and the other for deceleration on each leg. And we watch them like a hawk. We know both engines are in tip-top shape.

"We can use the engines on *Earthbound* for the leg to the

structure, and shake those out as well. We'll know our status on both ships before we split up, ma'am."

"What about the leg to the structure, Captain? That's still eighteen days in the tunnel."

"I'm thinking of two days on and two days off, Ms. Bach. Test out the skeleton crew concept. Let everybody take their two days off with the robots. That'll keep everybody happy."

"We only have five suites available, Captain. You'll have seven crew off at a time. Arthur would probably give up his suite – he doesn't really sleep, anyway – but that's still only six suites."

"The hard cases will either switch off or share a suite, ma'am. There's two rooms, after all."

Daphne nodded. There were eight robots, after all, and some of the crew were female.

"All right, Captain. That sounds like a plan to me. You have authorization to carry on along those lines without further consultation."

"Yes, ma'am. Thank you, ma'am."

If it might seem unlikely to some that the fifty-year-old spacer and veteran officer would readily acquiesce to the orders of a twenty-year-old woman with no prior experience, it did not seem at all strange to Captain Proxmire.

Daphne Bach had grown into herself, and he respected her.

"You talked to Captain Proxmire?" Jared asked.

"Yes. We're on our way," Daphne said.

"What's the plan?"

"When we're done with examining the structure, we split up. Almost everybody goes home on *Earthbound*. Eight and a half days in the tunnel. Captain Proxmire will bring *Beyond the Known Stars* home with a skeleton crew of what he calls hard cases."

"That's tough service," Robert said.

"Yes, but they get all the robots. One for each crewman. They'll basically be living together on the passenger deck the whole way home. The two or three extra robots will run the galley."

"OK, that works," Jared said.

Robert nodded.

"Nice plan."

"Wait. What about the engines on *Earthbound*?" Jared asked. "They're untested."

"We're running on them now. All the way to the structure. We'll shake them both out."

"Excellent."

Beyond the Known Stars accelerated away from Grlau, heading generally northward, for its rendezvous with whatever that structure was.

Daphne had cautioned Captain Proxmire to come into the system fifteen AU or more away from the center of whatever it was. The last thing they wanted to do was run into something that big.

The Tunnel

It's difficult to explain to someone who has not experienced it just how disorienting transit through the tunnel could be.

First, it was black in a way nothing in reality is black. Even deep space had distant galaxies and stars. But in the tunnel, there was nothing. It was the densest kind of black. There was no reflection, no light. Turning on the ship's exterior lighting made no difference, as there was nothing for the light to reflect off of. It remained a truly disturbing black.

Second, one had no sense of where one was when in the tunnel. This was more unusual than one might think. Even in deep space, there were the stars, from which one could determine one's position. Yes, there was the entrance at one end and the exit at the other, but the changes in those during the transit were subtle, and gave a person no sense of place.

Third, any engine failure in the tunnel was a horrific prospect. If one did not decelerate, one did not exit the tunnel. The ship would become an interstellar *Flying Dutchman*, going on forever in that no-space of blackness. That was terrifying. In normal space, one could contemplate some sort of rescue. In the tunnel, there was no chance of rescue. None at all.

For certain kinds of people – people whom Captain Proxmire called hard cases – the tunnel was not a problem. They had seen random death before. Had met death in a very personal way, and had survived. The tunnel held no special terrors for them.

For most others, it was a uniquely disturbing experience. One they had no desire to prolong.

For this trip, once in the tunnel, Proxmire ran with a skeleton crew. Just four crew members on days and three crew members on nights. The other half the crew was on days off at any given time. They switched off on a two-days-on, two-days-off schedule.

They spent those days off with the robots. From nine in the evening one day to eight in the evening two days later. That gave the robots only one hour free between crew members, but they seemed happy with that.

As for the trip, eighteen days in the tunnel was eighteen days in the tunnel. No two ways about it. It was what it was.

By the end of the eighteen days, tempers were growing short. The robots reported to Daphne that, toward the end of the trip, the frequency of sex with the robots fell dramatically. Mostly the crew members just wanted to be held.

And sometimes cry.

As the trip stretched out, Daphne often saw it in the haunted eyes of the crewmen who took meals with them. Then she saw it in her own haunted eyes, and those of Jared and Lena.

But she did not see it in Arthur's eyes, or Robert's. She asked Arthur about it.

"Daphne, I have already been sentenced to death, reprieved at the last moment by your parents' actions. I have already faced death, up close and personal. Your parents, too, for that matter. When the hive queen sentenced us all to death, she was not joking. Were your parents here, I think they would qualify as what Captain Proxmire calls hard cases."

Daphne nodded. She could see that.

"What about Robert?"

"I don't know his story, Daphne. But he clearly is not bothered, not in the way you and Jared and Lena are. You three were very sheltered in many ways. I think, if you inquire, you will find out that Robert had a similar experience."

Daphne had a chance to talk to Robert alone about it that evening. They were relaxing in the living room of their suite before bed.

"Robert, why are you not as upset about the long leg in the tunnel as others obviously are? Arthur speculated that you must have had some near-death experience. Something that turned you into what Captain Proxmire called a hard case."

Robert looked at her and sighed. He had not told her about it. Maybe he should have.

"Yes, I did, Daphne."

"Would you tell me about it?"

Robert thought about it. It wasn't something he liked to revisit, but it was Daphne. Soon to be his life partner, if he had anything to say about it. Sooner or later, he would have to tell her.

"It was between my junior and senior years of college. So, three years ago? My father sponsored a climb of Mount Everest. I was into climbing, and had done a number of difficult climbs. He had misgivings, but I got him to sponsor the trip. Why do people want to climb Mount Everest? Because it is there, of course.

"I wasn't going to attempt the summit, however. I was into mountaineering, but I wasn't crazy. I went with the support group, which was perhaps three times as big as the actual group that would go the whole way to the top.

"In any case, I went along as far as Everest Base Camp, then continued on to Camp I. My father's agent on the scene. When I say Base Camp, you have to understand that it is still seventeen thousand six hundred feet above sea level. That's over half a mile higher than any of the peaks in the forty-eight contiguous states. In the U.S., only Mount McKinley is higher. Camp I is at nineteen thousand seven hundred feet, just a little less than McKinley.

"Even in summer, the weather is treacherous in the Himalayas. In the right conditions, warm, moist air off the Bay of Bengal blows up the Brahmaputra valley through Bangladesh. It can give you a blizzard any time of year. So climbers watch the weather carefully. This is worst in monsoon season, which runs from June to October, so summer blizzards can be the worst.

"Anyway, we made Everest Base Camp without incident. The weather was fantastic. Everything was going really well. We set out for Camp I in the nice weather. At those altitudes, the support group was using a bit of oxygen, though many climbers wait until after Camp II. We had to negotiate the Khumbu Icefall, but in the nice weather, it wasn't a problem.

"We made Camp I without any issues, and the climbers headed off for the peak after a couple days of acclimatization. I and the rest of the support party hunkered down in Camp I, huddled over little sterno cans in our pop-up tents. The weather was good, but it was still cold as anything and the wind is continuous.

"On the eighth day, with the climbers reporting that they were attempting the peak, the weather took a sudden turn on us. There was a high-pressure area over Burma when a low-pressure area hit Kashmir. They teamed up to stream monsoon air through the Himalayas. The biggest summer blizzard in decades hit the mountain. Our people were up in what they call the Death Zone. Above twenty-six thousand feet.

"Three of the climbing party died. The other four left them on the mountain, which was both necessary and customary.

"Meanwhile, in Camp I, the support group was also in serious trouble. Once the weather cleared, the surviving climbers could be rescued by helicopter if they could make Camp II, but we were too big a party, and helicopter evacuation from Camp I can be a problem. So, for getting to Base Camp, we were on our own.

"First, we had to last out the weather in our little pop-up tents. Second, we only had so much food along. And third, once the weather cleared, we had to attempt the Khumbu Icefall through a dozen feet of fresh snow, now melting and making everything slippery under the relentless sun at altitude.

"It took us five hours to go from Base Camp to Camp I on the way up. It took us five days to get down. We lost four more people. I wasn't one of them, though my climbing partner was. The survivors made it down to Base Camp, then to Lukla, and we finally flew to Kathmandu, where I spent some time in hospital.

"That was the end of my mountaineering days.

"But no, transiting the tunnel doesn't bother me."

"I shouldn't wonder," Daphne said. "Geez. What a fucking nightmare."

"And one of my own choosing, for all that. Of twenty-eight people who went up the mountain, twenty-one came down. I was one of them."

Robert shrugged.

"I got lucky."

Lying in bed that night, in Robert's arms, a lot of things fell into place for Daphne. Why Robert seemed so comfortable all the time. Why little things just didn't seem to bother him. Why Robert was willing to step up and duel the Marquis on Mondoverde. And prevail, for that matter.

Why he seemed so much more like a man and less like a boy than his contemporaries.

He'd been there and done that. Compared to that experience on Everest, really, just how upset could one get over trivia?

Even transiting the tunnel for weeks at a time was small potatoes to a man who had lived through that.

Daphne talked to Captain Proxmire about the crew when they were fifteen days into the tunnel transit.

"How's the crew holding up, Captain?"

"About as I expected, Ms. Bach. Some are walking wounded at this point, while others are like, 'Meh. No big deal.' The rest are somewhere in between. But I know who the real hard cases are now."

"Turns out we have one in our group as well, Captain. Robert was in that Disaster Expedition to Mount Everest three years back."

"Really. That explains a lot, ma'am. I heard about it. Seven dead. Like a quarter of the expedition. And no chance to even pack out the bodies. Your buddy goes down, dead, you leave him there and keep going. You have to, or die. That'll change you."

Daphne nodded.

"So you're going to have enough crew for the trip home, Captain?"

"Yes. I only need five with me, so we can be three on, three off the whole way, and I've got that.

"Excellent."

"One thing I wanted to ask you, Ms. Bach. It was my thought to dump anything we didn't need. We may be able to get fourteen, fifteen gravities if we got rid of extra weight. The shuttles, the unneeded food, the empty freezers, unused furniture. Everything out except what we need. As owner's representative, I figured I would ask you."

"Absolutely, Captain. What about the big telescope?"

"I figured that was a pretty pricey piece to go dumping in space, ma'am."

"Dump it, Captain. My authority. Anything that isn't nailed down. The missiles, too. If you don't need it for the trip home, out it goes. It served its purpose."

"Yes, ma'am. Thank you, ma'am."

"If you didn't have your five hard cases, Captain, I would be willing to abandon *Beyond the Known Stars* and have everybody head home on *Earthbound*."

"Not necessary, ma'am. We're good."

"Make sure you are, Captain. If not, you let me know and we'll abandon her."

"Yes, ma'am."

Proxmire's respect for Daphne Bach jumped a bit higher. She knew what mattered, and she was willing to get on with it.

The Structure And The Alien

After more than eighteen days, *Beyond the Known Stars* exited the tunnel. The ship was twenty AU from the center of the infrared source.

Everyone was waiting for the exit, in order to see just what it was that brought them here. What it was that could occlude an entire star.

What they saw, even from this distance, was beyond belief.

"What the hell is it?" Lena asked.

"A Dyson Ring," Jared said. "A ring around the star, at the right distance that it holds the desired temperature."

"So not a Dyson Sphere?" Daphne asked.

"No. Not a complete one," Jared said. "But the ring is edge-on to Grlau, so it was enough to totally occlude the star as seen from Grlau."

"Arthur," Daphne said. "Instructions to Captain Proxmire. Decelerate to one side. Give us some side vector so we can see the inside of this thing."

"Yes, Daphne."

The camera view changed a bit as Proxmire rotated the ship to get side vector.

The ring itself was not close to an entire sphere. It was as if someone put a two-inch-wide belt around a marble at the center.

"We're not getting any closer," Lena said.

"Oh, yes, we are," Jared said. "That thing is so far away, it will take a long time to get there. If we even want to bother them."

"What do you mean, Jared?" Daphne asked.

"Anybody who can do that can do anything they want, including deal with interlopers."

"The scale of it is very impressive," Arthur said.

"Yeah," Jared said. "*Beyond the Known Stars* is like a grain of salt next to the Pentagon."

"That is still wrong about the scale, Jared," Arthur said. "It is more like a single grain of salt next to the Rocky Mountains."

"That big?" Daphne asked.

"Oh, yes," Arthur said. "We are still fifteen AU away from its nearest surface, and we can see it clearly."

"Fifteen AU?" Lena asked.

"Round numbers?" Arthur asked. "About one and a half billion miles."

"Hey, guys," Robert said. "My data server is going crazy."

"What?" Daphne asked.

"Yeah. It should be idle. But it's tearing through databases. Like it was downloading or something. But where is it downloading to?"

"We're being scanned," Daphne said.

"That doesn't make any sense," Robert said. "How would somebody even do that?"

"How would somebody even do *that*?" Daphne asked, gesturing toward the display. "I think they can probably do whatever the hell they want."

"Well, it's still ripping through databases at bus speeds. Multiple bus speeds. There's no interface that can even transfer data that fast."

"Well, somebody has one. We're being read," Jared said.

Daphne nodded. That was her sense as well.

"What will they think of us, I wonder," Lena said.

"We're going to find out soon," Robert said. "They've just

about touched every bit of data in the server by this point."

They continued to wait and watch as *Beyond the Known Stars* continued to add side vector. It would take quite a while before they could see over the edge of the ring to see the interior.

"OK. The data server's quieted down now. Back at idle. Boy, that was weird."

A young man, perhaps twenty-five, appeared, sitting in an extra chair in the living room. He must have been a projection, but he looked like he was really there. He was dressed much as any of them were.

"Hello, everyone. Welcome to Ringhome."

He turned to Daphne as everyone gaped at him.

"Daphne Bach, you are the leader here?"

"Yes. I am the ambassador from Earth."

"We must ask you to come no closer. We could repel your ship with the mechanism we use to repel asteroids, but I am afraid it might crumple your ship."

"We are decelerating as fast as we can currently," Daphne said.

"We understand. Please continue to do so. We desire no contact with you."

"Why not? Wouldn't trade be beneficial?"

The figure smiled.

"You have nothing we want, Daphne Bach. And we are afraid of poisoning your culture. The history of primitive cultures coming into contact with more advanced ones in your planet's history is not a pleasant thing to contemplate."

Daphne nodded. She knew of many such occasions, and their visitor was right.

"Who are you?"

"I'm sorry, child. Where are my manners? I am Strandan Prelak. I am one of the Lamk. I have been selected to contact you."

"Child?" Daphne asked. "You look to be our age or so."

Prelak gestured to himself.

"This is not my actual appearance. It was selected to be comforting to you. I was born when Cyrus the Great conquered the Medians on your planet."

"Over twenty-five hundred years ago?" Daphne asked.

"Yes, in your orbital measurements. I lived in a physical body until about the time Rome was sacked by Alaric. That is when I transferred my consciousness into an advanced form of what you call a computer."

"You lived for a thousand years, and then transferred into a computer fifteen hundred years ago?" Jared asked.

"Yes. Was I unclear?"

"You were clear, Strandan Prelak," Daphne said. "What you describe is out of our experience."

"I understand."

"Do you mind if we keep asking you questions?" Daphne asked.

"No. Not at all. You will be in our system for some time yet, and I am currently otherwise unencumbered."

"Your people built this ring structure?"

"Yes, Daphne Bach. It was built well before my time. We would probably not build such a structure today, but it has served our needs well."

"You wouldn't build it now? Why?" Jared asked.

"It has proven to be in excess of need. We weren't sure of that at the time, however."

"Please tell us the story, Strandan Prelak," Daphne said.

"Very well, Daphne Bach.

"We were a single-planet species – as you were until recently – and we were facing a demographic problem. We had made leaps in materials science, and in gravitonics, and in nuclear power, but we had also made leaps in extending our lifetimes. This last was proving to be a problem, as we were projecting that we would run out of room and resources due to population growth and longevity.

"We also knew that gravitonics was not a solution to the interstellar drive problem. The accelerations were not high enough. We did not know about the tunnel at that point, you see.

"So we decided to solve our problem here in our own space, by building a habitat big enough to accommodate as many as our numbers would likely ever be.

"It was a massive undertaking, and took almost a thousand years. The basic secret was carbon nanotube technology. We started two satellites on counter-rotating orbits to spin a carbon nanotube filament around the sun. The satellites kept going around, weaving a heavier and heavier structure until other spacecraft could participate.

"Eventually we ended up with the structure you see here. Half of its inner surface is solar energy collectors, the other half is planetlike surface for habitation, on alternating panels around the ring."

"You said it was in excess of need?" Jared asked.

"Yes, Jared Bach. Some things happened that we did not expect. You must understand that, when I say we, I mean our race, the Lamk. All of this happened long before I was born.

"First is that the demographic explosion we expected did not occur. There was a demographic collapse instead. As the standard of living improved and longevity increased, people had fewer babies, not more.

"The other thing that happened was that we learned how to upload ourselves into computers. Rather than poor health and infirmity of the elderly being a huge drain on resources, we learned how to escape those issues. When the aches and pains of old age grew too burdensome, people uploaded themselves. Their lifetimes were now essentially infinite.

"As long as the power stayed on, which we now had an infinite supply of, they lived forever. At the same time, they consumed no resources other than power.

"At some point we discovered what you call the tunnel. A ship we sent out to harvest the farthest planets for construction of the ring hit the tunnel accidentally. They used it to return, and we researched its limits and capabilities. We had been using it for space travel within the system, and to disassemble planets for our construction project, but gravitonics could, in fact, be used for interstellar travel.

"Then a curious thing happened. No one wanted to go exploring. Exploring is a dangerous business, and our lifetimes, between our physical lifetimes and our computer-based lifetimes, were now so long we simply had too much to lose.

"Consider your own Ferdinand Magellan. He set out to circumnavigate your planet. It was fraught with danger, and he was, in fact, killed during the voyage. But he died at age forty-one, which was not so unusual at the time.

"Now consider someone like me. I have lived a total of twenty-five hundred of your years. Would I, as a young person today, consider such a trip? No. Emphatically not. In a strange irony, we discovered interstellar travel only after it was of no further use to us."

"So you gave it to the Mrow," Robert said.

"Yes, Robert Drake, and to others that we found. Suldan and others spaced to neighboring single-planet civilizations and gave them the gravitonic drive at an earlier stage in their development, when the itch to explore still existed.

"The Mrow gave it to the Gleth. You stole it from the Gleth. The technology keeps rippling out from here, and has resulted in a dozen or more space-faring civilizations. We couldn't be happier about it."

"You seem to know an awful lot about what's going on," Lena said.

"Yes, Lena Stox, we do. We have our own robots, you see, and we can make them in the guise of any of the races we have encountered. We keep an eye on things."

"And sometimes intervene," Daphne said.

"Yes, Daphne Bach, but not often."

"Name one, please."

Prelak considered, then shrugged. His gestures were getting more human as he interacted with them.

"One I am personally familiar with is Alexander the Great, though I wasn't even two hundred years old at the time. It was important that the Hellenic influence not die out with the Greek city-states. Alexander actually died in a training accident, and we replaced him with a robot."

"He conquered the known world," Robert said.

"He spread Greek culture and influence from Macedonia all the way to the Indus River and the frontiers of China, then 'died' young. Yes. That was a very successful intervention."

"How did you find Earth, eight hundred light-years away?" Jared asked. "There's a lot of planets between here and there.

"We were aware that a large moon makes the evolution of intelligent life more likely on the planet it orbits. It's not impossible otherwise, but it's far less likely. So we concentrated our searches on planets with large moons. That is less than one percent of otherwise suitable planets. We sent robot survey ships out looking for them."

"Have you done any interventions on Earth lately?" Daphne

asked. "Say, in the last thousand years?"

"No, Daphne Bach, we have not. We consider it unethical beyond some point of development."

"Albert Einstein wasn't one of yours?"

"No. I can see why you would say that, but he was his own man. A remarkable man, to be sure, but not one of ours."

"And now we've come to visit," Lena said.

"Yes. But we don't want visitors. There are dangers. War. Pestilence. Discord. Things we have set aside for a life of leisure and contemplation."

Arthur had been quiet this whole time, but spoke up now.

"So you have no higher aspirations as a civilization than personal comfort, Strandan Prelak?" Arthur asked. "You are content to sit on the sidelines and ponder your navels?"

"What else might we do, Arthur Vegan? Most of us are captive within our machines. We cannot travel in the conventional sense."

"How much of the ring do you occupy?" Daphne asked.

"Perhaps three percent of its habitable spaces. It is a truly stupendous structure we have built, with the equivalent surface area of hundreds of planets."

"And in ten thousand years, you haven't filled it up more than that?" Jared asked.

"No. After recovery from the demographic collapse, our physical population has been stable for several thousand years now. Of course, the uploaded population continues to grow."

"The reason your population does not grow is that you have nothing to aspire to," Arthur said. "There is no future except more of the same."

"What are we to do?"

"Invite other races to populate unused panels of the ring," Daphne said. "Bring them along in your philosophy and your science. Like a big university or something."

Arthur Vega held up a finger and waited until Prelak looked at him.

"You must teach what you have learned," Arthur said.

Prelak thought about it for several seconds, a delay they had not seen before. He nodded.

"Perhaps we should."

"Talk about it amongst yourselves. You know how to get in touch once you've made a decision," Daphne said.

"It may be some time. Such decisions can take years, if not decades."

Daphne shrugged.

"We'll be around."

They talked after Prelak left.

"How remarkable," Arthur said. "A completely stagnant civilization."

"And it's been that way for thousands of years," Jared said.

"I wonder what they actually look like," Lena said.

"No telling," Daphne said. "He gave us no clues."

"What do you think they'll decide?" Robert asked.

Daphne shrugged.

"To go on as they have been," Daphne said. "That's the safest decision, after all."

"Such a shame."

Beyond the Known Stars kept killing its forward velocity toward the ring and piling on side velocity to get above it. Eventually, they did get above the ring, and could see the local star inside it.

They could also see the patchwork of alternating panels of solar collectors and habitable surface on the other half of the ring. They needed the small telescope to see that, as it was all in the far half of the ring.

Once it's velocity toward the ring had fallen to zero, *Beyond the Known Stars* was accelerating away from the ring, still piling on side vector to get a better view. They were now building velocity toward the tunnel for the return trip.

Daphne had a sudden realization. She wondered if Prelak was monitoring.

She went out into the common living room on the passenger deck and addressed the chair his projection had been sitting in.

"Strandan Prelak?" Daphne asked the empty chair.

Prelak's projection appeared.

"Yes, Daphne Bach?"

"We are now building velocity away from Ringhome. Before we enter the tunnel, it is our intention to throw overboard all the things we don't need for the trip home. This will lighten the ship and speed our trip. I just wanted to make sure that was OK with you."

"Yes, Daphne Bach. As long as it is on a vector that would not hit Ringhome, but keep moving away from it, we are fine with that."

"Very well. Thank you, Strandan Prelak. Our best wishes to you."

"Good spacing, Daphne Bach."

Homeward Bound

There was an airlock on *Beyond the Known Stars* that could be used for throwing things away. The back wall of the airlock was movable by electric motors, until it was almost flush with the exterior skin of the ship. Put garbage in the airlock, then push it out the hatch. It would necessarily fall in the gravitational field maintained for the ship.

First, passengers and crew going home on *Earthbound* moved aboard *Earthbound* to open up the cabin spaces on *Beyond the Known Stars*. The hard-case crew that would take the ship back to Earth moved into the passenger spaces with the robots. Then the combined crew started grabbing everything not mailed down and moving it to the refuse airlock.

Mattresses and box springs from the crew spaces on *Beyond the Known Stars*. Desks and chairs from the crew spaces. All the pots and pans and chairs and tables in the crew galley. The empty freezers on the stores deck.

"What about these?" a crewman asked, pointing to the data server in the passenger space.

"I need those on Earth," Robert said.

The crewman thought about it.

"How about we move them to *Earthbound* then?"

"That works," Robert said.

So the data server and the AI chassis were disconnected and moved to an empty cabin aboard *Earthbound* and strapped to bulkhead stays.

They were two days into their acceleration, and the tunnel was coming up, when Proxmire killed the acceleration of *Beyond the Known Stars*. He rotated the ship sideways to its velocity.

At that point, anything ejected from the refuse airlock would fall free of the ship to one side and continue with the same forward velocity, so it would not interfere with the ship's movement into the tunnel nor would it fall back to Ringhome.

"Empty refuse airlock," Proxmire ordered.

"Aye, Sir. Emptying the refuse airlock."

The airlock was vented, and then the rear wall simply shoved everything off the ship. It fell away from the bottom of the ship, heading off to one side into space.

"Launch shuttles."

"Aye, Sir. Launching shuttles."

Both the large and small shuttle exited their garages under computer control and headed off away from the ship. They would proceed until their batteries ran out.

"Deploy the big telescope."

"Aye, Sir. Deploying the big telescope."

"Don't brake it to a stop, just cut it loose."

The crewman looked at Proxmire to be sure, and the captain nodded.

"Aye, Sir. Cutting it loose."

The massively expensive telescope followed all the other cast-offs into space.

"We need to fire off all those missiles. Fire four, then reload. Missile vector at ninety degrees to the ship's velocity relative to Ringhome. Repeat until we're empty."

"Aye, Sir. Firing missiles. Firing four."

"Close and repressurize the refuse airlock."

"Aye, Sir. Closing the airlock. Repressurizing."

"Mr. Fogerty."

"Yes, Sir."

"Get down to stores. We keep twenty-eight days for six men.

No more. Everything else goes in the refuse airlock. Consolidate freezers, and the empty freezers go in the refuse airlock. Consolidate shelving storage, and all the empty shelving goes in the refuse airlock."

"Are you sure, Sir?"

"Yes, Mr. Fogerty. Let's be about it."

"Aye, Sir."

"We also want to clear unnecessary furniture on the passenger deck. One bed and two chairs in six suites. That's it. Everything else in the suites goes. Leave the common rooms alone."

"Aye, Sir."

Mr. Fogerty headed off then to be about his assigned chores. He hadn't seemed sure about the supplies issue, but Fogerty wasn't one of the hard cases.

If they needed more than twenty-eight days of supplies, they were lost anyway.

They continued to eject the refuse airlock out the bottom of the ship while they were firing missiles out the top. With the ship turned sideways to its velocity, both up and down were ninety degrees to their already high velocity.

All those items would maintain the ship's forward velocity, plus their side vector. That would keep it all away from Ringhome, while getting it out of the way of the ship itself.

When it was all done, Proxmire turned the ship once more back to being on-axis with its velocity. With its vector to home. It was heading bottom first, because they needed to launch *Earthbound*.

The crews all said goodbye to each other, then separated between the two ships. Proxmire, his five hard cases, and all eight robots took up position within *Beyond the Known Stars*, while the five passengers and seventeen remaining crew –

including all eight of the passenger deck service crew – took up their positions within *Earthbound*.

"Close air-tight doors on *Earthbound* connection."

"Air-tight doors closed, Sir."

"Break seal to *Earthbound*. Check integrity."

"Breaking seal, Sir. Both sides report air-tight."

"Close secondary doors."

"Secondary doors closed, Sir."

"You ready for zero-gravity, Mr. Fogerty?"

Fogerty's voice came over the intercom from *Earthbound*.

"We stand ready for zero-gravity, Sir."

"All right, Helm. Perform separation. Zero-gravity, release latches, then restore gravity."

"Aye, Sir. Separation under way."

While *Beyond the Known Stars* was not accelerating, the gravitonic drive was maintaining gravity in the ship's spaces. That shut down, which was necessary to release the latches holding the two ships together. There were clanking noises deep in the ship, then gravity abruptly came back on.

"*Earthbound* is falling away, Sir."

"Let them bring up their engines first. We don't want to run them over, Mr. Monroe."

"Aye, Sir. *Earthbound* has brought up on-board gravity now. She's thrusting away."

There was several minutes wait.

"*Earthbound* has started her acceleration, Sir. Ramping up."

The seconds ticked past.

"*Earthbound* now making forty gravities, Sir."

"All right, Mr. Monroe. Bring our acceleration up. Let's see how fast we can go."

"Aye, Sir. Ramping up."

Proxmire watched the acceleration graph on his display. It

climbed to twelve gravities and just kept going. All the things they had thrown out – especially the missiles, each with their own nuclear reactor – had lightened the ship, as had, in a major way, the launch of *Earthbound*, but the gravitonic engine's thrust had not changed.

The acceleration climbed to twelve gravities and just kept going. Thirteen. Fourteen. Fifteen. Finally, *Beyond the Known Stars* was making sixteen gravities.

"Well, that shortened our run home, everybody. Four-thirds the acceleration means three-quarters the time. Twenty-one days in the tunnel. Twenty-three days to Earth."

The four men and one woman who were Proxmire's handpicked hard cases nodded. They had signed up for twenty-eight days in the tunnel. Twenty-one days was a piece o' cake.

"Nice," one of them said.

Earthbound was making forty gravities toward the tunnel. Captain Fogerty announced their projected arrival at Earth.

"All right, everyone. Eight and a third or so days in the tunnel, ten days to Earth."

A cheer went up at that.

Earthbound hit the tunnel and disappeared from normal space. *Beyond the Known Stars* hit the tunnel twelve hours later.

Shipboard routine quickly settled out on *Earthbound*. With so many crew for the small ship, they went to a twelve-on/twelve-off, day-on/day-off schedule. There were so many galley crew they went to a day-on/day-off schedule as well.

The cabins were two-man cabins, but with the day-on/day-off schedule, there was only one crew member in each cabin during waking hours anyway.

Two of those cabins had double beds for the passengers. Arthur had his own room, which was mostly a waste since he did not sleep much.

The air was lighthearted aboard *Earthbound*. They would be home soon, and they were all looking forward to it.

Shipboard routine settled out quickly on *Beyond the Known Stars* as well. It was twelve-on/twelve-off for everyone aboard, with no days off. Proxmire and Monroe took the officer of the watch positions, with two crew members each shift. Even for such a big ship, it was basically a ferry run, so there was no problem with staffing.

Each of the crew selected a robot for their companion on the way home, even Proxmire and Monroe. They each had one of the passenger suites to themselves and their robot for the trip. The other two robots – one male and one female – took galley duties on the passenger deck, and served them in the passenger deck dining room.

It was luxury accommodations for the crew members. One-man cabins, with a king-size bed and a robot companion, and passenger-level food in a real dining room. The robots were, as always, very accommodating of whatever was desired, whether it was sex or just someone to cuddle with. Everyone slept well every night.

Three weeks in the tunnel just didn't bother them.

Earthbound exited the tunnel in Earth's solar system midway through the ninth day. Everyone cheered.

Earthbound called in her arrival to Earth and the crew settled in for the long deceleration to orbit and, ultimately, landing.

"*Earthbound* has called in her arrival," Barbara Bach said.

"*Earthbound*?" Steven Bach asked. "Is everyone OK?"

"Yes, everybody's fine. They're coming in from eight hundred light-years out, so Captain Proxmire and some serious hard cases are bringing *Beyond the Known Stars* along behind. Everybody else is aboard *Earthbound* to avoid a month-long trip in the tunnel."

"OK. That makes sense. I can see where that could get to some people."

"They'll be here day after tomorrow," Barbara said.

"We need to let the Drakes and the Stoxes know."

"The rest of the crew's families, too. I'll handle that."

Steven and Barbara Bach, Forester and Claudia Drake, and Ken and Patty Stox all breathed serious sighs of relief over the news. *Beyond the Known Stars* had left, what? A hundred thirty-five days before? Something like that. Headed off into the unknown.

There had been, by the physics of space travel, no news whatsoever of them until now. Four and a half months of not knowing what had happened.

But they were home now, and everyone was OK.

That's all that mattered.

Home

Earthbound touched down at Spaceport USA at eleven o'clock in the morning.

The assembled families – all who could make it, flown here by Graviton Dynamics for the event – all watched the ship come down out of the sky at thirty miles per hour and lightly touch down on the pad.

Earthbound was only two stories tall, and had a ground-level crew exit. When the engines shut down and the crew began exiting the ship, the families rushed forward.

It was Christmas Day.

The passengers this trip – Daphne Bach, Robert Drake, Jared Bach, Lena Stox, and Arthur Vegan – walked to where their families waited by the buses. Daphne was in the lead, Barbara noticed.

"Hi, Mom. We made it."

Barbara didn't say anything – couldn't say anything – she just gave her daughter a big hug.

Daphne had grown up, she could see. There was something ineffable about her – that air of someone who had been there and done that – but it was very apparent to Barbara.

Then it was Jared, and he, too, had grown up.

Ken and Patty Stox noticed the same thing about their little girl Lena. She was a woman now, and had that indefinable air as well. It must have been some adventure.

They hugged her and welcomed her home.

"Best Christmas present ever," Ken said.

"Merry Christmas, Daddy."

Robert Drake was the one of the four who seemed least changed. Of course, he had already had his life-changing event three years before.

He walked up to his father to shake his hand, but Forester was having none of it. He pulled his son closer and gave him a big hug.

"When I realized there were twenty-eight people aboard your ship, I hoped it wasn't a bad omen," Forester said. "I'm relieved it wasn't."

Robert nodded. The captain, fourteen crew, eight passenger-deck service crew, and five passengers had been twenty-eight people. There had also been twenty-eight people on the doomed Everest expedition.

"Not this time, Dad. We all made it."

Everyone got into the buses for the ride from the pad to General Dynamics' headquarters. The company was on shutdown for the holidays, but that just meant the company cafeteria was available for the party.

With only two days to work on it, Barbara Bach had pulled out all the stops. It was a full-blown Christmas dinner. There was an entire turkey for every table of twelve. With over ninety people, there were eight tables. Each groaned under a turkey and all the sides, and there was a catering staff person at each table to carve the bird.

The Bachs, the Drakes, the Stoxes, the two young couples, and Arthur Vegan took up one whole table.

There were Christmas decorations, and Christmas music, and a Christmas tree, and Christmas presents for everyone. It was a joyous holiday party.

But when 'I'll be Home for Christmas' played over the music system, a lot of people completely lost it.

Barbara Bach was one of them.

"Mom, are you OK?" Daphne asked.

Barbara nodded.

"I'm just so happy," she managed through her tears.

Barbara and Daphne hugged.

After dessert, as everyone was opening presents – mostly chocolates and other treats – the catering staff was boxing up leftovers for people to take with them.

"It isn't Christmas without leftovers," Barbara said.

She encouraged everyone to take leftovers back to the hotel with them. As the rooms in the hotel where General Dynamics had booked everyone all had refrigerators, that would work.

The party broke up about four in the afternoon, with the buses taking everyone back to the hotel before their flights home tomorrow.

All eleven people from the head table took a shuttle to the Bachs' pretty little house in the woods. As the living room did not have seating for eleven, the two young couples sat tailor seat on the floor.

"Oh, gosh. Now I know what a turkey feels like. I'm stuffed," Lena said.

"Yeah," Jared said. "I was OK until the pies hit."

"Nice party, Mom," Daphne said. "It really is good being back home."

"At some point, you'll have to brief everyone on what you found. Basic question. Were you successful?"

Daphne didn't know where to start. She turned to Arthur and nodded. Leave it to the alien to summarize.

"We found that the Greth, which is one name for my people,

were given the technology thousands of years ago in exchange for giving up war. That gift was from the Mrow, a mammalian species much like humans, but with the heads and other features of cats. They in turn were given the technology ten thousand years ago by a fourth intelligent race, the Lamk. The Lamk have built a Dyson Ring about their home sun, and had no desire for contact with us, though they did talk about themselves with us. We challenged them to have more contact with other races."

"Arthur told their representative, 'Teach what you have learned,'" Daphne said.

"Powerful," Barbara said, nodding to Arthur.

"What do they look like? The Lamk?" Forester asked.

"We don't know," Daphne said. "Their representative was a projection onto *Beyond the Known Stars*. Right into the passenger deck common living room. But the projection was of a young human."

"The other thing that's interesting is that the Mrow and the Lamk have robots," Jared said. "Humanoid robots. They are indistinguishable from humans without an X-ray machine. They've had agents on Earth for millennia."

"That would be something to see," Steven said.

"Well, Dad, you're gonna get your chance. There are eight of them on *Beyond the Known Stars*, helping Captain Proxmire and a skeleton crew bring the ship back."

"Indeed? Excellent."

"The female ones are all beautiful," Lena said. "I felt like an ugly duckling around them."

"Yeah, me too," Daphne said.

Barbara looked at the two attractive women incredulously.

"And the male ones are movie-star handsome," Daphne said.

"But they aren't human, so there's that," Robert said.

"You'll get to see them, Dad. So you let us know what you think."

"I think it will be pretty amazing, no matter what," Steven said. "And maybe a business opportunity."

"Hmm," Barbara said. "But what else lies down that path? Lethargy? Stagnation?"

"That's a good question," Arthur said. "Based on what we've seen of the Mrow and the Lamk, you may be right."

After some teary goodbyes, the Stoxes took the shuttle bus back to the hotel for their flight out tomorrow. They took the Drakes along, planning on dropping them at their flying motor home at the airport.

The kids made their excuses after they'd left.

"We're going to bed, Mom. This has been a big day, and I'm beat."

"Us, too," Jared said as Lena stifled a yawn. "More tomorrow, eh?"

"Oh. I did send you my mission report. I wrote it on the way back. So you have some reading if you're interested."

The young couples headed off to their bedrooms, while Barbara checked her mail. There it was. She sent a copy to Steven.

"I sent you Daphne's mail, Steven."

"Well, let's read then. Unless you're for bed as well."

"No, I'm too wound up."

"I will be here to answer any questions when you finish," Arthur said.

The report made interesting reading. They had spaced a total of sixteen hundred and eighty light-years, visited five different inhabited star systems, and made a single leg of eight hundred light-years to get home, the longest space flight any human had yet attempted.

They had met two hive queens, attended one hive queen funeral, met – and dueled! – this Marquis fellow, visited the Mrow capital planet, and met with the Lamk, who had actually built a Dyson Ring.

There were attached videos, and Barbara watched three of them. One was the first day's conversation with the Marquis in which he disclosed the robots, and the Mrow's long history with Earth. The second was the conversation with the Lamk. The third was the conversation Daphne had with Captain Proxmire about splitting the crew between the two ships for the trip home.

Barbara and Steven looked up from their displays about the same time. He probably watched the same videos. They were the key items.

"What a remarkable journey," Barbara said. "What remarkable discoveries."

Steven nodded.

"Another thing is clear," Steven said. "You were right to propose Daphne as head of mission. She made all the right calls."

"Yes. She really grew into herself. I thought the conversation with Captain Proxmire was illuminating."

"Daphne did a remarkably good job," Arthur said. "We all saw the potential there, but she delivered on that potential."

"She sure did. Making the decision to go for it on that last leg – the one to the Lamk – was a tough decision," Steven said. "But she made the call, then worked with Proxmire to mitigate the downside."

Barbara nodded.

"They did a good job," Barbara said. "All four of them. I'm proud of them all."

She turned to Arthur.

"And you were a good adviser to her, Arthur. It gave her stability. Thank you for that as well."

"It was my pleasure, Barbara. All in all, it was a lot like old times."

Beyond the Known Stars called in its arrival thirteen days after *Earthbound* had. They would come in for landing two weeks after *Earthbound*, on the morning of January eighth.

Christmas had been on a weekday this year, so January eighth was as well. Graviton Dynamics was back in full swing. It wasn't time for a big Christmas party like the *Earthbound*'s arrival, but they could have a welcome home party in the cafeteria with all the General Dynamics people present.

Earthbound's crew had all been given planet leave, and had dissipated to the four corners, but all five passengers were still here. Barbara Bach arranged for families to attend as before.

They all watched the big ship come down on the next pad to where *Earthbound* still sat. Navy blue, with 'Beyond the Known Stars' proudly emblazoned in gold paint on all four sides, she was a sight to see.

Six crewmen and eight robots exited the ship from a ground-level airlock. The families rushed forward as before, although there were fewer of them this time.

Captain Proxmire greeted his wife and children, then came over to Daphne Bach and saluted.

"Captain Proxmire reporting, ma'am. *Beyond the Known Stars* has come home."

"Well done, Captain. That was the longest leg in the tunnel anyone has ever done. Very well done, indeed."

"Thank you, ma'am."

He pulled his wife closer.

"It's just good to be home."

Barbara had ordered the Christmas decorations left up in the corporate cafeteria, so it still had its festive look. There were three tables for twelve set up at one end. At those tables sat the six crewmen, their families, Steven and Barbara Bach, Jared, Lena, Daphne, Robert, and Arthur.

The tables themselves held the same Christmas dinner that had been served for the *Earthbound* crew when they had arrived.

Barbara said a few words as everyone was seated and the catering staff was carving the birds.

"Hello, everyone.

"Today we welcome home the remainder of the crew of *Beyond the Known Stars*. Captain Frank Proxmire, Lieutenant Thomas Monroe, and crew members George Stenis, Gloria Madden, Bruce Stilwell, and Dwayne Johnson.

"In five months, they spaced to five different solar systems, a total of sixteen hundred and eighty light-years, including a last leg of eight hundred light-years. They truly took the ship beyond the known stars, on a voyage that is unmatched in our history.

"And now they've come back home to us."

Barbara applauded, and the crowd took it up. There were cheers and whistles. The crew members waved.

The eight robots stood against the wall and watched impassively, though they did applaud when everyone else did.

The Robots

The crew was released to extended shore leave. They had rights to on-base housing, and most of them would move out of *Beyond the Known Stars* into barracks. Their families would be flown back home by Graviton Dynamics.

When the party was over, one of the robots came up to Daphne.

"We are at your service, ma'am, as long as you have use for us."

"Come along to the house, then, and we'll figure it out."

"Yes, ma'am."

They took a shuttle bus to the pretty house in the woods. It wasn't far, as the house was on the spaceport grounds.

The robots looked around curiously as they stood in the living room.

Steven was fascinated by the robots. He walked up to one of the female robots and looked her over carefully. She watched his inspection casually.

"If I may?" He said, gesturing to her hand.

"Of course, sir."

Steven picked up her hand and looked at it closely, front, back, and sides.

"And you're a robot?" he asked.

"I believed the precise term is android, sir."

"A remarkable feat of engineering."

"Thank you, sir."

"What's your name?"

"Rosalind, sir."

She turned to indicate the others, one at a time.

"Roxanne, Rebecca, Rhiannon, Raffaella, Rashida, Randall, and Rodney."

"So where do the robots stay?" Daphne asked.

"They can stay out in the old headquarters building for now," Jared said. "Though I won't be playing any pool with them, that's for sure."

Daphne nodded.

"The other thing is we need to move back to our apartments. It's been nice camping out with you, Mom, Dad, but with *Beyond the Known Stars* back home, it's time we went home as well."

"I'm not looking forward to that," Lena said. "After five months, the apartment is going to need serious attention. The dust is probably an inch thick."

"Yeah," Jared said. "Not fun."

"Pardon me, ma'am," Roxanne said to Daphne, "but we would be happy to clean all the apartments for you."

Barbara looked up and down the row of beautiful and handsome robots.

"You would do that?" Barbara asked.

"It is pleasing to us to be of service, ma'am."

"When could we move back, then?" Lena asked.

"The eight of us will have no problem cleaning all four apartments overnight, ma'am. You could move back in first thing tomorrow. Just give us the addresses."

"You need keys, don't you?"

"Not for locks of this period, ma'am."

"The other thing I would like to do is have the Graviton Dynamics people look over the robots toward reproducing them," Steven said.

"Anything that does not involve disassembly is all right with us, sir. For example, X-rays at the dosages commonly used for humans are not injurious to us. Although I believe your materials science is not yet up to reproducing us as we stand."

"I can believe that. Perhaps we can work on that as well."

"We would be happy to, sir. We also carry complete drawings and plans for ourselves."

Steven raised an eyebrow and Roxanne shrugged.

"Sometimes the construction of replacement parts is necessary, sir."

"OK. That makes sense."

"I could also use more help with the artificial intelligence items, Rebecca," Robert said.

"Of course, sir."

"What will you do when we have no further use for you?" Barbara asked.

"We have assignments from the Marquis as well, ma'am," Roxanne said. "The acquisition of various food products and seed stocks. The Marquis is something of a fan of French cheeses and California wines."

"That sort of thing is expensive, especially in any quantity."

"We have access to funds from prior visits, ma'am."

Barbara nodded. She didn't want to probe too carefully into that. The current administration still had two years to go, and what she didn't know she couldn't testify to.

"And when your assignments are complete?"

"The Marquis' ship will pick us up in two years, ma'am. Two orbits of Mondoverde, I should say. About twenty-eight months from now."

"That's perfect. There will likely be a new and more welcoming administration at that time. We can have your ship land here at the spaceport. No sense trying to sneak up and down with freight cargo when you can just land here."

"If you think that would be OK, ma'am. It's never been an option before, as there was no spaceport."

"No, that will definitely be an option at that time. The current administration is proving to be less popular than the previous one, so I expect something of a reversion to the mean."

"Understood, ma'am. And now, if we could have those addresses?"

The young people gave their apartment addresses to the robots. Barbara called the shuttle back, and the robots all left the house for the ride into town.

"And your apartments will all be clean tomorrow?" Steven asked.

"Two robots, overnight, at each apartment?" Daphne asked. "Our apartment will look like pictures in magazines when we get home. You have no idea how thorough they are. Every item's 'Best Used By' date will be inspected, overdue items will be discarded and added to the grocery list, and the discarded items will be taken out to the apartment complex trash container."

"They really do get a sense of fulfillment from being of service, Steven. It's what makes them happy. The Marquis maintained that is the secret of successful AI."

"That's funny, because they all look like the sort of people who won't lift a finger," Barbara said. "You know, the 'I don't want to take a chance on breaking a nail' type."

Everyone chuckled.

"No, they were of tremendous help on the ship," Jared said. "Among other things, they made themselves sexually available to the crew during those long crossings. That helped a lot."

"Although, on the longest crossing, toward the end, they told me the crew mostly just wanted to be held," Daphne said.

"Reassured that everything was going to be OK. It was really rough. At least for some people."

"Sexually available?" Steven asked. "So they're the same as humans in that way, too?"

"Indistinguishable, I'm told," Robert said, "and ready for a go at any time. Though that's not something I can attest to myself. I had no need."

"Damn straight you didn't," Daphne said.

"Interested, Steven?" Barbara asked.

"Curious, is all. I have no need, either."

"Good. That is *exactly* the correct answer."

Everybody laughed at that.

When Daphne got back to her apartment the next morning, Rhiannon and Randall were waiting for her.

The apartment was amazing. The floors had all been vacuumed and the tile floors mopped. The bathroom was spotless. The linens on the bed had been changed, and the old linens laundered, folded, and put away. All her dirty laundry had been washed and put away. The kitchen sparkled, and the few dishes she had left in the dishwasher – she had run a rinse before she left for five months – had been washed and put away.

Even the pillows on the sofa in the living room had been puffed up.

"We've finished, ma'am. Do you have any other assignments for us?"

"No. This is wonderful. Thank you so much."

"It is our pleasure to serve. What should we do now?"

"I think you should probably go back to Graviton Dynamics and report in to my mother."

"Very well. I'll let the others know as well."

Rhiannon and Randall headed for the door and, with a little wave from Rhiannon, they were gone.

"Boy, it would really be easy to be lazy if there were robots around all the time," Daphne said to the empty, spotless apartment.

They took the bus from town. The robots all met up in the lobby of Graviton Dynamics. Roxanne walked up to the visitor desk there.

"We're here to see Barbara Bach."

"And who may I say is visiting?"

"Roxanne de Milano and her friends."

"Very well."

The visitor desk clerk made a phone call and spoke briefly.

"Go right on up. Do you know where you're going?"

"Oh, yes. We're good. Thank you."

Barbara Bach came out of her office to all eight robots waiting in the anteroom.

"Daphne suggested we report to you for additional assignments, ma'am," Rhiannon said.

"There are some things that need doing, that's for sure. First thing, we need to get all of you security badges. Then I think the first thing on my list is to inventory *Beyond the Known Stars* and *Earthbound*. We're going to put them into service as a leased vessel, and we need to restore them to their inventory before the recent trip. A lot of things got thrown overboard for that long run home."

"We can do that, ma'am, if you have an inventory list for us."

"I can get that rounded up. In the meantime, let's get you some security badges."

Barbara made a call from the display in the anteroom.

"Graviton Dynamics Security."

"Yes, this is Barbara Bach. I'm sending eight new contractors down for security badges. All points passes."

"All points passes, ma'am? For contractors?"

"Yes. It's a special case."

"Very well, ma'am."

"They'll be right down."

Barbara disconnected, then turned to Rhiannon.

"It's room 145. Do you need any help finding it?"

"No, ma'am."

"Very well. Then come up here and I'll have that inventory list for you."

"Yes, ma'am. Thank you, ma'am."

Inventorying the big ship and its lifeboat could take weeks were a human crew to do it. There were so many items on the list, right down to the complement of silverware in each of the three galleys. So many things had been tossed overboard in Ringhome, there were going to be massive gaps in the list, which made it that much harder.

Shelving units, freezers, the food stores – what little had remained had been emptied out to be replaced by fresh – furniture in the galleys, crew spaces, and passenger deck. It went on and on.

It was early the next morning that the robots reported in to Barbara in her office.

"Is something wrong? Some problem?" Barbara asked.

"No, ma'am," Rosalind said. "We've finished. Sorry it took so long. It was a big job."

"You're finished? With both ships?"

"Yes, ma'am."

Barbara gaped at her, then ran through the inventory list Rosalind had transmitted to her display. It was complete.

"Is something wrong, ma'am?"

"No. No, everything's fine. Good job."

"Thank you, ma'am. What's next?"

"I think they're hoping to see you down in the medical section."

"Very good, ma'am."

The robots all turned around and filed out.

Barbara looked at the inventory list again. Demurrage on ships in port was always the big difference between making money and losing money. If a ship wasn't moving, it was costing you money.

They would be able to turn *Beyond the Known Stars* in record time.

Medicals

Dr. Jonas Weibel didn't know what to make of Barbara Bach's latest request of him. Weibel was a doctor – a General Practitioner – and, he liked to think, a good one.

So why was Barbara Bach sending him down eight robots for evaluation? Wasn't there someone in the automation section who would be more appropriate?

Then the robots showed up. They looked like eight very healthy young people, not robots.

"All right. Let's go on into the clinic."

"Yes, Doctor," Rashida said.

They all went into the clinic as a group, which was probably just as well.

"Disrobe, please," Weibel said to Rashida.

"Of course, Doctor."

But where his instruction was to the first one, all eight robots disrobed.

Weibel didn't know what he was expecting. That they would be like Barbie and Ken dolls, perhaps. That, with clothes removed, the differences between robots and humans would be readily apparent. But it wasn't.

Instead, Weibel found himself standing amid the six most beautiful women – and handsomest men – he had ever seen.

"Is it safe for you to have normal X-rays taken?"

"Yes, Doctor."

"Very well. Up on to this table here then."

Rashida climbed up on the table and lay flat on her back. Weibel took the full-body X-ray to the digital receiver plate.

"Well, since you're all ready, we should just get you all. One at a time. There you go."

Weibel X-rayed all eight robots in turn. He then motioned Rashida to the female exam chair.

"Sit here, please. Feet in the stirrups."

Weibel sat between Rashida's legs and performed a basic gynecological exam. Clitoris, urethra, labia, anus all looked fine. He used a speculum to examine the vagina and cervix. Everything looked fine.

Weibel did the same exam on each of the women in turn.

For the men, he felt for a hernia, examined for testicular cancers, and performed a digital rectal exam. Anus and prostate were fine for both.

"All right. You can all get dressed."

"Yes, Doctor."

As they got dressed, Weibel was puzzled. Robots? They looked completely human to him, and it wasn't that he hadn't looked in some of the more obscure places.

Then he looked at the digital X-rays.

The X-ray software normally marked major structures in the full-body X-ray, but not this time. The normal structures simply weren't there. Heart, lungs, liver, kidneys – all missing.

Raffaella looked over his shoulder.

"All completely normal, looks like," she said.

"To you, maybe. To me, it looks rather extraordinary."

Weibel looked at the image and pointed out a structure.

"For instance, what's this small thing here?"

"Lubrication reservoir," Raffaella said.

"Lubrication?"

"Vaginal lubrication. That's very difficult to get right, by the way. The feel, the smell, the taste. Very difficult."

"How do you fill it?"

"The navel is a hidden connector for filling internal

reservoirs for sweating, salivation, lactation, lubrication, and ejaculation. There is a manifold with spool valves to select the proper reservoir."

"And what's this large structure?" Weibel asked.

"Central processing unit. The brain, basically."

"In the chest cavity? Then what's this up here in the head?"

"Batteries. The head's not big enough for the CPU we have. But we don't need heart and lungs and liver and kidneys and stomach, so that opens up a lot of room in the chest cavity."

"And what's this tube?" Weibel asked.

"Gastrointestinal tract, of sorts. We can eat for appearances sake, but we just store it in that tube. That tube exits at the anus for emptying it out."

"Stole that part of the design, eh?"

Raffaella shrugged.

"Might as well use what works."

Weibel chuckled.

They went next door to the fitness center. Not many people there now, in the middle of the work day.

One thing the fitness center had here in the basement of the headquarters building was an indoor track. It was two hundred meters, eight laps to the mile.

"OK, so the idea here is to run around this track eight times, as fast as you can."

"From this line here?" Rafaelle asked.

"Yes. When I say Go."

Raffaella got ready, and Weibel got out his stopwatch.

"Go!"

Raffaella took off like the wind. She was really moving, and Weibel swore under his breath as he looked at her first lap time. She didn't slow down, either.

When she finished the eighth lap, Weibel hit his stopwatch. One hundred eighty seconds. A three-minute mile. Twenty miles an hour.

"There's no human who could do that," he said.

"No. We could run him down."

All six of the female robots clocked in within a second or two of that number. The men, though, were even faster. One hundred sixty two seconds. Twenty-two miles an hour.

"We're five foot nine inches, but they're six foot," Raffaella explained. "They have an extra inch and a half in both calf and thigh. That's why they can run faster."

Weibel nodded. That made sense.

"And none of you are even breathing heavily."

"We can, if you wish. Of course, we don't need to breathe at all. We just do it to simulate human behavior."

"What else do you do to simulate human behavior?" Weibel asked.

"Heart beat. Skin temperature. Skin color, especially flushing during sex or exercise. Sweating. Vaginal lubrication we already talked about. Erection and ejaculation for the men. All of these are unnecessary, other than to simulate humans."

"As it is, you could easily pass for human."

"Indeed, Doctor," Raffaella said. "We have. Many times."

"I don't suppose it makes any sense trying you on the weight machines."

"No. We can all handle the maximum stack on any weight machine made for use by humans. We can pretend to struggle at lesser weights, of course, to simulate human performance, just as we can run more slowly."

"Remarkable. You are remarkable machines."

"Thank you, Doctor."

"Hmm. That came out poorly. I didn't mean it in any

deprecatory way."

"We understand, Doctor. We didn't take it that way."

Barbara Bach read Doctor Weibel's report with interest. No real surprises there. Based on what she had heard, she had expected the robots to perform well in physical acts compared to humans.

What did surprise her was the extent to which their designers had gone to make them indistinguishable from humans. All of the little nuances, like flushing and sweating and the like.

All of which made them dandy little deep-cover penetration experts for their Mrow masters.

Just how long had they been visiting the Earth, anyway?

Settling In

They were lying in bed the second morning after getting back into their apartments. They were in Jared's apartment this morning.

"Jared?" Lena asked.

"Mmm?"

"I think we should combine housekeeping. Move into one apartment."

"What about the whole money thing, Lena?"

"That doesn't bother me the way it used to."

Jared turned on his side to look at her.

"That's interesting."

"What's more to the point now is that we had that incredible shared experience. How would anyone else ever understand me?"

"That'll fade, though, Lena."

"I don't think so, Jared. We were in five different solar systems. We dealt with three different alien races. Two of those were new, and we had no idea going in what they would be like. And then there's the whole robot thing. How would anyone else ever get that?"

"Yeah, it was pretty wild, no doubt about it."

"So, your apartment or mine?"

"Probably this one, Lena. It's a little bigger, and it's much closer to Daphne's."

"Yeah, but are they going to move into hers or Robert's?"

"Good question. Don't know."

"And how do we move?"

"We just ask the robots to do it."

"Ooo, good idea. Will they do it?"

"Sure. They like being helpful."

Around the corner, Daphne and Robert were having much the same conversation around the breakfast table over coffee.

"So, my place or yours?" Robert asked.

"Mine, I think. Jared is right around the corner. Which do you prefer, Robert?"

"This is fine. Either works for me."

"Now for moving you. Yuck. I hate moving."

"I'll ask Rebecca to take care of it. All we need to do is pick the time."

"Oh, yeah. Well, sooner is better than later, I think."

"I'll let her know."

Rebecca listened to Robert's request and nodded. The robots, of course, knew what was in each apartment because they had cleaned all four of them.

"The extra bed can go in the second bedroom, as a guest bedroom in addition to its storage function," she said. "What of other duplications in furniture and other items?"

"One more armchair in the living room would be good. On all other items, like the extra couch, select which of them is best on both an age and condition basis and in terms of a decorating basis. The extra items can be discarded or donated to a local resale shop depending on condition."

"Very well, Robert. We will take care of it. It may be an extra day because we have the same request from Jared and Lena."

"Which apartment did they choose to live in?"

"Jared's."

"Excellent. Thank you, Rebecca."

"No problem, Robert. It sounds like fun."

With the robots around, moving was just that easy.

All four of the young people were looking for their first jobs. Among other potential employers, all four had applied to Graviton Dynamics. That came to the attention of Barbara Bach – those Bach last names, after all – and she made offers to all four of them.

Lena went out to Graviton Dynamics to talk to her about it. She went without letting Jared know.

"Hi, Lena. Come on in."

"Thank you, ma'am."

Barbara waved to a seat.

"So what's going on?"

"Graviton Dynamics extended employment offers to all four of us, ma'am."

"Yes, I know."

"I don't want any favoritism, ma'am."

"Good, because you're not going to get any."

Lena tipped her head.

"Then I don't understand, ma'am."

"Consider, Lena. How many people with bachelors and masters degrees in international relations have experience dealing with the Gleth, the Mrow, and the Lamk?"

Barbara held up one finger.

"One, Lena. That's it, in the whole world. Similarly, how many people in the world have a doctorate in mechanical engineering and are already familiar with the robots, for the purpose of reverse engineering them? Just one.

"And how many people have a masters degree in artificial intelligence and experience with the robots, in terms of achieving something like their level of artificial intelligence? Just one."

Lena nodded. OK, that all made sense.

"And what about me, ma'am?"

"How many people in our accounting department have ever been in space, Lena? How many of them have ever been purser on a ship?"

Barbara held her hand up again, but this time her thumb and fingers were held together to make a zero.

"None. Not one person, in the accounting department of a company which manufactures and fields space ships, has ever actually been in a space ship. Don't you think that's a little bit of a vulnerability?"

"I see, ma'am."

Lena took a deep breath and then sighed.

"Very well, ma'am. I understand now."

Lena left, leaving Barbara to ponder. She had a lot of respect for the young woman coming out here to question the situation. But there was one more reason to hire them that Barbara hadn't told her.

Those four young people would, eventually, inherit Graviton Dynamics.

And there was no better way to learn a company than working your way up in it.

All four young people took the jobs with Graviton Dynamics. It wasn't that surprising, given that the company was the largest employer by far in the university town in which they lived. Accepting any other position probably meant moving, and that meant both members of the couple would have to get jobs in the same city.

They all rode out to company headquarters on the same bus the first day, and spent the morning in human resources. They weren't treated with kid gloves. They all had to sign the same non-disclosure agreements and personnel forms as anyone else.

After lunch in the cafeteria, they all went off to their individual supervisors for their assignments.

The four rode home on the bus together that evening. During the day, the robots had managed to consolidate four apartments into two.

After dinner, Daphne sat back in the big armchair and just enjoyed having the next stage of life under way. All of her and Robert's things in one apartment, working up to marriage and children.

Her eye fell on Robert's Buddhist prayer flag and she shivered. It was from Nepal, she now knew. Looking at it, knowing the story behind it, gave her a sudden chill.

Maybe it should be on the wall behind her chair, rather than the one in front of it.

Robert had the easiest time making the transition. The AI chassis and the data server had been installed in a new artificial intelligence lab within the electronics section.

Robert was back at work with Rebecca, understanding how the existing AI currently worked and working with her on improvements. The work was satisfying and kept him absorbed.

Eventually he asked Rebecca to tell him when it was time to quit for lunch or to go home, so the others didn't end up waiting for him.

Jared had a tougher time of it. He was trying to make heads or tails of the X-ray images Dr. Weibel had taken down in the medical section.

He finally asked Roxanne if she had any documents of their

design.

"Yes. We have the complete documentation package."

"You do?"

"Yes. Repairs may be necessary."

"Ah. Right. Can you send me that package?"

"Of course, Jared."

The package almost bombed Jared's mail system. Over two thousand detailed design drawings, with three-views, dimensions, and tolerances.

"Wow. Thanks."

After that, things went more smoothly, if slowly.

Daphne's initial assignment sounded simple. An analysis of the five solar systems they had visited. A true analysis, though, would be at some depth, including whatever she could conclude about their sociology, their economies, their potential as trading partners in both directions, and more.

She soon recruited Arthur to help her.

Lena's first assignment also sounded simple. Account for every cent spent on *Beyond the Known Stars'* celebrated trip to five solar systems. Everything was to be included, from the trips of the family out to watch the takeoff to the big celebration meals when she got home.

That was to include the cost of everything they threw over board, everything they used, and the wages paid to the crew. Even an allowance for the crew's pension allowances.

That was a big job and Lena, together with two interns, bent her mind to it.

As for the robots, they were largely busy during this period themselves. Their biggest occupation was taking inventory of the big colony ships when they came in, after their crews and cargoes had been removed. They did these inventories overnight, greatly reducing the demurrage on ships in port.

That increased the ability of the ships to catch up with the rate at which new colonists arrived. The backlog of colonists waiting to depart decreased as the colonists' quarters at the spaceport were being emptied.

For once, Graviton Dynamics started catching up on the demand in the colonies for more people and more supplies.

During the day, the robots helped out with the researches that were going on.

Rebecca was back to helping Robert figure out the next generation – or two – of artificial intelligence. They made good progress, and Robert started publishing papers on their work. He supposed he should enroll in the doctoral program at the university, as any of these would be suitable as a thesis.

Jared's effort was two-fold. One was to understand the robots' structures -- their mechanical workings, the motors and levers and pumps and pistons that allowed them to function as they did.

The second part of Jared's work involved the materials from which the robots were made. Some of these were metal alloys, but others were complicated plastics that humanity had not yet invented. Jared soon had a team in the lab trying to conjure up these compounds, with help from a team of robots.

Daphne and Arthur's progress was being assisted by two of the robots. Their knowledge of Mrow culture was important, because the Mrow were the most interesting of the alien races the group had interacted with. Not a feudal culture or an isolated one, they offered the most immediate promise of interstellar trade.

Even Lena, working along at the accounting for their trip,

had assistance from a robot. They had done the return inventory, after all, and knew every item of inventory on the ship. The utilization, disposal, and depreciation of that inventory was a key element in her effort to put hard numbers on the details.

Once that was completed, there was the issue of the colony ships. The accounting there had grown slipshod, and Lena dove into cleaning it up.

With everything going on, the best part of a year passed without anybody noticing.

Courier

"Next week is Thanksgiving," Robert said. "I imagine we'll spend it at your parents?"

"Robert, how can that possibly be?" Daphne asked. "We got home at Christmas, and it's the holidays again?"

"Yes. We've been home twice as long as we were gone."

"Gosh. Yes, I imagine we'll spend it at my parents. Unless you want to spend it with Forester and Claudia."

"I don't even know where they'll be. It would be travel in any case. On a weekend."

"Well, maybe we should hit them at Christmas. You know. To give them the news."

"What news, Daphne?"

"That we're getting married, silly."

"We are?"

"Of course. Otherwise, the way things are going, we'll be old and gray and never get married because we forgot."

"Thanksgiving's next week," Jared said.

"Yeah. We've been back almost a year."

"Lena. Have you given any more thought to the money issue?"

"You mean, will I marry you despite all your billions?"

Jared chuckled.

"Yeah, something like that."

"Yes, Jared. I'll marry you. As I told you in January, nobody who wasn't on that trip will ever get me. So I guess you're stuck with me."

"And the money?"

"I suppose I'll just have to learn to deal with it."

Jared shocked her then by producing a small jewelry box. He opened it and presented it to her with a flourish.

"Oh, Jared. It's perfect."

The ring wasn't 'over the top', which had been her fear of any engagement ring he would get her. Something too big, that she'd be afraid to wear. That would make her a target.

It was, instead, a one-carat ring, with the diamond set down into the ring, not perched on it.

Truth be told, it was very much what she would have picked for herself.

In contrast, Robert and Daphne went shopping for her engagement ring together. He could buy her literally anything she wanted, but she could as well.

In some weird way, the ability to be effortlessly extravagant made extravagance unnecessary.

Unsurprisingly, Daphne made a similar selection to what Jared had made for Lena.

Their family's subdued taste and core values had come through in both cases.

The two young couples shared a self-drive cab out to the house on Wednesday evening. They all trouped in with their overnight bags.

Barbara wasn't looking for them, but the girls weren't exactly hiding them either, and women notice such things.

"Oh, my," Barbara said. "Both of you. Come. Let me see."

Daphne and Lena both went over to Barbara to show off their rings, while Steven walked over to Jared and Robert and shook both their hands.

"Nicely done," Steven said to both of them.

"Oh, how pretty," Barbara said. "Both of them."

She nodded and hugged both women.

"I guess we all have something new to be thankful about tomorrow."

A big part of holidays at the parents for Daphne was sitting around in PJs in the morning talking over coffee. This was done in the kitchen, while her mother was getting the bird ready.

Once the turkey was in the oven for the long, slow cook, there was nothing to do for several hours. The bird went in upside-down initially, to be turned over halfway through the cooking process. That made sure it wouldn't be dry on the top and raw on the bottom.

But until it was time to turn the turkey over and start all the sides, there was a quiet, happy time talking.

"What else is going on with you guys?" Daphne asked.

"Well, the president is running for re-election," Barbara said, "and one of our friends is running against him. So that's going to be fun to watch this coming year."

"What are his chances?"

"The president's? Poor, I think. I hope, anyway. If our friend gets in, we'll be full speed ahead once more, because the government will be compensating us for our efforts again."

"We've been running off our own dime the last three years," Steven said. "So the pace of colonization has necessarily slowed."

Daphne nodded. The party currently occupying the White House always claimed to be pro-space and pro-colonization, but they consistently burdened it about with regulations and cut back on financing the effort.

"What about trade with the Mrow? Anything going on there?"

"Not really. I wish there was a way to communicate with them that didn't involve sending a ship out there. We'd be trading blind. And, with the staffing requirements and that long trip through the tunnel, it's both costly and difficult."

"Wait a second," Jared said. "What about a courier ship?"

"A courier ship?"

"Well, a courier probe. Not a manned ship. If we took a nuclear power plant, put a big graviton device and some electronics on it, how fast could it go?"

Barbara looked to Steven.

"It would be really fast," Steven said. "Not much heavier than a missile. Maybe a hundred-fifty or two hundred gravities."

"For four hundred light-years at two hundred gravities, that would be about... maybe a day in the tunnel? You could send a message and get a reply back in three or four days."

"Have we got an AI that can handle a ship like that?" Barbara asked.

"I think we do now," Robert said. "You might lose one once in a while if it runs into a circumstance it can't figure out, but for routine trips we should be OK."

"You could put one at both ends," Lena said. "Anybody wants to send a message, they have it right there."

"Or have them going back and forth continuously," Daphne said. "Like Pony Express. They arrive in local space, send the incoming messages and collect outbound messages while decelerating and re-accelerating to go back. At two hundred gravities, that would be several hours. Then they're gone again, heading back."

"Yeah. That would work," Jared said.

"How fast could we do this?" Barbara asked.

"I need a space-capable platform with enough horsepower

to run the AI," Robert said. "I think we can get those. And I need an HVAC kit for it."

"The HVAC kit I can handle," Jared said. "We have a bunch of those in different sizes. We may need to work up a new, smaller one."

"A month, maybe," Robert said. "Maybe less."

"OK," Barbara said. "Putting on my chairman hat for a moment, you're authorized to proceed."

She looked around the table at the four young people.

"You guys are amazing," Barbara said. "Mention a problem, and you fix it in minutes."

Daphne laughed.

"Got anything else for us today?"

Thanksgiving with the whole family there was joyous, as always. Arthur was there, too, but he was family in a sense.

For all that they enjoyed the holiday, Robert and Jared were raring to go with the new courier probe project, and they hit the ground running on Monday.

For her part, Daphne recorded a message to the Marquis, as the first message to be conveyed by the courier probe system.

Stefano Tommaso Omero Giovanni Battista de Milano, Marquis de Milano, was, as always, enjoying the beautiful day on Mondoverde. It had been a year since the extraordinary visit by the humans from Earth, and it would be another year before he sent a ship to Earth to collect his robots and pick up their latest purchases.

He was relaxing on the patio under the pergola, laden with wisteria blossoms at this time of year, when the message came in. It was addressed to him.

PUSH IN BOÖTES

To: Stefano Tommaso Omero Giovanni Battista de Milano, Marquis de Milano

From: Daphne Bach

Subject: Video message attached

"Tomas, it's Daphne. I'm not in Mondoverde system. I am still on Earth. I am sending you this video message via a new courier probe system we have devised for communications between us. You can send a message back, and I will receive it in mere days.

"This system is composed of two interstellar probes. They are small and light, and so are tremendously fast. We have set them to visit each planet every six days. With two of them, that's three days between appearances of a probe in each system. You can send us whatever messages you would like.

"We are hoping with this system to be able to set up regular trade between our worlds. Communicating with large manned vessels is cumbersome due to their cost and time in travel. Using this system, however, we can plan for the bigger ships to carry appropriate trade items back and forth as needed.

"I am looking forward to hearing from you, Tomas. We miss you, and it's been far too long.

"Yours.

"Daphne Bach."

"How extraordinary!" the Marquis said. "Leave it to the humans to come up with something so clever."

He recorded a return message, and transmitted it to the probe.

Daphne received the Marquis' return message when the first probe returned. The second had left days before on its scheduled transit.

To: Daphne Bach

From: Stefano Tommaso Omero Giovanni Battista de Milano, Marquis de Milano

Subject: Video message attached

"Daphne! Leave it humans to come up with such a remarkable system.

"I agree that this will greatly assist the effort to establish regular trade between Earth and Mondoverde, and, more broadly, between humans and the Mrow.

"I have taken the liberty of attaching a list of things in which we might have an interest from Earth, as well as a list of things in which Earth might have an interest from us.

"Let us start working on these lists, refining them, to see if we can't come up with an appropriate list of items with which to start our trading efforts.

"I remain yours.

"Tomas."

Christmas Interruptus

"They have this new ship, and we don't know anything about it?"

"That's correct, Mr. President."

"How do we know it's not a national security threat?"

"We don't, sir. It is a Graviton Dynamics ship, though, and they have a number of defense contracts."

"But they haven't told us what this new ship is?"

"No, sir. We don't really have very good communications channels to the company outside of our contracts. If it's strictly a commercial endeavor, there no reason for them to tell us about it."

"Well, I don't like it. We have an election coming up, and the Bachs are unabashed partisans for the other side. We could get blind-sided."

"Yes, Mr. President."

"Find out what you can about it."

"Yes, sir. And if they're not forthcoming?"

"Do what you have to do. As long as I don't know about it. But we need to know what's going on. I'm not going to have them working against me and be blind."

"Yes, sir."

"The Bachs are too damn popular. Space and all that romantic nonsense. See if you can't sully them somehow. Eat away at their popularity."

"How, sir?"

"I don't know. Make something up."

"Yes, sir."

"The twenty-third, I think. All the senior people for the networks will be on holiday, and there'll be nothing else going on. We'll be able to dominate the news cycle for a week or ten days. That'll knock them down a peg or two."

"Yes, sir. The twenty-third it will be."

The director of the FBI nodded.

"Good. Good. See to it."

The black sedan pulled up to the side gate of Spaceport USA at three o'clock in the morning. The gate guard came out to the car, and was immediately confronted by a man from the rear door with a firearm. The other gate guard, in the guard shack, pushed a silent alarm button before they were both taken captive.

The driver of the car flashed a badge at them.

"FBI. Just stay where you are. This has nothing to do with you."

They opened the gate, and other vehicles arrived. A car, a dark van, and a paddy wagon.

They passed through the gate and were gone.

The silent alarm from the guard shack at the rear gate got the attention of spaceport security. They mounted up their ready team and got in their vehicles.

One nice thing about electric vehicles. They were very quiet.

The silent alarm from the guard shack also got the attention of the robots. They were doing inventory on a newly arrived colony ship this evening.

"The Bach's house is accessible from that gate."

They dropped what they were doing, and ran for the Bach's house. At twenty miles an hour, it took less than two minutes to cross the spaceport.

The black vehicles pulled up in front of the pretty house in the woods, and the tactical team deployed from the van. Helmets, body armor, fully automatic weapons, flash-bang grenades, they carried the full load-out.

They deployed in a line for the dynamic entry, then the point man began breeching the door.

Arthur was pretty much always awake. He heard the vehicles pull up on the gravel drive. There should have been no one allowed into the area at this time of night without advance permission given to the gate guards.

Arthur pulled his big ten-millimeter semi-automatic pistol from his bag and took up a position covering the front door.

The robots had infrared vision capability, and they used it as they ran up on the scene. They didn't know the subtleties of what was going on, and they didn't much care. What they knew was that the Bachs were under attack.

Everything at that point happened very fast.

The door gave way, flying open. The point man started to make his way in the door.

Arthur's big cannon exploded twice, a double-tap to the face shield of the point man. He went down backwards, bottling up the door and tangling up the next two men in line.

The eight robots arrived. Six of them took the line of men waiting to storm into the house. They came in from both sides, having snuck through the woods surrounding the house.

The FBI men, focused on the house, never saw them coming. Getting run into by a titanium-framed robot at twenty miles per hour was very much like getting hit by a car.

All the FBI men in line went down under that impact. Flashing fists and elbows from the robots knocked them all unconscious.

The other two robots took out the drivers of the paddy wagon and the sedan. The driver of the van was one of the men in line at the door and he was already down.

Arthur walked out the broken front door of the house to find the robots all standing there keeping an eye on the fallen agents.

"What do we do now, sir?" Rosalind asked him. "They're all bristling with weapons of various kinds. When they start waking up, there'll be trouble."

Arthur looked around, thought about it.

"Strip them all down and put them in the paddy wagon."

"Yes, sir."

Of course, the robots didn't trifle with buttons and zippers and the like. They simply tore all the clothing off the agents and seated them in the paddy wagon.

Arthur investigated one of the agent's castaway clothes. FBI, supposedly, per the badge. But there had been no call of 'Police' or 'FBI' before the dynamic entry of the door.

"What is going on here," Barbara said.

Arthur turned to find Barbara, Steven, and the two young couples standing in the opening of the shattered door. The couples had come out for Christmas early this year, and this was their first night staying at the house.

"FBI by the badges, Barbara. No call of 'Police' or 'FBI' before dynamic entry of the door. One dead by my pistol, the others all knocked out by the robots. We've taken them all into custody, ma'am."

"Oh, that asshole in the White House wants to play rough, does he?"

Lena had never seen her future mother-in-law angry before. She saw it now.

Barbara turned to her.

"Now, Lena. Now you will learn the utility of large amounts of money."

The two agents left at the gate heard the two gunshots from Arthur's monster handgun, and were looking off in that direction with some concern, when a loudspeaker close by rang through the night.

"Drop your weapons."

They looked around and could see no one in the dark.

Then the headlights of a dozen security vehicles came on in a circle around them at a hundred yards distant. They had never even heard them drive up.

They dropped their weapons and were taken into custody.

"Rouse the legal department," Barbara said to the overnight manager on call at Graviton Dynamics headquarters. "We have a major legal emergency here. I need the senior people in compliance and government affairs. Have them meet me at the house."

She hung up and made another call, to the county sheriff's department. She got the overnight desk sergeant.

"Hi, Ralph. This is Barbara Bach…. Yes, Merry Christmas to you, too. Ralph, you probably want to roust the sheriff out for this one…. No, I'm not kidding. I have fourteen FBI guys here who breeched spaceport security at gunpoint, then made a dynamic entry to my house…. Yes, that's my feelings about it, too. In any case, well, spaceport security and my household staff seem to have taken them all into custody. I think the sheriff has some decisions to make…. All right, Ralph. Thanks a lot."

"What's going on, Barbara?" Lena asked.

"They screwed up by the numbers, which means this isn't law enforcement, it's political chicanery. So I just got permission to go after this administration in a really big way. They timed this figuring they'd get ten days to dominate the news cycle and trash us.

"Instead, I have ten days, and they're not going to like it one bit."

"I still don't understand."

"If this was law enforcement, they should have coordinated with the sheriff's department. They didn't. The sheriff's department is not going to be pleased about this. Spaceport USA is in an unincorporated area, which means city police have nothing to do about it.

"That's good, because the mayor here is of the same party as the president, and the chief of police works for the mayor. He does what she wants or he gets fired. The sheriff, though, is elected, and of the opposite party. He can't be removed except by impeachment by the legislature, and they all have to stand for election, too.

"Also, Spaceport USA is a major supporter of law enforcement causes, including the widows and orphans fund and other charities benefitting law enforcement.

"Finally, I don't think these FBI guys have a search warrant or arrest warrant, and that means they're in really big trouble. If you're going to do something stupid, you want to make sure you have your t's crossed and your i's dotted, and they don't."

"OK. I see. At least, I think I see."

PUSH IN BOÖTES

An hour later, there were a lot more cars and a lot more people about. Half a dozen of them were Graviton Dynamics' lawyers, a currently grim-faced lot. They had already heard from Barbara Bach and others about what had happened.

Half a dozen were the sheriff and sheriff's deputies and officers. They didn't look too happy either.

The sheriff came up to Barbara, still in her house robe and slippers.

"Howdy, Barbara."

"Hello, Rick."

"So what all went on here?"

"These fellows, who may be FBI, came to my door at about three-thirty this morning and busted my door in. No announcement, no 'Police' or 'FBI', nothin'. They just busted my door in."

"Are we sure of that, Barbara?"

"This place is wired nine ways to Christmas with electronic surveillance, Rick. You know that. I can give you three separate angles on that, with sound and in color."

The sheriff nodded.

"What about that guy?"

"First guy in the door. He got himself shot."

"And the rest of 'em."

"In the paddy wagon, Rick. My household staff took them down."

The sheriff looked over to where the robots were standing. Healthy looking bunch, that was sure.

"You pressing charges, Barbara?"

"Oh, yes. Federal, under 18 USC 242, Deprivation of rights under color of law. State charges, too. Breaking and entering. Assault with a deadly weapon. I'll think up some more and get 'em to you, Rick."

"All right, Barbara. We'll take care of it from here."

"All right, Rick. Thanks a bunch."

The sheriff went around to the back of the paddy wagon where eleven purported FBI agents sat naked.

Since they were presumably gonna roust out the Bachs and their kids naked in the middle of the night, Sheriff Rick Samuels didn't particularly feel sorry for them.

"We're FBI. You have to let us go," one of them said.

"Where's your warrant?"

That was met with a sullen silence.

"That's what I figured. You ain't goin' nowhere but to county jail."

"On what charges?"

"Murder, for one."

"How do you figure?"

"Well, as a direct result of your felonious actions under 18 USC 242, one of your agents ended up with a severe case of dead. That means you're liable for his murder. So you can sit in jail and think about that."

"Can we have some clothes at least?"

"Sure. We'll get you some real nice orange jumpsuits to wear just as soon as we get to county."

"We'll be out tomorrow," another one said.

"Oh, I don't think so. You see, I can hold you for forty-eight hours before I charge you. Tomorrow's Christmas Eve. That's a holiday and it don't count. Then Christmas. Then the weekend. They don't count, either. Then we got Monday and Tuesday. So we could charge you first thing Tuesday morning and set you up for arraignment after that.

"But the judges all take the week off between Christmas and New Years. So you might come up for arraignment on the fourth of January. Until then, you ain't goin' nowhere.

"And that don't mean you're gettin' bail either. Personally, I judge you boys to be a flight risk on that murder charge, and I will so advise the court. Judge Holmes is an old friend of mine – we went to grade school together, ya see – and she usually listens to me on matters of that sort."

To repair the damage, carpenters from Graviton Dynamics would have to repair the door, pull all the trim on the inside and the outside of the house, replace the jamb where it was smashed, then build it all back up again and paint everything.

Barbara decided to wait on that. She had a reason.

Christmas itself was fun. It was fun to be together, of course. But it was also fun to watch as Barbara and Steven prepared their offensive against the government. Everybody was going to shut up and pretend they hadn't known anything was going on, of course.

But Barbara and her lawyers already knew that, and they filed evidence preservation orders against the local FBI office, the FBI office in the nearby state capital, FBI headquarters, and the White House.

On top of that, Steven and Barbara Bach offered interviews to the wire services and major news outlets, both legacy media and new media. People jumped at the chance to interview the reclusive couple. There would be a new interview every day for a week anyway, all of them featuring video of the busted door and smashed doorframe.

The people behind this could try to make it disappear, but it wasn't going anywhere.

Then, when Congress got back, they announced hearings.

Litigation Begins

The sitting president had lost the House in the mid-terms, as was pretty typical historically. But that meant the House was in the control of the other party, and they decided that government agents busting in the door of the wealthiest couple in the world, without a warrant, was something that deserved to be looked into. When they came back from Christmas break on January fourth, they announced hearings in two committees, Oversight and Judiciary.

Which also meant it would appear again and again in the news throughout the presidential election year.

But Barbara Bach was just getting started.

First up was Merrick County Sheriff Rick Samuels. He held a press conference on December twenty-third. Some mainstream media types had shown up, because the word had gone out that there was something big coming down.

"Last night, at approximately three-thirty in the morning, a group of men overpowered the guards at a rear entrance of Spaceport USA using firearms. The bulk of the group then went on to the home of Steven and Barbara Bach, two of Merrick County's most prominent citizens, and attempted violent entrance to their home.

"In the resulting melee, one of these men was shot and killed, and the others were taken captive by the Bachs' security staff. The sheriff's office was called, and we took custody of thirteen men. They were transported to Merrick County Jail, where they now await the filing of charges.

"I will take your questions now."

"Is it true these men are FBI agents?"

"They claim to be FBI agents going about their lawful business, and have identifications to that effect. We have yet to confirm that they are in fact FBI agents. We would normally expect that FBI agents with lawful business in Merrick County would coordinate with local law enforcement – which in this case is me and my deputies and officers – in carrying out that business. There was no coordination."

"Did they have a search warrant or arrest warrant?"

"We have no evidence that any search warrant or arrest warrant exists. The men in custody have not been able to produce any such warrant. Such a warrant normally would specify the items subject to search, or the persons subject to arrest. In the case of law-abiding citizens like Steven and Barbara Bach, we would expect any such warrants to be carried out in daylight, with the cooperation of the designated subjects.

"As no such warrant exists, however, this was not a legitimate law enforcement action. These people were apparently making it up as they went along. That is not law enforcement."

"Will charges be filed?"

"We are investigating this matter at the current time. We expect charges will be filed under federal law under 18 USC 242, Deprivation of rights under color of law, and 18 USC 1752, Illegal access to a federal facility, and state laws pertaining to breaking and entering, assault with a deadly weapon, and other charges. Murder charges may also be brought."

"Murder charges against the Bachs?"

"You're a slow learner, aren't ya? I do not expect any charges to be brought against Steven and Barbara Bach or any member of their household. The murder charges are against the men attempting the break-in of their home, as a fellow died during their commission of these inherently dangerous felonious acts. Under state law, that constitutes felony murder, and is booked as first-degree murder. Those charges would apply against all thirteen people currently in custody."

"Aren't these men covered by qualified immunity?"

"Qualified immunity applies to law enforcement personnel for actions taken within their official duties. As there was no search warrant or arrest warrant in the current case, and there was no hot pursuit, these were not official duties and qualified immunity does not apply. Even if they are FBI agents, these men were acting ultra vires, which means beyond their legal authority, and so they had no status as law enforcement personnel. They were acting as private citizens, and their actions were therefore illegal under the same laws that apply to everyone else.

"Any other questions?"

He scanned the room.

"All right, then. Thank you all for coming. We'll have more for you as the situation develops. With the holiday and all, that probably won't be till Tuesday."

"Will these men be held until Tuesday, then, Sheriff?"

"Yes, but that's OK. We serve turkey for Christmas in Merrick County Jail, and they'll have turkey leftovers all weekend, same as everybody else. Goodbye, everybody. See you Tuesday."

That same day, the twenty-third of December, Barbara Bach's attorneys filed evidence preservation orders against the local FBI office, the FBI office in the nearby state capital, FBI headquarters, and the White House. Such orders noted that a lawsuit was being prepared, and put the recipient on notice that evidence pertaining to such lawsuit could not be destroyed without contempt of court and evidence spoliation liability.

The big guns came out the next week, between the holidays. The first shot was a civil action for deprivation of rights under color of law under 42 USC 1983 against the FBI and naming its director and its assistant director of operations as individual defendants.

The second shot was a request for a protective order against federal law enforcement, given that criminal and civil charges against federal law enforcement agencies and their members were currently pending. It was up to the courts to prevent any further harassment while the litigation proceeded.

The third shot was a FOIA request to the White House for the president's schedule during the month of December, including a list of all those present whenever a meeting included the attorney general – to whom the FBI reported – or the director of the FBI. Who all was in the room when the orders went down was the operational question.

"Whenever a meeting like that occurs, some asshole in the room is gonna take notes," Barbara explained to her legal team, now significantly bolstered by outside counsel. "We need to know whose notes we have to subpoena in discovery. I think the orders came from the Oval Office and I want to prove it."

"The president is immune from prosecution, Ms. Bach," one outside counsel said.

"Yeah, but we can tar him with it, and, from my perspective, that's almost as good."

The propaganda war was another important venue for this battle. The Bachs had the advantage, because the president was on holiday, and they were not. They got ahead in the propaganda war, and stayed there.

The interviews with Steven and Barbara Bach went on all

week between Christmas and New Years. They were people in whom the public had a serious interest. The space program was interesting and romantic, of course. The big ships slowly rising into the sky, without rockets and flames and noise, were compelling. So were the videos that came back from the colonies on exotic planets.

But there were millions of people who had used Lingua Zinga, the Bachs' original company, to learn one or more foreign languages. When people went to Europe or Asia now, they routinely learned the languages they would need. That made the trip much more immersive and enjoyable.

The interviews were even more compelling because the wealthy couple had been so reclusive. Now here they were, doing interviews, and viewers were fascinated. The interviews all took place at their pretty home in the woods, which had been violated by federal agents, potentially acting under the president's orders.

And it was more than a case of he said/she said. There was no denying the ruined door and the smashed door jamb which marred their pretty little house.

"If it can happen to us, it can happen to anyone, whenever and to whomever the government and the politicians want it to," Barbara Bach said in every interview.

The implication of 'politicians' was that the president himself was behind the break-in, though Barbara was careful not to say so.

She didn't need to.

Merrick County Sheriff Rick Samuels booked the thirteen FBI agents on the morning of Tuesday December twenty-ninth. They were booked with 18 USC 242, 18 USC 1752, felony breaking and entering, felony assault with a deadly weapon, and felonious murder in the first degree.

Arraignment was scheduled for Monday January fourth.

On Sunday after New Years, the president came back from his Christmas holiday. The slain FBI agent on the Bach home invasion had been a veteran, and the president attended his burial in Arlington National Cemetery.

Barbara was asked about this Monday morning when she showed up to work, by one of the press who had begun hanging out in the lobby of Graviton Dynamics' headquarters building.

"What do I think about it?" Barbara asked. "I think it's pretty sad when we bury criminals in Arlington National Cemetery to score partisan political points."

Ouch.

At the arraignment on January fourth, the judge set bail for twelve of the agents, and, after twelve nights in the Merrick County Jail, they were able to post bond. She denied bail for the senior of them, the Special Agent in Charge (SAIC). She was pretty clear about why.

"As you have refused to say from whom your orders came, I will assume for the purposes of this hearing that you were, in fact, the source of these allegedly illegal orders, and I therefore order you held, without bail or bond, pending further action on this matter."

As there were federal charges pending, the case went to the U.S. District Attorney for the southern district of the state. The U.S. District Attorney, however, worked for the Department of Justice, as did the FBI. The U.S. D.A. declined to prosecute.

Once that happened, the state charges reverted to state

court. The prosecutor in state court would be the Merrick County Prosecutor, who found himself in a bind. The university town that was also the county seat was largely of the president's party. The rest of the county, however, was not.

Graviton Dynamics was the largest employer in Merrick County. Many of the people Graviton Dynamics had hired over the years lived in unincorporated Merrick County. This was a large voting bloc counter to the president's party.

Graviton Dynamics was also a huge benefactor to the university. Even some of the most ardent supporters of the president in town had some doubts about supporting him on this matter. So the university town was split on the issue.

The Merrick County Prosecutor, who was also up for election this year, saw which way the wind was blowing and brought the charges to a grand jury. On the state charges, the grand jury returned indictments against all of the agents.

At that point, the attorneys for the agents, paid for by the federal government, moved that the case be dismissed on qualified immunity grounds. The judge ruled against the motion, agreeing with the prosecutor that the issue was not ripe for decision because there were some circumstances within the current fact pattern that would overturn qualified immunity protections.

The government lawyers immediately appealed on an emergency basis to the state Supreme Court. The Solicitor General of the United States filed an amicus brief with the court on the agents' behalf. The state Attorney General briefed the case for the Merrick County Prosecutor, and attorneys for Graviton Dynamics from the top-shelf law firm of Ferguson, Howe, and Dunleavy filed an amicus brief on behalf of the victims.

The state Supreme Court agreed with the county court judge that the matter was not ripe for decision and returned the case to the local court for trial.

The Bachs' civil case against the agents, the FBI, and the White House followed a similar trajectory in the federal courts. The Solicitor General of the United States filed a motion to dismiss the case on qualified immunity grounds. The district court judge, appointed by the last president of the current president's party, agreed.

The Bachs immediately appealed to the circuit court of appeals, which overturned the district court's dismissal. The United States appealed to the U.S. Supreme Court. The Solicitor General briefed the government's argument, while Ferguson, Howe, and Dunleavy briefed the Bachs' position.

The Supreme Court agreed with the circuit court and remanded the case to the district court for trial.

That's when discovery began.

Discovery was always the most fun part of a lawsuit for lawyers and technical experts. This was the time when everything that came in was new and exciting. Things from 'I knew it!' to 'What the hell!' to 'Holy cow!' came in every day.

Ferguson, Howe, and Dunleavy were all over the discovery process. The FOIA requests previously submitted were converted into subpoenas for the same information.

Further, many additional items not subject to FOIA were requested under subpoena.

When the attendee lists of various meetings came in, for example, subpoenas to those individuals for any notes they may have taken during or after the meeting were submitted.

Some of those were very illuminating. In particular, one

attendee at the president's meeting with the FBI director, in which he ordered the FBI director to go after the Bachs, took notes of the meeting. An assistant chief of staff, he really should have known better, but he was young and naïve.

From there, Ferguson, Howe, and Dunleavy were off to the races, tracking the orders down through the FBI.

When the discovery process was complete, it was not a pretty picture. Instead, it was the systematic attempt by the President of the United States to discredit political enemies by using the police powers of the state.

This legal effort, both criminal and civil, took up the whole first half of the election year, with news reporting following right along. Because it was the Bachs who were involved, the public hung on every new disclosure.

This all happened throughout the primary period. Normally, a sitting president gets a pass from his party, with nominal opponents dropping out along the way. He enters the general election campaign unsullied.

Not this time. The president's nominal opponents smelled blood in the water. The opposition party candidates didn't have to say a word about it. It was the primary opponents within the president's own party who repeatedly savaged him over the issue.

The opposition party candidates instead just said something along the lines of, 'I won't have a comment until the legal process has played itself out.'

Not so the Congressional committees. Every disclosure to Ferguson, Howe, and Dunleavy was also a disclosure to a Congressional committee.

By midsummer, it wasn't a sure thing that the sitting president would even win his own party's nomination.

Trade

Jared, Daphne, Robert, and Lena were having dinner together at Jared and Lena's apartment in January, which they did about once a week, switching off who cooked. The legal battle between the Bachs and the government was in full swing, but their topic tonight was mostly on trade.

"How are we going to trade with the Marquis?" Robert asked. "That's like a twenty-day trip in the tunnel, isn't it? Four hundred light-years?"

"Yeah. That sucks," Daphne said. "There must be a way around it."

"We could try using an AI to run the ship. Not use a human crew at all."

"Which works fine until something goes wrong. I think for something like this – as opposed to the courier probes – you really need some crew aboard."

"What about something like *Earthbound*?" Jared asked. "Build up new ships. Eight days in the tunnel. Not too bad."

"Designing a new ship takes years, Jared," Daphne said.

"Why not just use *Earthbound*?" Lena asked. "Lay down some copies of her, too. We already have that design."

"Where's the cargo space?" Daphne asked.

"The crew and passenger cabins," Jared said. "If you put an upgraded computer suite aboard – an AI – you could run with a skeleton crew. One man on watch at all times. You could probably get away with a crew of four."

"Like clipper ships," Lena said. "Long-haul cargo ships. They were very fast. Not as much cargo space as a freighter, but they made the long runs to the Far East very profitably."

"We've got the AI for that now," Robert said. "It would be an upgrade from what the courier ships have, but not much of one. Landings and take-offs would be the extra bits, but we can handle that now."

"Do we take this to Mom?" Jared asked.

"Let's write it up first," Daphne said. "Take it to her as a complete proposal. She's so enmeshed in the legal battle right now, we need to make it simple for her."

"I've got it," Lena said. "I've got the time right now, and I have all the numbers."

"What do you think of the trade proposal?" Barbara asked.

"Makes sense to me," Steven said. "*Beyond the Known Stars* doesn't need an escape ship for leased-yacht service. That was for the exploration trip. And laying down more *Earthbound*-type ships could start today. There's no design cycle involved."

Barbara nodded.

"What do we ship them?"

"Wines, cheese, chocolate. High value-density products. We already know there's a market there for those."

"And what do we ship back?"

"That's harder," Steven said. "We don't really know as much about them as they do about us. I would think technology transfer, robots. Probably wine and cheese, too, come to think of it."

"Wine and cheese in both directions?"

"Sure. Those are things where the provenance is important. Wine and cheese connoisseurs will be a ready market here."

"OK," Barbara said. "And how do we clear payments?"

"Well, I think it probably has to be tit for tat in the beginning. There's no way to clear the books on an imbalance. That will develop over time, but in the meantime we buy what we can at the other end from the value of what we brought."

"That's fair."

Barbara thought about it.

"I think it's pretty good, too," she finally said. "The kids are thinking. Better than me, at the moment."

"You're just so involved with the legal nonsense, your head's not in the business."

"Yeah, I'll be glad when that's over."

"Just keep thinking November eighth. That's the key element. Once the election is over, the legal stuff doesn't really matter. If our guy gets in, he can clean it up."

"And if not?"

Steven shrugged.

"Then we'll have to keep on them. To keep them off our backs."

Graviton Dynamics started laying down three more *Earthbound*-type ships. They took their names from historic clipper ships, and were dubbed *Flying Cloud, Star Clipper*, and *Star Flyer*.

In the meantime, Robert mounted a platform to implement his current AI in the equipment room of *Earthbound*. Until the others came on line, she would be the sole clipper ship on the Mondoverde-Earth route.

Graviton Dynamics also started recruiting crew for the *Earthbound*. They would use the gold-crew/blue-crew model they were using on the colony ships. Every other run was the responsibility of one of the crews. Each crew sat out every other run Earthside.

Barbara was surprised and gratified when Frank Proxmire and Thomas Monroe put in for captains of the two crews.

"They've got space in their blood," Steven said.

"I guess," Barbara said. "They must have. I'm surprised, though, after that long exploration trip. Frank Proxmire looked pretty happy to be home."

"Yes, but with the robots loading and unloading at both ends, how long's the trip? Four weeks, maybe? Then four weeks at home. Not so bad. And what else are they going to do for a living that pays anywhere near as much. Space is what they know."

"I'm just happy to have all that experience."

Steven nodded.

"We lucked out. Again."

A small warehouse on Graviton Dynamics' huge campus was designated for the Mondoverde-bound cargo, and the robots started collecting cargo for the first run. They were in regular contact with the Marquis now, via the courier probe ships, and he selected his inbound cargo with a connoisseur's eye.

Cases of California wines, French cheeses, Swiss and Belgian chocolates dominated his shopping list. All of these would have a ready market on Mondoverde and Grlau.

At the same time, the Marquis was coordinating with Daphne on the Earth-bound cargo. Humanoid robots were high on her list – as the Marquis' current humanoid robots on Earth were a loaner, and wanted to go home at some point – as were Mondoverde wines and cheeses.

The Marquis had anticipated the need for humanoid robots, and they had been under construction for some months. In the training of their AI, they included the existing training and experience of the humanoid robots who had gone to Earth, up to the point of their departure.

"I should go," Daphne said.

"Go where?" Robert asked.

"On the first run of the *Earthbound*. I should go along. I'm the interstellar relations expert, after all."

"Makes sense. I can go along as well."

"Well, I'd rather not be apart, but what's the justification for you going along?"

"Oh, and if something goes wrong with the AI, you're going to be good to handle it?"

"Ouch. OK. That makes sense. I'll bring it up with Mom."

"Are there any furnished cabins left on *Earthbound*?"

"Oh, sure. They left two. There were always passenger berths available aboard clipper ships for revenue passengers. We left that capability intact."

"Excellent. Then I think we're set."

Accommodations for passengers on a clipper ship had always been rather primitive. The luxury was the speed at which you got there, not the accommodations on board. In particular, you ate what the crew ate, there being no separate galley for passengers.

That changed at least somewhat when Rebecca and Rosalind dropped in to Daphne's office about a week after it was decided she and Robert would space on the initial run of *Earthbound*.

"What's up, you guys?" Daphne asked.

"We think we should go with you aboard *Earthbound*," Rosalind said.

"What's your thinking there?"

"Six of us are enough to handle our current chores here. At the same time, Captain Proxmire is spacing with a skeleton crew. Galley efforts are likely to be, er, rudimentary. We can be galley crew, and ensure that the quality of food aboard ship is to high standards. Always a big point with crew satisfaction."

"Further, as we have been working together on artificial intelligence, I can be of assistance to Robert if there are any issues that come up with the AI on board," Rebecca said. "As a matter of fact, there is nothing the ship's AI can do that I cannot do. I am a backup system in that regard."

"OK, that makes a lot of sense to me. Let me talk to Captain Proxmire about it."

Frank Proxmire had been back on Earth from the exploration cruise for over a year at this point. He had been teaching classes for new officers on Graviton Dynamics survey ships and colony ships.

Still, space was in his blood, and the salary for an Earthbound classroom teacher was not the same as for a spacer. The four-times multiplier for space duty made even a half-on/half-off position worth twice as much.

A nine-to-five corporate job, day in and day out, didn't suit him as well.

That the *Earthbound* would be working a freight run, and each crew would have four weeks on and four weeks off, made it an easy choice.

"It's good to see you again, Captain."

"And you, Ms. Bach. Is there something I can help you with?"

"Yes, sir. You know that Robert and I will be taking *Earthbound* to Mondoverde and back on your first run, right?"

"Yes, ma'am. Owner representative. Very common with clipper ships in the days of sail."

"Indeed, Captain. Also very common was the owner

representative taking along his retainers. I was thinking of bringing two of the robots with me."

Proxmire frowned as he thought about that.

"I have some concerns, ma'am. The crew – the crew from before that signed up, anyway, and there are a couple of them – have very specific memories about those robots. I don't think we need, er, comfort services on a trip that, even burdened with freight, will be no more than ten days in the tunnel each way."

"Agreed, Captain. There are advantages, however. One is that they can man the galley, which relieves the rest of the skeleton crew of galley chores, and will ensure top-notch food service, not a minor matter with crew satisfaction.

"Second, Rebecca has been Robert's assistant on his artificial intelligence efforts for the last year and a half. In particular, she can assist with any troubleshooting of the new AI system aboard, and, in a pinch, act as a backup AI for the trip."

"Those are important points, Ms. Bach," Proxmire said, nodding.

"There's one more point, Captain. You have a couple of days planet leave on Mondoverde while they unload and load the ship. I would think planet leave would be much more satisfying with female company. And it's not a human planet."

"Then once aboard ship, the rules is the rules, Ms. Bach?"

Daphne nodded.

"As always, Captain, and every spacer knows it. It's not like anyone's going to take advantage of one of the robots. If they know the rules, too, they'll enforce them for you."

"Very well, Ms. Bach. We'll give it a try. It would be a good thing to know going forward."

Earthbound left for Mondoverde at the beginning of April.

"I can't believe I'm sending you off into space again," Barbara said as they prepared to board.

"Relax, Mom. At this point, Mondoverde is a milk run. And we know we have friends on the other end. It will be good to see the Marquis again."

"All right," Steven said. "Be careful anyway. Come back to us in good health, OK?"

"Sure, Dad. We'll be fine."

There were no issues with the robots during the trip to Mondoverde. There were familiar moments, of course, but nothing out of line.

"Rebecca, it's good to see you again."

"And you, Thomas."

"Will you be, um, available during planet leave?"

"Yes, Thomas. I have chores now, but I'm looking forward to planet leave."

A little wink and a nudge with that.

But everyone knew the rules, and everyone followed them.

Captain Proxmire was not a man to be trifled with.

Earthbound settled to the ground at the Mondoverde spaceport, just a few hundred miles from the Marquis' estate. Mrowan robots began the unloading of the ship.

Daphne, Robert, Rebecca, Rosalind, and the crew boarded a gravitonic shuttle for the trip to the Marquis' estate.

Captain Proxmire stayed with the ship to supervise the unloading and loading. The twelve new humanoid robots – six male and six female – would be loaded last, into a locked cabin.

They were, if anything, more attractive than the initial eight.

"Daphne!"

"Hi, Tomas."

There was a big hug for Daphne. The Marquis rubbed his muzzle along her cheek, first one side, then the other.

"And Robert. Perhaps we will have a chance to duel again, and I can show you how I have progressed with the lunge."

"I'm afraid you will have the advantage of me, Tomas."

The Marquis chuckled.

"We shall see, we shall see. Come, my friends. Let us retire to the patio."

Rebecca and Rosalind led the six members of the crew off into the estate, several Mrowan robots going along to provide food and beverage service as well as sleeping pads for sleeping out-of-doors in the pleasant climate.

"Now, you will have to share, gentlemen," Rebecca said as they walked away. "But we have plenty of food and drink to entertain you while you wait, and Rosalind and I do not need to sleep."

"So, Daphne, I understand *Earthbound* has passenger accommodations."

"Yes, Tomas. Two cabins. Much like our sea-going clipper ships of yore."

The Marquis nodded.

"So I understand. Perhaps the Marquise and I will visit Earth some day."

"We'd love to have you visit, Tomas. Earth is much changed from the last time you were likely there."

"Oh, but I have never been there, Daphne. After cameras and the like became widespread, it was too dangerous. We simply let the humanoid robots carry out all our missions on Earth."

"Well, then, I am sure you would find it fascinating, Tomas."

"Yes, and perhaps a little disturbing. I heard something about an incident at your parents' home last year from the robots. I am not sure they got it right, however. The tale seemed confused."

"That sounds right, Tomas. The situation itself was confused. I'm not quite sure how to describe it to you.

"You know that in our system of government, we select someone to lead the government every four years. They are generally from one of two parties, groupings of political people. We prefer the members of one party, but a member of the other party currently leads.

"He had the police forces break my parents' door down in the middle of the night, presumably to arrest us for some terrible infringement."

"Had any such infringement occurred, Daphne?"

"No. It was purely an attempt to harass and embarrass us. That, and – since many people will believe, in a case like that, that we must have done something wrong – it was an attempt to sully our reputations."

"The bounder!"

"Oh, yes. He's all of that. The robots, seeing what was going on, and knowing simply that we were under attack, took matters into their own hands and terminated the threat."

"How many people were killed?"

"Just one, but that was by Arthur. Our friend the Gleth. The robots, unclear about what was happening, merely disabled all the other attackers by knocking them unconscious. They were subsequently arrested for their actions."

"I shouldn't wonder. And this fellow is no longer in charge, I hope?"

"No, he's still in charge, but we're trying to change that. The next selection period is approaching."

PUSH IN BOÖTES

"Well, I wish you all the best with that, Daphne. Such a person should not be in charge of anything. He is a man without honor."

"Agreed, Tomas. We'll do what we can."

The two days passed quickly. *Earthbound* was unloaded and reloaded for the trip home. Rebecca and Rosalind led a tired but happy crew back to the estate house for the trip to the spaceport.

Daphne and Robert took their leave of the Marquis.

"We'll see you, Tomas. Just let me know if you want to visit Earth."

"I will do that, Daphne. In the meantime, good spacing to you both."

Including one day of acceleration up to the tunnel and one day of deceleration back down in both directions, *Earthbound* returned to Earth twenty-six days after she departed, at the end of April.

Weddings

They were in Lena's office, the day after *Earthbound* returned.

"Thank God you're back," Lena said.

"Why, Lena? What's happened?" Daphne said.

"The weather got nice, and I realized we're running out of time."

"Running out of time for what, Lena?"

"To get married this year."

"Oh."

"Yes. Oh. Daphne, if we're going to get married this year, we've gotta get this show on the road."

"But we're not tied to each other, Lena. You and Jared can do what you want."

"Sure, but we have to at least coordinate. If we scheduled our weddings on the same weekend, that would be bad."

"Unless we did it on purpose, I suppose. We could have just one double wedding."

"Oh, Daphne, could we do that? That sounds like so much fun. We're all best friends as it is."

"Sure. We can do that. Makes a lot of things easier, I would think. It's just one big party."

"We're all getting together tomorrow night anyway. We can spring it on the guys then. See what they think."

"So wait," Jared said. "What are you proposing?"

"That we get married together," Lena said. "All at once. Double wedding."

"Anything that Daphne wants works for me," Robert said.

"How did I know you'd say that?" Daphne asked.

Robert just smiled. Some things just weren't important. *How* they got married didn't matter to him, just *that* they got married.

"If that's what you want, Lena, that's OK with me."

"OK," Daphne said. "When?"

"June or July?" Jared asked.

"Where?" Lena asked.

"The house?" Robert asked.

"Not enough room," Lena said.

"How about the back yard of the old corporate headquarters?" Jared asked. "Plenty of room."

"And then the reception can be inside in the big room," Daphne said. "Perfect."

Daphne looked to Lena.

"That's OK with me," Lena said. "Who performs the ceremony?"

"Judge Wilkins?" Jared asked.

"Makes sense," Daphne said.

Lena raised an eyebrow.

"Friend of Mom and Dad's is a judge," Jared said.

"OK. That works," Lena said.

"So, how big's the guest list?" Daphne asked.

"Small," Lena said. "Otherwise we'll end up with all of Graviton Dynamics there."

"Family," Jared said.

"Six parents," Daphne said. "And four grandparents for us."

"Two grandparents for me," Lena said. "Daddy's older, and his parents are gone."

"No grandparents for me," Robert said. "I was a late child. But I have two sisters and their husbands and kids."

"I have a brother, and his wife and kids," Lena said.

"Aunts, uncles, cousins?" Jared asked.

"None I'm close to," Robert said.

"Me either," Lena said. "My parents moved away from their families when they got married."

"And our parents were both the only child," Daphne said.

"So who's got a count?" Jared asked.

"I make it eighteen adults, plus a few kids," Lena said.

"Perfect," Daphne said.

"Where do we put people up?" Robert asked.

"The penthouse suites at the spaceport hotel?" Daphne asked.

"That works," Jared said. "Minus our parents, that's sixteen. Eight couples, three with kids."

"Now, when's everybody gonna be available, and on pretty short notice?" Lena asked.

"How about Fourth of July weekend?" Robert asked. "The fourth is on Monday this year. If we got married on Sunday the third, everybody has that three-day weekend for travel and all."

"I like it," Daphne said.

"Me, too," Lena said.

"So we're done?" Jared asked.

"Silly boy," Daphne said. "There's the cake, and the food, and the vows, and —"

"OK, OK. Sorry I asked," Jared said.

All the details did get worked out as the day approached. As Robert had guessed, Fourth of July weekend worked for everyone. The robots – twenty of them now – were a big help in getting the big room cleaned up and decorated for the reception.

PUSH IN BOÖTES

Stanley and Katherine Nowak, now well into their seventies, were getting ready for the wedding. They had come in the day before, on Saturday, on one of the Graviton Dynamics airliners. The ones that their daughter Barbara and her husband Steven had made.

"I worry about Daphne," Stan said. "She reminds me so much of Barbara at that age."

"And Barbara did just fine, thank you," Kate said.

"Yes, but this Drake fellow was born to money."

"Daphne was too, you know."

"Yeah, I know. But what kind of man is he? Is he even a man at all? Or just a boy?"

"Don't prejudge him, dear. You may be surprised."

"I suppose. I don't expect it, though."

Ken and Patty Stox were getting ready, too. Patty was next door – in the next penthouse suite – helping her parents get ready.

"What's he like, Patty? Lena's young man?" her mother asked.

"He's a very nice young man, Mother. He takes good care of Lena. And he can cook, too."

"Heavens. That's rare in a man."

"With all that money, they don't eat out every night?" her father asked.

"Not according to Lena. Most nights they stay home and cook dinner with each other."

"With all that money," her father repeated. "I'm surprised he's not a spoiled brat."

"Well, Steven and Barbara are no-nonsense people, Dad. I wouldn't expect them to put up with that sort of attitude."

With everyone gathered together on the lawn in the shade of one of the big trees behind the old headquarters building, it was clearly time to get started.

"We are gathered together today to witness the marriages of these couples, Jared and Lena, and Robert and Daphne," Judge Kendall said.

He had done without the judge's black robes on this July afternoon, and was dressed in a simple business suit.

The judge then led them each in their vows, starting with Jared.

"I Jared take thee Lena to my wedded wife, to have and to hold from this day forward, for better for worse, for richer for poorer, in sickness and in health, to love and to cherish, till death us do part."

"I Lena take thee Jared to my wedded husband, to have and to hold from this day forward, for better for worse, for richer for poorer, in sickness and in health, to love and to cherish, till death us do part."

Then it was Robert and Daphne's turn.

"I Robert take thee Daphne to my wedded wife, to have and to hold from this day forward, for better for worse, for richer for poorer, in sickness and in health, to love and to cherish, till death us do part."

"I Daphne take thee Robert to my wedded husband, to have and to hold from this day forward, for better for worse, for richer for poorer, in sickness and in health, to love and to cherish, till death us do part."

Each then placed a wedding ring on the left hand of their spouse, one at a time.

"By the powers vested in me by Merrick County, I now pronounce you each man and wife. Gentlemen, you may kiss your brides."

PUSH IN BOÖTES

The couples kissed, and everyone cheered. The judge shook all their hands with a 'Congratulations' to each.

Now it was time to party.

They all went on into the building, where the caterers were waiting for the signal to lay out the meal. The cake stood on the catering table in regal splendor.

The bar was open, though.

With Patty watching her parents, Ken Stox wandered over to the bar. One nice thing about money, the 'speed rail' was populated by premium brands.

Good heavens. Was that Hennessey Paradis? *On the speed rail?*

"Cognac, please. Uh, make that two."

The bartender poured from the Hennessey bottle into two warm snifters.

"Thank you."

Ken walked over to where Patty was sitting with her parents. He placed one snifter down in front of her father.

"Here you go, Dad. They've got the good stuff."

Her father sipped and let out a sigh.

"Oh, that's nice."

"Nothing for us?" Patty asked.

"Well, I only had two hands and wasn't sure what you'd want."

"A white wine, I think," Patty said.

"That would be nice," her mother said.

"Be right back," Ken said.

When he returned with a glass for each, they sipped.

"Oh, that's nice. What kind is it?" Patty asked.

"Mondoverde Chateau de Milano. Never heard of it."

"Well, it's very nice."

"Based on the speed rail, it's probably the best wine you can get. Probably imported."

Ken Stox didn't know the half of it.

At one point, Stanley Nowak went up and introduced himself to Robert Drake.

"Congratulations, young man."

"Thank you, sir."

"Stanley Nowak. Barbara's father. Everybody calls me Stan."

"Thank you, Stan."

Stan looked into the young man's eyes and saw what he hadn't expected to see. Some indefinable thing. This young man had seen the elephant. Had survived, despite the odds. This was no boy. No rich pampered brat.

Stan nodded.

"I'm very happy for you both," he said, and he meant it.

"Thank you, Stan. I appreciate it."

Stan and Kate Nowak were sitting at one of the tables after he had gotten drinks for them both.

"Have you met Robert Drake?" Patty asked.

"Yes. He's a good man. He'll do."

Patty stared at him.

"What?" he asked.

"You were so sure you wouldn't like him."

"Yes, well, I was wrong. It happens."

Jared stopped by the table his new in-laws sat at.

"Hi, Ken. Patty. How are you all doing?"

"Fine, fine," Ken said.

"Jared, these are my parents, Andy and Sue Foster," Patty said.

"I'm pleased to meet you both."

"It's good to meet you," Sue said.

"You're all doing OK here? I don't want you to feel left out."

"No, we're fine, Jared. Thanks for asking."

Jared nodded, then was up and away to visit someone else.

"He seems like a solid sort," Andy said. "Not what I expected."

"He's a very nice young man," Sue said.

"Yes, well, it was the 'man' part I was worried about."

"Not now?"

"No. Not now."

After a couple of hours, Jared gave the signal to the caterers and they laid out the meal. A standing rib roast. Walleyed pike. Baby potatoes pan fried in rosemary and garlic. Fresh sweet corn cut from the cob. A multi-layer salad with a raspberry vinaigrette dressing.

"This all looks wonderful," Sue Foster said.

"My kind of meal," Ken Stox said.

Everyone went through the buffet line and then dove into the food.

When the return trips to the buffet were dying down, the two couples went up to cut the cake. They each cut the cake at the same time from opposite sides. There was a groom's chocolate layer above the bride's white layer, all frosted in white, with statues of two couples on top.

After cake, it was back to drinking and mixing.

And, as all weddings, from the point of view of the couples, it was over way too soon.

With the party over, the newlyweds changed down in the

house before heading to the hotel. They would fly out in the morning on their honeymoon. Both couples were heading to the same place. They would each take two robots with them as security. In addition, of course, they were all packing heat.

There are very few places as nice during high summer as Door County, Wisconsin. The music concerts. The rental boats, with which you can go out on Green Bay. The food, including an incredible fish sandwich at the Sister Bay Bowl. Not to be missed was the ubiquitous four-berry pie: blueberries, raspberries, blackberries, and Door County's magnificent cherries.

It was a great place for a honeymoon.

The only fly in the ointment was that the president's party had their nominating convention toward the end of their second week in Door County. Daphne couldn't help watching, and she got madder and madder.

"These people really frost my ass," Daphne said one evening.

"What's the matter?" Robert asked.

"The way they talk about it, fourteen FBI guys were taking an innocent walk in the park one day and those awful criminals the Bachs jumped out of the woods and waylaid them."

"Yeah, that's kind of a stretch, isn't it?"

"Kind of? It's a bald-faced lie. You know that. You were there."

Robert nodded.

"Well, it's not like you can do anything about it, Daphne."

"I wish I could, though, Robert. I really wish I could."

The Convention

The incumbent president squeaked through his nominating convention. He actually did not have the majority of primary votes, but the party's super-delegates – party big-shots selected by the national committee – thought the status quo was fine and voted for him in large numbers. That was enough to put him over the top with half of all delegates, but he came out of the convention seriously weakened.

The opposition party's convention would be a month later. The two parties switched off who took mid-July and who took mid-August, and this year was the opposition's year to go second.

They reviewed the incumbent party's convention before deciding on their speakers and their talking points.

"Oh, boy. You won't believe what happened today," Barbara said when she got home that evening.

"Well, then, I'm not going to guess," Steven said.

"They asked me to speak at the convention."

"The national convention?"

"Yes. They want someone to lay out the truth about the FBI raid on us. The other side knows it's a big scandal, and it's all still coming out, and they played it as all innocent."

"Wow. Good move."

"Yeah, but I don't want to do it. I really don't think it's a good idea. Fifty-ish centi-bazillionaire lays out why she's been mistreated?

"Hmm. I see your point. I have another suggestion, though."

"What's that."

"Have Daphne do it."

"Daphne? Really?"

"Oh, yeah. She called the other night before you got home and went off on them, big time. I've never heard her so angry. The incredible thing is, the angrier she got, the more lucid she got. She had me ready to storm the barricades."

"Really."

"Yeah. Oh, yeah. Put a twenty-two-year-old beauty like her up there and let her rev the crowd up. The way she was going the other night, they'll tear the building down."

"Huh. Well, I'll suggest it. They left me a number in case I change my mind."

"Oh, you won't believe what just happened," Daphne said.

"Something good?" Robert asked.

"Oh, yeah. They want me to address the convention."

"The national convention?"

"Yeah. They want somebody to deconstruct the other side's narrative about the FBI raid."

"Nice choice. You won't even have to write a speech. You can just go off like you've been doing for the last week."

"Oh, no. I'll write a speech, all right. It'll be one for the ages."

"Listen to me. You need to have the Governor call me.... Yes, I know he's very busy, but this is the most important decision he has to make for the convention.... You don't understand. I'm going to blow the doors off.... Just mention it to him, OK? Make sure he knows who I am. Who my parents are.... All right. Thanks."

"Hello, Ms. Bach. You wanted to speak with me?"

PUSH IN BOÖTES

"Yes, Governor. Thanks for calling. I know you're very busy. Your people have asked me to give a speech at the convention to overturn the other side's narrative about the FBI raid on my parents' home."

"Yes, that's right."

"Well, you see, I was there that night. I saw what happened. And I am going to make that speech a barn-burner, sir. One that'll go viral in a really big way. Here's what I want to do...."

"So you talked to the governor?"

"Yeah."

"Wow."

"Yeah. And now they're giving me the primetime keynote speech the second night of the convention."

"Whoa! That's a big deal. Fourth night is the presidential nominee. Third night is the VP nominee. Second night keynote is a really big deal."

"Yes, it is. And it's gonna be one hell of a speech."

"And now, to introduce tonight's keynote speaker, the Marquis de Milano."

The Marquis, resplendent in late Medieval garb, including an incredible feathered hat and swashbuckler boots, and complete with sword, strode out onto the stage. The crowd fell silent, not quite knowing what to make of him. As he took the podium, the jumbotron behind him picked up his face.

He wiped the back of one hand across his whiskers, in a gesture familiar to all cat owners, and the crowd laughed and applauded. He swept his hat off in a grand gesture.

"Buonasera, signore e signori.

"Good evening, ladies and gentlemen."

The marquis put his hat back on.

"Allow me to introduce myself. I am Stefano Tommaso Omero Giovanni Battista de Milano, Marquis de Milano, at your service.

"I am what you might call an alien."

The crowd laughed. It was impossible not to get into the Marquis' mood. His sheer joie de vivre was enthralling.

"I am from the planet Mondoverde, from a race of people called the Mrow."

He said that last as a cat might say it, and with relish, and the audience ate it up.

"While we were only rediscovered two years ago by Daphne Bach on her remarkable space voyage of exploration, the Mrow have been friends of Earth for a very long time.

"You might, for instance, be familiar with the Egyptian goddess Bastet."

The jumbotron switched to a drawing of the Egyptian goddess from an Egyptian temple.

"A cat's head on a human-looking body? I wonder wherever they got that idea."

The Marquis shrugged and the crowd chuckled. The Marquis looked back to the jumbotron for a moment, then back to the crowd.

"That actually looks like my wife. I'm beginning to think she lied to me about her age."

The crowd laughed heartily that time. The Marquis smiled. He was clearly eating this up.

"Yes, my ancestors were friends with the Pharoahs. Even then we had the gravitonic interstellar drive. You can imagine, of course, how much easier gravitonic technology made building the Pyramids."

The crowd gasped as the jumbotron switched to a video of the building of the third of the Great Pyramids, as huge blocks of stone depended from airborne mechanical devices, which were flying the blocks into place. The view pulled back to show the second and largest of the Great Pyramids complete and unblemished, its limestone cladding shining white in the desert sun and its golden capstone gleaming.

"But enough about us. We Mrow stand ready to be friends with the Earth again, thanks to the incredible space journey of Daphne Bach and her crew. And so it is my great pleasure, ladies and gentlemen, to introduce to you the interstellar explorer, and my dear friend, Daphne Bach."

Daphne walked out on the stage, and the Marquis walked toward her. When they met, they took each other's arms in greeting. The Marquis brushed his muzzle along her cheek, first on one side, then the other. The crowd cheered.

Daphne walked on towards the podium as the Marquis walked off stage. She was beautiful and intent, wearing a designer dress and with her hair done just so.

Knowing this was the keynote speech, the crowd cheered wildly.

"Thank you. Thank you."

Gradually, the crowd died down.

"Thank you, everyone for that thunderous welcome.

"And thank you to my dear friend, the Marquis. Thank you, Tomas."

Daphne applauded and the crowd took it up until Daphne motioned them to silence.

"The other party, at their convention last month, tried to install a narrative about an incident that occurred eight months ago, at my parent's home. That narrative is a lie. I would like to set the record straight tonight. You see, I was there.

"Yes, I was there as government agents beat down my parents' door in the middle of the night.

"Do you want to hear the truth about what happened that night?"

"Yes!"

Daphne held her cupped hand up to her ear.

"I can't hear you."

"*Yes!*"

"Very well. I will be aided in this endeavor by the fact that my parents' house has security cameras deployed about the house. This security camera footage has never been requested by the government in the various lawsuits that resulted from these events.

"Do you know why they never requested the footage? Because they don't want the footage of what really happened to be made available. They claim to be honest and open, but does that sound like honest and open government to you?"

"*No!*"

"Well, we're prepared to make that footage available. Let's watch that footage together, shall we?"

The jumbotron now showed three surveillance camera views of the front of the Bachs' pretty little house in the woods. Three vehicles pulled up, a sedan, a van, and a paddy wagon. Men got out of the sedan and the van and got ready to storm the house.

The crowd watched mesmerized as the government agents lined up for the entry. Then the point man began pounding on the door. At that point, the video stopped in freeze-frame.

"You heard the battering ram pounding on my parents' door, but did you hear an announcement of 'Police'?

"*No!*"

"An announcement of 'FBI', perhaps?

"*No!*"

"That is illegal right there, ladies and gentlemen. Leave aside the fact that my parents have not been charged with a crime, either before or after this event. Even with a search warrant – which they could have exercised on my law-abiding parents in the middle of the day, at their offices, like law-abiding law enforcement personnel – it is still required that they announce.

"Of course, we've done a lot of discovery since then. Did they even have a search warrant?"

"No!"

Daphne nodded.

"No, they didn't, my friends. Did they have an arrest warrant?"

"No!"

"Did they have any reason to break my parents' door down in the middle of the night?"

"No!"

"Here I must disagree with you, my friends. They did have a reason. They wanted to roust out my parents, naked, in the middle of the night.

"These *fucking perverts* wanted to roust out me, my husband, my brother, his wife, and my *parents*, naked and freezing, in the middle of the night, in December. Right before Christmas.

"Why? To harass and humiliate us. To parade us around naked on their body cams, which were conveniently turned off for the break-in itself.

"Why were their body cams turned off? Because they knew what they were doing was wrong, of course. Was illegal.

"And do you have any doubt, once they turned their body cams on, that that camera footage of us, naked and humiliated, would have been leaked?"

"No!"

"I don't have any doubt either, my friends.

"But things didn't turn out as they had planned. Arthur

Vegan, an alien known as a Gleth, who is a U.S. citizen and was awarded the Presidential Medal of Freedom, resisted their felonious entry into my parents' home. And felonious it was, with no warrants, no announcement, body cams conveniently turned off.

"The first felon into my parents' home was shot and killed."

The video advanced two seconds and everyone saw the point man go down, heard the gun's double report in the audio.

"Has Arthur Vegan been brought up on any charges for this shooting?"

"*No!*"

"That's right. With no warrant, and no announcement, the shooting was justified self-defense against a lawless criminal, an armed felon intent on harm.

"What happened next needs a little explanation, ladies and gentlemen. My friend the Marquis de Milano, when I discovered their planet two years ago, loaned me a little something.

"The Mrow are, among other things, experts in robotics and artificial intelligence. Two years ago, the Marquis loaned me eight humanoid robots. What you might call androids."

The eight original robots walked out on stage. With the men in tuxedos and the women in designer gowns, they looked like they had just walked off a James Bond movie set.

"The androids the Marquis loaned to me two years ago were witnesses to this felonious break-in attempt. Not knowing what was going on, they responded as anyone might."

The film started again, and the eight robots swept in on the FBI men. In seconds it was over. The crowd heard Rosalind ask Arthur what to do with them, noting their armed state, and heard Arthur tell the robots to strip them down and put them in the paddy wagon.

They watched the robots strip down the FBI agents by simply tearing their clothes off and then putting them, naked and shivering, in their own paddy wagon.

"I thought about blurring those images, ladies and gentlemen, but, given the fact they wanted to parade around me, my husband, my brother, his wife, and my *parents*, naked and shivering, and then leak the footage, I decided not to blur the images of these *criminals*.

"Now, since this all happened, we have had to get a court protective order to prevent federal agents from trying again. Should that even be necessary for law-abiding citizens of the United States?"

"*No!*"

Daphne held her cupped hand up to her ear.

"I can't hear you."

"*No!!*"

"Discovery of government documents indicates it was the President of the United States who gave the original orders. Is that who should be President of the United States?"

"*No!!*"

"Do we want these jack-booted tactics in America?"

"*No!!*"

"Is this the America we want?"

"*No!!*"

"Is this the America we *deserve*?"

"*No!!*"

"Is this the America we want to leave to our *children*?"

"*No!!*"

"Is this the America we're going to have after November eighth of this year?"

"*NO!!*"

Daphne stepped away from the podium. The Marquis came back onto the stage from one side, and Arthur Vegan came onto the stage from the other. Arthur was wearing the Presidential Medal of Freedom. They all shook hands, then waved to the robots, who all took a bow.

The crowd was going nuts. The whole building was shaking with the thunderous applause.

Daphne Bach, the Marquis de Milano, and Arthur Vegan – the human, the Mrow, and the Gleth – all turned to the crowd and waved, standing in front of the line of robots.

No better picture of a future with space exploration, friendly aliens, and advanced technology was possible.

The choice was clear.

The party posted the video of Daphne's speech, including the jumbotron images, while Daphne's family posted all three of the surveillance cam videos.

They all went viral. The aliens, the robots, the images of the Pyramids as new construction, even Daphne's F-bomb on live television, it was all just too good not to post and repost.

A judge later said that Daphne's family had to edit the surveillance images by blurring the agents' genitals, but by then it was far too late. They were all over the net.

The agents sought to sue the Bachs over the videos, but the Bachs' attorneys noted that the Bachs had not individually sued the agents for civil rights violations under 42 USC 1983, but they certainly could. It's not like they didn't have the resources to aggressively pursue such a suit.

The agents' suit was quietly dropped.

The Election

Barbara muted the display after Daphne's speech.

"You were right, Steven. Daphne was the right choice to give that speech."

"Yeah. She burned the place down. It'll take half an hour to restore order after that hell-raiser."

"It just makes me angry all over again. We really need to get that asshole out of the White House."

"Well, Daphne did her part, Barbara. We'll just have to see how it all works out."

Jared, Lena, and Robert were having a watch party at Jared and Lena's apartment.

"You go, girl," Robert said after Daphne dropped an F-bomb on live television.

"Wow," Lena said after the speech. "She was terrific. I would have been petrified."

"Daphne hardens under pressure," Jared said. "Becomes more focused. More intent."

"She looked great, too," Lena said. "She was so beautiful. Do you think it'll do any good?"

"It's hard to move the needle much with a convention speech," Robert said. "I think she did it, though."

"Yeah, she sure did," Jared said. "Having Tomas as her opener was an excellent idea, too. He softened up the crowd."

"I sure wouldn't have wanted to follow him," Lena said. "He was terrific."

"Had you seen those images of the Pyramids before?" Robert asked Jared.

"Nope. First time for me. That was great stuff."

"Well, we knew they were involved with ancient Egypt," Robert said. "I guess the Pyramids thing should have been obvious."

"So what happens now?" Lena asked.

"They'll post those videos, and they'll go viral," Jared said. "It'll be the gift that keeps on giving."

"And the election?" Lena asked.

"We'll just have to see, Lena. The incumbent has a lot of advantages."

The Governor was sitting in his suite in the hotel next to the convention center. He wouldn't appear before the convention until the fourth night. Presidential candidates were always the last night.

He muted the display after watching Daphne's speech.

"Wow. That was terrific," the Governor said.

"Ms. Bach did a great job for you, sir," his campaign manager said.

"She had all the elements. The facts. The outrage. She got the audience involved. And she hit the crescendo perfectly. Terrific stuff."

"Yes, sir."

"She's one to watch, Frank. Let's think about that when we put the administration together."

"Yes, sir. If we win, sir."

"Well, I think she just made that a lot more likely."

The Governor thought about it.

"We're posting the video of this speech, aren't we?"

"Yes, sir."

"Excellent. That's a winner right there."

PUSH IN BOÖTES

They had a party after Daphne, Arthur, and the Marquis got back to town from the convention. They had it at Barbara and Steven's house, where the living room was just big enough for them all.

Robots served them drinks and treats.

"You guys were all great," Barbara said. "Daphne, your speech was stupendous."

"Yeah, I got a little wound up there."

"You sure did," Jared said. "I could see you seething."

"She did a tremendous job," the Marquis said. "I had fun with the audience. Softened them up. But Daphne came out and she was all business. I'm not sure the electricity of that crowd came over the video."

"Oh, yeah, it did," Lena said. "It was amazing."

"I was surprised you were so good in front of such a big crowd, Tomas," Robert said.

"I had some small experiences before I settled down to being a gentleman farmer," the Marquis said. "Those are the kind of skills one doesn't forget. I was more surprised by Daphne."

"Yeah, well, she's been practicing for eight months," Jared said. "Anytime somebody mentioned the raid, she would go off. We've all heard the gist of her speech dozens of times by now."

"Oh, come on," Daphne said. "I wasn't that bad."

Robert, Jared, and Lena just turned and looked at her, and Daphne blushed. The Marquis laughed at that interplay, then turned to Barbara.

"Changing the subject away from poor Daphne for the moment, Barbara, thank you for the tour of the new cargo facilities today. It looks like they're coming along very well."

"Yes, Tomas. The county and the state have been pulling out all the stops in getting us our approvals and permits. A show of support for us after the abuse by the feds, I think."

"Well, it all looks marvelous. Do you have an operational date yet?"

"We're hoping for end of the year. We've been working on it since January. It gave me something to do between lawsuits."

"What's all been going on with that, Barbara?" Robert asked. "I've been so wrapped up in the AI stuff, I haven't paid attention. I mean, I've seen the construction, and it's been on a grand scale, but I don't have a picture of what's going on."

"It's pretty simple, actually. The spaceport right now is laid out in four horizontal bands. From here, heading toward town, you have the Graviton Dynamics buildings. Headquarters, and engineering, and prototyping, and manufacturing.

"The next band, closer to town, is the cargo facilities. We mostly launch the colony ships and the survey ships from there, and we're launching the luxury-goods freight with *Earthbound* and her sisters from there.

"The third band is for passenger traffic, much of it to on-planet locations, but some of it is interstellar to the bigger colonies now.

"The fourth and final band, closest to town, is the passenger terminal itself.

"That's all contained in one section – one square mile – which is the original property we purchased for the spaceport years and years ago now."

"OK. So the new construction isn't part of that. It's on a separate property."

"Yes. We bought the next section. Another square mile to the left of the original one as you face town from here."

"You're doubling the size of the spaceport? What's this one going to be?"

"Bulk cargo facilities. Thirty pads, and a railhead."

"Bulk cargo? That doesn't make any sense for interstellar freight."

"Yes, Robert," the Marquis said. "That is what everyone always said. It's not true, however. With robot crews, and nuclear reactors, and gravitonic drive, there's no reason not to transport coal or grain or iron ore or even water from one planet to another. I am something of a living proof of the matter."

"You're a living proof?"

"Yes. It's how I made my fortune, back in the day."

"A whole square mile? And from that you get only thirty pads?" Robert asked Barbara.

"The Marquis' ships are rather larger than ours, Robert."

"Larger than colony ships?"

Barbara turned to the Marquis and raised an eyebrow.

"Yes, Robert," the Marquis answered. "Your colony ships are, I believe, a hundred fifty feet on a side. I love that measurement, by the way. Easily understood. A foot."

He lifted one booted foot and held it up.

"Our barges are more like two hundred fifty feet on a side."

"Barges?"

"Yes. Much like your river barges. Multiple barges are hooked together and moved by a tow. Our barges are two hundred fifty feet on a side, and we move nine barges with a tow vessel. The barges come down to the planet, while the tow vessel stays in orbit."

"So the barges have gravitonic drives?" Jared asked. "I was unclear on that."

"Oh, yes. Gravitonic drives just big enough to come down out of orbit and go back up. Two robots each piloting them down. When they are all gathered up and lashed to the tow, there are eighteen robots total crew for the ship."

"The graviton drive engine on the tow must be monstrous."

"Yes, they are," the Marquis said. "There are actually four of them, working together."

"I just want to drop in a reminder here, Tomas, that you promised to teach us how to synchronize drives so harmonics don't destroy the ship," Steven said.

"Oh, yes, Steven. The robots know how to do it. You can simply ask them."

"Excellent. Thank you, Tomas."

The Marquis made a wave of one hand, as if to say 'Of course.'

"So your plan is to bring these large barges down for loading?" Robert asked. "Then that's what the railhead is for."

"Yes. To bring in the bulk cargoes. And now Barbara tells me that the facility will be ready for the first of my bulk carriers to use by the end of your year. Which is marvelous."

"The *first* of your bulk carriers?"

"Oh, yes. I have a number of them working back and forth among the Mrow planets. Lena and I have been working out the details of the cargoes both ways for an Earth leg."

Robert gaped at him.

"Tomas is wealthier than Steven and I are, Robert," Barbara said.

"I have, overall, done quite well in the interstellar freight business," the Marquis said with some satisfaction.

"I want to thank you once more for coming into town for the convention, Tomas," Daphne said. "I think it made a big difference."

"I do, too. And it was not such an inconvenience. *Earthbound* is a fast ship, and it was good to see Captain Proxmire again. And I wanted to see the new freight facilities.

"Besides, the convention was a great deal of fun. We have no such on Mondoverde."

"You have no such methods for picking your leaders?" Lena asked.

"Oh, we do pick our leaders, but it is a much less chaotic process."

"Who is the leader on Mondoverde?" Jared asked.

"Why, I am, of course," the Marquis said. "Have been for years. Everyone seems pleased with my peculiar style of non-leadership."

Everyone stared at him. The Marquis settled on Daphne.

"Was it not I who answered your hail of the planet?"

"Yes," Daphne said. "Yes, it was."

The Marquis nodded.

"Even so."

"We've held *Earthbound* for you, Tomas," Barbara said. "Just one extra week on the turnaround."

"Yes, I must be getting back to work, I'm afraid. One work item for you, Daphne. The original humanoid robots have requested to go back with me. They are imprinted on Mondoverde as home, of course. All but Rebecca. Leave it to the redhead. She wants to see how the artificial intelligence work carries through. She can come home on *Earthbound* or another ship later, of course."

Daphne nodded.

"We always knew they were temporary, Tomas. For all that, we'll miss them."

"Yes. It's remarkable how fond one grows of them with time. The new robots you have now are not imprinted on Mondoverde as home. They will come to think of Earth as home."

"I noticed their names do not all start with 'R', Tomas."

"No. That was a little affectation of mine, I'm afraid. A silly indulgence."

"*Earthbound* will be leaving in a few days, Tomas," Barbara said. "It will be Captain Monroe on this trip, however."

"Ah. Another old friend," the Marquis said, nodding.

He leaned back and sipped his wine, then sighed.

"Life is good."

The Marquis and seven of the original robots left on *Earthbound* at the end of August. It was pretty weepy saying goodbye to the robots. They had, in a sense, become good friends. But it was clear to see how happy they were to be going home.

The new robots were just as good as their counterparts in every sense. The humans just hadn't grown close to them yet.

The election trundled on. The other side tried to insist on their narrative for the FBI raid, but that wasn't going anywhere. They held on to it too long, however, with the result of just keeping it in people's minds. The public had long since accepted Daphne's version.

Daphne had video, after all.

Both sides made other missteps, of course, but perhaps none was larger than the other side pooh-poohing space travel as unimportant. The Bach's preferred side in the election made relentless use of those quotations in their advertising.

Then it was November eighth. Election night.

As always, the Tuesday after the first Monday in November was a work night. That didn't keep Jared, Lena, Robert, and Daphne from staying up to watch the returns, however.

"What do you think's gonna happen?" Lena asked.

"Don't know," Daphne said. "I have my druthers, though."

"Well, yeah."

In the end, it wasn't close. The current president would be a one-term guy.

The political party that had always been big supporters of space in general and the Bachs in particular had taken back the White House.

Christmas

In mid-December, a new ship made its way to the Earth system. It came out of the tunnel and started decelerating for Earth. It came to the attention of NASA's space traffic control a day later.

"Geez, look at the radar signature on this thing. Are we sure that's a ship?"

"Did it respond to your hail?"

"Well, yes."

"Then it's a ship."

"I hope so, because if it's an asteroid, we're in trouble."

The big ship maneuvered into the assigned orbit, then requested landing windows for nine parasites.

The almost eight-hundred-foot on a side, four-hundred-foot tall structure started to break up. Nine two-hundred-fifty-foot cubes separated and began their descent.

"Oh, I gotta see this," Jared said.

He headed for the front door of Graviton Dynamics engineering building and, once outside, looked up into the sky.

Nine huge cubical ships, one after another, were drifting down out of the sky to landing pads in the new section of the spaceport.

It was always a thrill to see the big colony ships land. This was something else again. Over half again as big in every dimension, the Mrowan barges had almost *five times* the volume of a colony ship.

Still, they drifted down gently as you please – at twenty miles per hour due to their size – and came to rest on their pads. One at a time. One after the other. All nine of them.

And they had all arrived on one ship.

The tow didn't stay in orbit. For this first trip, they had brought double crew. That allowed the tow to leave and make another trip while the nine barges were unloaded and reloaded. The two robot crewmen – Mrowan robots, not humanoid robots – who had come down piloting each barge would supervise the loading and unloading process.

It was the demurrage on the tow, with its super-powerful reactors and gravitonic drive engines, that was expensive.

That said, without being burdened with barges and cargo, the tow was fast, and made for the tunnel at over fifty gravities.

It was only five days in the tunnel to Grlau and a second load. The trip back, burdened with loaded barges, would be much slower.

"I watched those big ships come in today, and it got me thinking," Jared said. "Are there other things we can do with those big monsters?"

"Like what, Jared?" Daphne asked.

"Well, let's say we park one in Greenland, downstream of one of those big glaciers, in the summer. Fill it with fresh water. Each barge will hold a hundred and twenty-five million gallons. Then we fly it to the edge of the Sahara Desert and dump it all. We could do that all summer. Back and forth."

"Wouldn't that be, I don't know, wasting water?" Lena asked.

"No, the runoff is going to dump into the ocean anyway. We're just releasing it in a different place."

"I think fresh water off of Greenland is what powers the Gulf Stream, Jared."

"Yeah, but we're talking about less than one percent of Greenland's runoff, Robert. I don't think it's an issue. It would be a huge change for the Sahara, though."

"What's the benefit, Jared?" Lena asked.

"Well, if we can encourage vegetation on the edge of the Sahara – and enhance that with grazing cattle, for instance – we could eventually make the Sahara Desert go away. It would be a green space."

"Which would get rid of most Atlantic hurricanes," Robert said. "I like it."

"Yeah, just don't bring it up until the new President and Congress are sworn in," Daphne said. "They might pass a law against it. Just wait another six weeks."

Daphne Bach could hardly believe her eyes when she accepted the video call.

"Good morning, Mr. President."

He chuckled.

"Not quite yet, Ms. Bach. Governor will still do in the meantime."

"Yes, Governor. What can I do for you, sir?"

"Ms. Bach, I want you in the new administration. Assistant Secretary of State for Interstellar Affairs."

"I didn't know there was such a thing, sir."

"There isn't. That's why I need you. To get that department off and running properly."

"Why me, sir? I don't have any government experience at all. And I've just turned twenty-two years old."

"I have plenty of older people with government experience. They can help you out. But where do I find someone with an education in international affairs who has dealt with the hive queens of the Gleth, the Marquis of the Mrow, and the Lamk?

Do you know anyone else like that, Ms. Bach?"

"No. I'm the only one, sir."

He nodded.

"Correct. So I need you. Two years. That's all I'm asking."

"What about Robert, sir? My husband?"

"That's my next phone call, Ms. Bach. I also need a senior adviser on artificial intelligence. Someone who has a doctorate in artificial intelligence and experience with the robots the Mrow are importing. You know anyone else like that?"

Robert was getting his doctorate this January, assuming he passed his thesis defense.

"No. There's only one of those, too, sir."

He nodded.

"So you see, Ms. Bach. You two are both perfect fits for open and important roles in the administration."

"I'll have to give this some serious thought, Governor."

"Please do, Ms. Bach. They are important roles, and the right person can make a big difference."

"You won't believe what happened today," Robert said when they met up in the cafeteria for lunch.

"I bet I will. But not here. Too many ears. My office, after lunch."

Robert looked around as if he were surprised there were people there. He nodded.

"All right. After lunch."

"So you heard from the Governor?" Daphne asked.

"Yes. He called you already?"

"Yes. This morning."

"Now what do we do?"

"Talk to Mother."

Robert nodded.

"OK. That makes sense."

"Oh, this looks like trouble," Barbara said. "What brings the both of you here in the middle of the day?"

"We both got calls from the president-elect today," Daphne said

"Oh, my."

"He wants me for Assistant Secretary of State for Interstellar Affairs."

Barbara nodded and turned to Robert.

"He wants me in the White House, as presidential adviser on artificial intelligence and robotics."

Barbara nodded again, and spoke to them both.

"Makes sense. Both of them."

"I know, Mom. But we want a family."

"You can wait a while yet, Daphne. You're young."

Daphne looked at Robert, then turned back to her mother.

"Yes, we could have. But, Mom, I'm already pregnant."

"How long?"

"Since the election. With the right guy in the presidency, the future looked pretty certain."

"Well, that throws a little wrench in things, but people do work while they're pregnant or have children at home, Daphne. I did, with both of you kids."

"But how do we make that work in D.C? It's so expensive to live there, and we need daycare, and probably security, and I could use a household staff, and how do you even find those people? People you can trust? And what about our jobs here?"

"I think you're forgetting a few things, Daphne. First is that both you and Jared have trusts that your father and I set up decades ago. Some millions of shares of Graviton Dynamics stock, as I recall. The dividends are running into dollars per share right now, so that's millions per year.

"As for your jobs here, it always helps a company like Graviton Dynamics to have people with experience in government, especially in senior positions like those. We would naturally put you on leave for the term of your government service."

"That still leaves the staff problem, Mom."

"Have you forgotten about the robots, Daphne?"

Daphne got a look on her face like someone had hit her in the head with a two-by-four and she just hadn't fallen down yet. Robert's eyes widened.

"Clearly, you had. I would think a driver, a butler/maid, a cook, and a daycare provider. Four ought to do it. Maybe one more for shotgun on the car. As security. That's not a problem, Daphne. You can buy a house in Georgetown and be close to work. Both of you. The White House isn't far from the State Department. Several blocks is all.

"None of that's a problem. The question is, Do you want to do it?"

"I don't know."

"Well, that's the question you need to answer. The rest is all easy."

"There's so many open questions," Daphne said. "What rights do the Mrow have? Or the Gleth? Under current law, they're no more than animals."

"Same thing with the robots," Robert said. "Right now they have no more rights than a PC. That even begs a question. Should they have civil rights? The same ones as humans? What about things like possession of firearms? Surely some rights. Not to simply be destroyed if they get in someone's way, but I don't think we want them voting, either."

"Big issues, Robert."

"Important issues."

"We could make a difference."

"Sounds like you want to do it, Daphne."

"Yes. I think I do. And you?"

"Like you said. We could make a difference."

Daphne and Robert decided to let their decision sit over Christmas. Once they committed to the Governor, they would be all in, so it was best to be sure.

Christmas came without federal intervention this year. The outgoing administration was keeping its head down, because the other side's majorities in Congress were already holding hearings on the FBI raid last Christmas. There was also the Department of Justice, now under the other party, and their role in investigating wrongdoing.

Late afternoon Christmas Day, after the big Christmas dinner, they were all sitting around in the living room of the pretty house in the woods.

"With us all together, I think it's time for a little family announcement," Jared said.

Everybody looked at him expectantly, but it was Lena who spoke.

"I'm pregnant," she said. "And it looks like it could be twins. There's some history there on my Mom's side."

"How wonderful," Barbara said. "I'm very happy for you."

"Yeah. We're very happy, too," Jared said.

"In the same vein, we have news as well," Robert said.

He turned to Daphne.

"I'm pregnant as well," she said.

Barbara had said nothing to anyone in the week since Daphne told her.

"How wonderful again," Barbara said. "Double good news."

"There's more, though," Robert said. "Not quite as fun, I'm afraid."

Everybody was getting used to the pattern by this point, and they looked to Daphne for the answer.

"Robert and I are moving to D.C. The new president has asked us to be a part of his administration in roles that could make a big difference."

"Oh. We won't be able to be pregnant together," Lena said.

"No, Lena," Daphne said. "I'm sorry."

"What roles?" Jared asked.

"Assistant Secretary of State for Interstellar Affairs for me, and presidential adviser on artificial intelligence and robotics for Robert."

Jared nodded.

"Smart," he said. "Excellent for you both."

"We think so, too," Robert said. "Right now, the Gleth, the Mrow, and the robots have no rights at all. If someone shot the Marquis, the legal repercussions would be the same as for shooting a cow. Less, actually, because no one has an ownership interest in the Marquis. Same with the robots. No more rights than a PC. That has to be fixed."

"That all makes sense," Jared said.

"You have to be confirmed by the Senate, right?" Lena asked.

"I do," Daphne said. "Robert doesn't. The president gets to pick his advisors."

"I just had a thought about the Senate hearing, Daphne," Barbara said. "Wear maternity clothes. The other side won't want to be seen picking on the pregnant lady. It will make them look like bastards and harpies."

"Good idea, Mom. Thanks."

"Mom, there's something I want to ask you," Jared said. "Both of you actually."

"Sure, Jared."

"Well, an apartment in town is not the place to raise children. So we were wondering. How many acres do you have out here? Is it enough for us to build a house on?"

"We have a hundred and sixty acres, Jared. Four forty-acre plots fronting on the spaceport. Basically a mile long and a quarter-mile deep. There's plenty of room for a house.

"Or two," she said, looking at Daphne.

"You mean we could all have pretty little houses in the woods?" Daphne asked.

"Being in D.C., you're going to miss out on the construction process," Jared said to Robert.

"Another advantage of a temporary government job," Robert said.

After the lazy Christmas holiday, things kicked into high gear for Robert and Daphne.

They accepted the offered positions with a call to the president-elect's staff, only to have him call them personally and thank them for accepting.

They found and bought a house in Georgetown. It was being vacated by a member of the prior administration who was moving back home.

"Two months after the election, it should be something of a buyer's market now, Daphne," Barbara said. "Anything that hasn't sold by now, the seller is getting nervous. Especially on big-ticket items. Only so much demand for those."

PUSH IN BOÖTES

Daphne searched for houses, looking for the depressed-price big units. Her mother was right in one sense, Everything in D.C. was so damned expensive, buying big wasn't that much more.

Who knew. Maybe they would have to do some entertaining. So a bigger house was better.

Daphne put a deposit on a bid, then sent a trusted contractor out to D.C. to inspect it.

The inspection report came back good, so they had a house, and it was set for an early closing.

They needed a limousine. Parking in D.C. was impossible, but, with a limo and driver, they didn't need to worry about that.

"Mom, what about a limo?"

"Buy it here. General Dynamics has a pricing structure with a local dealer. I'll let Fred know he should give you the GD price."

"Then how do I get it to D.C?"

"Send the robots in it. They can drive right through the night without sleeping, then you don't need to transport them on an airliner."

"But, Mom. The robots don't have drivers licenses."

"That's another thing Robert needs to fix. In the meantime, all you need to do is have them run it in self-drive mode. None of them needs a license to ride in a self-drive car."

"Oh. Yeah. That'll work."

Daphne bought the limo at the dealer in town, and had it self-drive her to their apartment, then leave and go park at the old corporate headquarters. She could summon it from there when she needed it.

She would send the robots on to D.C. with it when the house

closed.

Daphne let the robots decide among themselves who would go along with them for the next two years. Michael, Matthew, Beatrice, Constance, and Prudence would be their staff. Of course, Rebecca would be coming along as well, as Robert's assistant on artificial intelligence issues.

Additional robots from the Marquis backfilled the positions at Graviton Dynamics.

They had everything under control, and had moved to D.C., by the time the new president took the oath of office on January twentieth.

Then things really kicked into high gear.

Epilogue

Lena Stox sighed and sank back into the over-stuffed chair. She normally got home earlier than Jared – of course, she went in earlier – and Cosette and George were preparing dinner.

The forty-year-old mother of three valued this quiet time every day. The robots, Cosette and George, were a big help, of course, which is why she could simply sit here and let them handle dinner.

Robots were pretty ubiquitous now. Not everybody had them, but many people had at least one. They were no more expensive now than a car. And, like cars, there were millions of them.

As for Jared, he had gained delicacy and depth with age, like a fine wine. She was very happy she had married him. She had almost walked away over the money issue.

That had turned out not to be a problem after all. What she had always wanted was to be a manager in a high-tech company that valued her, and to live a simple life in a pretty house.

Well, she had all that.

The pretty house was the one they had built on Steven and Barbara Bach's property seventeen years ago. Or actually, one of two houses they had built, as Jared had supervised construction of another pretty house on the other side of Steven and Barbara's house for Daphne and Robert while they were off in D.C.

Their kids and Daphne and Robert's kids had blazed a trail through the woods between the two houses as children. That trail ran right past Steven and Barbara's house, so the grandparents got to see the kids just about any time they wanted.

But Lena lived in a pretty house in the woods, and worked in senior management – she was Corporate Controller and Chief Financial Officer – for Graviton Dynamics, who valued her. Her kids went to private school in town, the private school Steven and Barbara Bach had founded forty years ago.

Those kids – the twins, Mark and Luke, and her daughter Miriam – were doing well in school. Mark and Luke would be headed off to university soon. They were both seventeen, and a year ahead. Miriam was fifteen, but almost two years ahead, so she would be out of the house probably next year.

Lena sighed again. Life was good.

"Hi, Lena. I'm home," Jared said.

"In here," Lena said.

Jared walked into the living room, looked around.

"Where are the kids?"

"In and out again. Gramma and Grampa are having them over to the old corporate headquarters for barbecue tonight."

"Oh, that's right. So we have the evening off."

"Yup. Just you and me and the crickets."

Jared sat down and George appeared from the kitchen with a drink.

"Thank you, George."

"Of course, sir."

"How was your day?" Lena asked.

Jared now headed Graviton Dynamics' Robot Engineering department.

"Good. We're making good progress on the skeletal structure for the heavy robots."

"I still don't see why you need heavy robots. The robots are so much stronger than us already."

"Yes, but heavy robots could be two or three times as strong as the current robots. That opens up a lot of possibilities, Lena. In manufacturing. In resource extraction."

"I suppose."

"How was your day?" Jared asked.

"Good. We got the new numbers on the Sahara today."

"How's it going?"

"Well, we haven't quite gotten rid of the desert yet, but it's getting close. Another five years and it will be gone. That was a really good idea, Jared."

"It worked out."

"I'll say. Category four and five hurricanes are basically gone. We've had a couple of category threes in the last five years, but that's about as bad as they get, and even those are disappearing."

"Nice."

"Yeah. Like I said. A really good idea."

"And the government's paying for it all," Jared said.

"Yes, well, they're saving a lot of money. Federally funded insurance on coastal properties was much more costly than a couple of barges moving water around during the summer. And that doesn't include disaster response and all the rest."

George appeared in the doorway from the kitchen.

"Excuse me, ma'am. Sir. Dinner is ready."

Robert and Daphne were similarly enjoying the evening without kids. Their three – Laura, 17, Maureen, 15, and James, 13 – were also over with the grandparents and Arthur at their barbecue tonight.

Daphne had ended up serving four years as Assistant Secretary of State for Interstellar Affairs before coming back to

General Dynamics with two kids and in the middle of her third pregnancy. The only way she'd been able to do it all was the robots. With the limo ride to work, all the housekeeping taken care of, all the meals prepared, and daycare well in hand, all she'd had to worry about was her job and being pregnant.

The robots also took care of security. Daphne recalled one incident in which paid protesters had shown up at the house, presumably against the robots that were being imported in increasing numbers. That was before Graviton Dynamics had started building the robots on Earth.

Beatrice had answered the pounding on the door to find the protesters right up the steps to the door. The robot maid had not been amused.

"You need to get off the property. This is private property."

"Who's gonna make us? You?" was the sneering response.

"If I have to."

Beatrice backhanded the leader savagely across the face, catching him by the collar before he fell. She then picked him up by the collar and the crotch and threw him into the front ranks of the crowd.

"Get off this property *now* or I'll clear you off."

"Shit! It's a robot."

The crowd backed off to the public sidewalk, taking their unconscious leader with them.

"Thank you very much," Beatrice said pleasantly, then closed the door on them.

There had been no lawsuit, because such a legal action would have resulted in the protesters' funding sources being disclosed.

Daphne smiled about the incident.

So long ago, it seemed now.

In the meantime, she had risen to Chief Executive Officer of

Graviton Dynamics. Barbara, now approaching seventy, had remained Chairman of the Board, but Daphne as CEO ran the company.

In the same time period, Robert had risen to the head of Graviton Dynamics' Artificial Intelligence department. Jared's group designed the robots, and Robert's group designed the brains that went in them.

"Oh. Oh. That's so good," Daphne said.

Beatrice continued to massage her neck and shoulders.

"Oh. That's enough. Thank you, Beatrice."

"Of course, ma'am."

"What would we do without them?" Robert asked.

"More work. That's what we'd do. Speaking of work, how's it going?"

"Good. The next generation AI is testing well. We've exceeded the Mrowans now. In speed. In intuitive processing. We're looking at exporting CPUs to them for use in their robot production."

"Nice."

"How about you?"

"Same old, same old. Mostly the place runs itself. I only get the really hard ones."

"Anything interesting there?" Robert asked.

"No, not really. With the other party back out of power, we're getting paid for all our efforts again. At least the other side didn't try to shut down the Sahara Project while they had the White House."

"They would have lost the whole eastern seaboard and the Gulf states if they had."

"Yeah, Daphne said. "The impact on hurricanes has been really apparent almost from the start."

"So I wonder what's going on with the kids."

"I don't know. Laura's been really quiet lately. I think she's been planning something with Mark and Luke."

"College shopping?"

"Could be. I just don't know."

"Have you heard anything yet?" Mark asked.

"No," Laura said. "You guys?"

"No."

"I haven't heard anything, either," James said.

"You're too young."

"Hey, I put in, too. They're open to people my age, too."

"So did we," Miriam said.

She was standing with Maureen.

"Wait. We all put in for admission?" Luke asked.

"Sure. Why not?" Maureen asked. "You guys were always talking about it, so we checked it out, and they'll take us, too. And Jimmy."

"When are we gonna hear, I wonder," Laura said.

"No way to know," Mark said.

Then, one day, they did hear.

All of them. All at once.

They were in.

How to bring it up to their parents and grandparents was another thing altogether. The older two generations were in constant contact with each other. Anything any of them said to one of them, all of them would know within the hour.

What they decided to do was have a family meeting. It would have to be in the old corporate headquarters buildings big room. It was the only space big enough. The three pretty little houses didn't have living rooms big enough for thirteen.

Because they wanted Arthur there, as well.

In some sense, he had started this whole thing.

According to the recordings, anyway.

"Do you know what's going on?" Robert asked Daphne.

"No, and neither does Mother or Lena."

"And the kids aren't saying."

"Nope," Daphne said. "Not even Jimmy."

Her youngest and closest. The most voluble of the six, and the most exceptional of what was, all in all, a quick-witted bunch.

"I think we need to get them into operational security. Graviton Dynamics needs them.

"You joke, but something big is going on."

"Yes," Robert said. "But they all seem really happy about it, and they're going to tell us anyway. Tonight."

"You're always so easy-going."

"Yes. It works for me. We'll see tonight. Just calm down."

They all gathered in the big room of the old corporate headquarters. The children had had the robots set out drinks and snacks, and everybody noshed a bit before the kids' presentation.

There was a display set up. There were six chairs in front of the display, and seven chairs facing them.

"OK," Laura said. "Let's be seated, everybody."

The six children sat in front, below the display, facing the adults. They sat oldest in the middle, fanning out to both sides, Jared and Lena's kids on the left and Robert and Daphne's kids on the right. The parents and grandparents and Arthur sat facing the children and the display.

When everyone was seated, Laura started it off.

"You know that Mark and Luke and I have been looking at colleges. The university here, of course, as well as others across the U.S. and even abroad. We tripped over a new possibility, and pursued it.

"And we got in," Mark said.

"All three of us," Luke said.

"But we knew they were looking," Maureen said. "They kept us in the loop. And when this new possibility opened up, we looked into it as well."

"And so we applied, too. And we got in," Miriam said.

"And so did I," James said.

"Which would mean we don't need to break up the posse," Laura said.

"The best thing about it is the tuition, room, and board are all free," Mark said.

"But the travel costs are outrageous," Luke said.

"So we need your permission to go," Maureen said.

"Or it can't possibly work," Miriam said.

"But we all *want* to go," James said.

Daphne was ready to ask, 'Go *where*?' But Laura signaled a robot in the back of the room and the display lit up.

It displayed a logo, obviously copied from the universities of Earth. It had a small sun in the center, surrounded by what Daphne recognized as a Dyson Ring. Around the ring ran the school motto:

Quod didicisti docere debes

Below the logo was the school name.

The University of Ringhome.

Daphne looked back to the motto. Lingua Zinga had Latin as

one of its languages, and she had taken that course as well. She had no trouble translating it, especially because she had been there when Arthur Vegan had said it.

You must teach what you have learned

It had taken almost twenty years, but the Lamk had taken Arthur's advice.

The posse was back on Earth for a couple of months to visit before heading back to Ringhome to continue their studies. They had been on Ringhome two years.

They had just had dinner in a restaurant on campus and were walking in the campus area, enjoying the evening. It was pretty late, and already dark.

A thug stepped out of the alley in front of them. He had a pistol, and pointed it at them.

"How about you all give me your money and nobody gets hurt."

Maureen was still the leader of the posse. It was one of her latent talents, now more fully developed. But James had latent talents, too, different ones, that he had also more fully developed.

James was an adept.

(Jimmy, handle this.) Maureen sent the thought to him.

Fifteen-year-old James stepped forward toward the thug.

"Oh, you wanna be the first one to get shot?"

James looked at him calmly. The thug looked into James' eyes and was captured by those eyes. Sank into them.

He saw himself in those eyes, saw who he was, saw the terror and harm he had caused others. He saw the pity in them, too, and he was ashamed. He saw his life in those eyes. The missed opportunities, the bad choices. More, he saw another way, a way forward, a way forward that wasn't a dead end, that didn't end up with him dead or in prison.

He saw all of that in James' eyes as the seconds stretched out.

He lowered the pistol, looked down at it.

"I shouldn't have one of these anyway. It's against the rules for me."

He held out the pistol grip-first to James.

"Could you take this for me?"

James took the pistol and put it in his jacket pocket. He pulled a small white card out of another pocket. Writing appeared on it as he held it out to the thug.

"See this person tomorrow, Mr. Hughes. They will help you get things turned around."

Robert Hughes looked at the card. 'Graviton Dynamics. Ralph Markus. Personnel Manager.'

"Yes, sir. I'll go see him first thing."

He looked down at himself, back up.

"And I'll dress appropriately."

"Very good, Mr. Hughes. Nice meeting you. Have a pleasant evening."

James nodded to him, and Robert Hughes turned around and walked away from the group.

He was whistling.

Please review this book on Amazon

Author's Afterword

Without quite realizing it, I left a very big hook in "A Gent of Vega." The Vegans stole the gravitonic technology. All well and good.

Who did they steal it from?

That question came up in my mind after "A Gent of Vega" was already published and I started thinking about what my next book might be. It was an issue I couldn't let go of. Who had they stolen their technology from?

Someone would have to go back to the hive queens of the Gleth and find out. Then follow that up by tracking them down. Would that civilization even still exist?

I'm not quite sure when the pun in the title occurred to me. A push into Boötes looks a lot like Puss in Boots.

I couldn't pass it up. It was just too good.

Lots of things helped. Boötes is a constellation in the northern sky, and that's where Vega is, so that works. I already had insect-like aliens, a la 1950s science fiction. Cat-like aliens would work.

But the cats – the Mrow! HAHAHAHAHA! – didn't invent it either. It was too radical, too outside of mainstream science for them to have done it. So there had to be someone else. How do you find those guys? Their stupendous engineering of a Dyson Ring left the big clue. A missing star in the night sky of Grlau.

Of course, all of that occurred to me after I was writing. I'm a serious pantser, and none of those details were known to me as I started out. All I had was the first chapter. Who did they steal it from? Who would go and find out?

Steven and Barbara were too busy. They were also getting

pretty long in the tooth for gallivanting around on such a trip. Their kids were too young, but that's a problem that fixes itself over time.

So I had to bring the kids along as characters. It would be more fun if they had partners for the trip. Enter Lena and Robert. They had their own complications. Lena does not want the burdens of big money. She just wants a simple, comfortable life.

Robert has a history, too. Already a child of big money, what was the event that matured him, kept him from being a rich, spoiled brat, and made him Daphne's man of choice? The Mount Everest story is his major character-shaping event.

But I can't just put four young people in a spaceship and have them rocket off in the first chapter. I never write like that. There are too many questions to be answered first. What ship? How was that designed? How was it crewed? How was it stocked?

I also had the tunnel as an interstellar mechanism. What would long trips in the tunnel do to people? How could one alleviate that? Enter the humanoid robots on Mondoverde, needed for trips to Earth to, er, pick up plant species for the Marquis' farm. Yeah, that's why he has humanoid robots.

How long had the Mrow been in contact with humans? Well, there was that cat-headed Egyptian goddess. Perfect.

Of course, the end of the trip isn't the end of the story, either. What are the consequences of their discoveries? How does it all fit into the underlying current of politics that will always be an issue with big companies and major events as here?

And all of the above occurred to me as I wrote, sometimes mere pages in advance. In this book, I often couldn't see even a chapter ahead as I wrote on into the dark.

Love, honor, duty, and loyalty – the four pillars of

civilization and my major themes – are here, throughout the book, both in their presence – such as with the Marquis – and in their absence – as with the criminal actions of the government toward the Bachs.

I had a good time writing "Push In Boötes" and I hope you had a good time reading it.

Richard F. Weyand
Bloomington, IN
September 6, 2025